PURGATORY CURVE

For Kenny
02-09-2019 Buffalo
CO
Ernest Francis Schanilec

By Ernest Francis Schanilec

Also by Ernest Francis Schanilec

Blue Darkness
The Towers
Danger in the Keys
Gray Riders
Sleep Six
Night Out in Fargo
Gray Riders II
Ice Lord
Rio Grande Identity

PURGATORY CURVE

Copyright © 2004 by Ernest Francis Schanilec
Second Printing, July 2012

Author - Ernest Francis Schanilec
Publisher - J&M Printing, Inc. - PO Box 248 - Gwinner, ND 58040 - 1-800-437-1033

International Standard Book Number: 1-931916-29-2

Printed in the United States of America

ACKNOWLEDGEMENTS

I THANK MY EDITOR Clayton Schanilec and my reader-critics: Vern Schanilec, Faye Schanilec, Artith Hoehn and Joanne Leinen.

Additional thanks to Lieutenant Michael Hanson of the State Patrol; Tim Gordon, sheriff of Becker County; Brian Nelson, New York Mills chief of police; Tim Olson of Burlington Northern Santa Fe; Captain Paul Goecke of the Detroit Lakes Police Department; Brian Schlueter, sheriff of Otter Tail County and Scott Fox, chief of police of Pelican Rapids. By providing details of operations, the above mentioned greatly contributed to the quality of this novel.

Thanks to Ron Goodman for providing the locomotive photo of the cover. The same thanks goes to Brian Nelson for allowing the New York Mills police car to be photographed.

Thanks to attorneys Phil Haus of Otter Tail County and Paul Grinnell for advice on legal proceedings.

Thanks to Dean Haarstick, owner of Vergas Equipment, for his expertise on corn heads for combines.

DEDICATION

PURGATORY CURVE IS DEDICATED to all the men and women of the armed services. Also to local law enforcement agencies of Minnesota including the State Patrol, Becker County Sheriff's Department, Otter Tail County Sheriff's Department and all the city law officers within those two counties. Those people risk their lives to keep the rest of us save and free.

1

SULLY HAD PRESSED THE BUTTON to activate the whistle as they rounded a curve two miles from New Dresden, while approaching from the southeast. A 260-ton diesel locomotive powered the fifty-six-car freight train…their speed registered at close to fifty miles per hour. Although the next crossing was used very little, it was on their blow-the-horn list. After pressing the button, he kept his fingers near it as they approached Main Street in New Dresden.

Brian, the conductor, munched on popcorn and communicated with Canadian National Railway central. He enjoyed the colorful run on that September fall day in central Minnesota. Brian looked up and saw the top of a grain elevator projecting above the splashes of fall colors. That old building in New Dresden must have been there for more than a hundred years, he thought. He glanced at Sully, who had just pressed the button…two longs, a short and another long blared as the small town came into view.

After the horn sounded, Sully exclaimed, "Jesus, Brian, push the brakes, there's a pickup truck on the tracks!"

Brian knew he needed almost three thousand feet of track to bring the train to a stop. Unless the truck got out of the way real quick, it was going to get hit.

Popcorn flew as Brian lunged and grabbed the brake handle, pushing it forward and up with all his strength…metal wheels skidding on the metal rails screamed intensely.

"Come on, baby, slow down!" Brian yelled.

"We'll never stop in time! Prepare for a hit!" Sully shouted.

TOM HASTINGS HAD COME OUT OF THE HARDWARE STORE and stood on the sidewalk. Hearing the train whistle, he knew there was going to be a traffic tie-up while the train rumbled through town. He glanced to his right and saw the double red lights flashing on the crossing post. The long white and red gates begin to lower.

He looked to his left and saw a semi-truck with large green lettering on its side making a wide turn onto Main Street. It narrowly missed brushing against a car that was parked a bit away from the curb. The semi is going to be the first vehicle to arrive at the tracks to begin the wait, he thought. It's one of many *Daggett's*.

Tom looked toward the tracks…my God, there's a pickup truck trapped between the barriers! He swallowed hard and watched as a person leaped from the driver's side of the cab and rolled onto the pavement just beyond the rails. It appeared to be a young man who got up and quickly moved toward a cluster of bushes.

"Oh, thank God, the guy got out," Tom said loudly.

He put both hands over his ears to prepare for the noise when the train hit the pickup.

Suddenly, an earsplitting bang, followed by an excruciating screeching sound reverberated through the small town. A drift of diesel exhaust reached Tom's nostrils as the engine gritted and grunted while attempting to stop.

Pieces of metal flew in all directions from the deadly impact as the pickup truck crumbled and the wreckage got pushed down the track.

"Did you see that?" yelled a man who ran up to Tom.

"Yeah, I saw it—whoever was in there jumped out just before the truck was hit."

"Oh yeah? You saw someone jump?"

People from all directions flowed to the scene of the accident after the screeching stopped. The bulk of the wreckage was out of sight, a considerable distance down the tracks. Tom followed the growing clusters of people that began moving anxiously down the railroad right-of-way toward the front of the train.

Before the first person from the approaching group of onlookers arrived at the wreck, the two operators of the engine had come down the ladder of the locomotive and looked at the wreckage. One of them brought both hands up to the sides of his head. The person leading the posse of local onlookers slowed as he approached the trainmen.

Sully turned toward the approaching people and exclaimed, "Do you have a rescue unit? We need one right away! There's someone in there—in the wreck!"

THE SOUND OF THE FIRST SIREN HEARD BY THE ONLOOK- ERS didn't last long, since if came from the local rescue unit housed only three blocks away. The two people, who had arrived with the blue and white rescue vehicle, attempted to access the person in the wreckage. They gave up in frustration when not being able to nego- tiate the mangled, twisted metal that trapped the body. Besides, they knew the victim had to be dead.

A short time later the fire truck, driven by Matt Nelson, rumbled up Main Street and bumped its way down the railroad right-of-way toward the wreckage. Four fire department volunteers ran to the scene. Two of them took charge of the hose that Matt had prepared for use. A flume of black smoke exhaled from the engine area of the wrecked pickup.

Within half an hour, the rescue crew gave way to welders, who had arrived and backed their unit close to the tracks. They had been working in the neighborhood and responded to a call from Matt Nel- son. After setting up their equipment, they began the agonizing task of cutting away metal to free the body. Close to an hour had gone by before the two welders signaled the crew of an ambulance that had arrived earlier.

Two men approached carrying a gurney. They were assisted by a third crew member in removing the body from the wreck. Some of the bystanders gasped as the body got lifted onto the gurney. After the rear doors of the ambulance closed, Tom and the other bystand- ers watched the vehicle bob up and down while cautiously working its way back to Main Street. There was no need for a siren as it trans- ported the mutilated remains of the body out of town.

Matt Nelson, owner of the hardware store, remained on the scene along with other fire fighters. They continued to spray liquid on the smoking wreckage.

Sheriff Torfin Allan Peterson, from the county seat town of Big Lakes, arrived with one of his deputies and they took charge of the removal of what remained in the pickup truck. "Anybody here know who it was—in the pickup?" the sheriff asked.

"Ben Talbot," Matt answered. "He and his brother have a hog farm east of town."

Main Street, to the north, had been closed to traffic for over an hour. Floyd, the barber, paused next to Tom while walking his way back to the barbershop…his bad hip hampering progress. "Did you see it happen?" he asked Tom. "The screeching of metal on metal was God almighty awful. My shop shook when the train hit the pickup."

Floyd had lost his left arm to cancer while Tom lived in Minneapolis. The sleeve of Floyd's shirt is pinned up neatly, Tom thought. The quality of his haircuts didn't suffer one bit as Tom had noticed last week.

"Yeah, Floyd, I did see it happen. Something I will never forget. The pickup just sat there as the train barreled into it."

"Poor Ben must have had a heart attack or something. Surely, he would have gotten out, otherwise."

"Floyd, there was someone else in the pickup. Whoever it was, jumped out before the train hit."

Expressing doubt on his face, Floyd looked up at Tom and said, "Someone else. How could that be? No one would abandon Ben. He doesn't have an enemy in the world."

Tom shook his head slowly. "Don't know, Floyd."

Speaking in hushed tones, the onlookers gradually drifted away from the wreck site. Tom overheard one of them say, "I can't believe this. Ben was just fine when he was in the grocery store. I'd just talked to him."

THE HIGHWAY GOING NORTH is going to be blocked for quite some time, Tom thought. Driving his pickup back through the other end of town, he took an alternative road. Using roads that wound around ponds and small lakes, it took an extra half an hour to arrive at his home.

The population of New Dresden had changed very little during short period of time Tom lived in Minneapolis…only one person. It remained at close to six hundred. His social life had taken a downturn since moving back. Julie, his closest friend for almost two years, had moved to Colorado to be with her daughter who was ill. Tom felt lonely and sad arriving back at his house on Thursday, the day of the accident.

He had just lost another friend. Tom enjoyed visiting with the Talbot brothers when he assisted them in learning computer accounting at their home.

Tom approached Medicare age. He felt thankful for being healthy, something he worked at almost every day. If not on the tennis court, he remained active maintaining his grounds. The greenway area, which surrounds the tennis court, needs mowing at least once a week during the summer, he said to himself. The trails through the woods are ideal for hiking early spring, and until the snow came. During the winter months, I enjoy x-country skiing on the trails almost daily.

He currently worked on cutting up some dead, fallen trees. Soon he would have the wood split and stacked…winter is just around the corner, he thought.

BEN TALBOT, WHO HAD LOST HIS LIFE on that colorful September day, had reached the age of seventy six on the 4th day of the previous month. Born and raised in the New Dresden community, he and his brother Ralph had operated a hog farm east of town along the state highway.

They inherited the farm and animals from their father. By utilizing their skills at fixing older machinery, they were able to keep expenses low. Ben had been more skilled than his brother at welding and machinery repair. Ralph's pride and joy was the tractor he had bought only two years ago. It wasn't new, but it had a heated cab.

Ralph felt deep pain because of the loss of his brother. He walked out to the pond behind the corn bins, knowing life would never be the same. He had sorrowful thoughts of preparing dinner and eating alone.

After the hogs were fed and bedded down for the night, Ben and Ralph usually enjoyed a quiet dinner, together. Ralph did the cooking and prepared the table. Ben took care of the cleanup and washed the dishes. After hearing the last plate clatter into the cabinet, Ralph would bring out their business ledger and lay it on the kitchen table.

Ben had always brought over two steaming cups of tea and they would sip and enjoy reviewing the ledger entries and totals. After they were both satisfied with the numbers, Ralph would place the ledger next to the computer on a desk in the corner of the room. Carefully working his fingers over the keyboard, he inputted the new figures. Ralph glanced at a business card lying on the desk. He smiled and thought about his computer mentor, Tom Hastings…that guy has helped us a great deal.

The previous day, they had sold six hogs. Ralph carefully filled out a deposit slip, which he would deliver to the bank during his next visit to town. Even though their profit margins at times had been limited, Ben smiled when he looked at the certificates of deposit's statement.

"Darn near eight hundred thousand, Ralph," Ben had said to his brother the day before the train accident.

"When it gets to a mill, let's sell the hogs," Ben responded with a laugh.

Ralph had become depressed since his brother died. I miss my brother terribly, he thought. I'll never have dinner with him again. Who's going to do all the fixing? He walked farther out beyond the farmstead.

The rolling landscape of their farmland was pockmarked with small ponds speckled with water lilies at that time of the year. Tall cattail reeds, water milkweeds and goldenrod crowded the ground next to the water. The ducklings learned to become expert flyers as they skittered from pond to pond…migration season approached.

He stayed out until almost dark and watched a small flock of geese coming in from the field. They landed in a pond where they would spend the night.

Walking back to his house, Ralph's mind drifted back to the phone call. *An accident! Ben has been killed.* Tears flooded his eyes. Why it was just minutes ago that I saw Ralph's blue pickup turn onto the state highway. I remember jotting down *butter*, adding it to Ben's shopping list.

The phone call had come from Matt Nelson, owner of the hardware store. Ralph remembered dashing out to his pickup and not being able to find the keys. After searching frantically for five minutes, he found them on the kitchen table.

Speeding toward town, Ralph noticed the speedometer pushing fifty after rounding the big curve near the city limits. He held his breath when seeing the train that had killed his brother.

Parking and climbing over the couplings of two boxcars, he had gotten there in time to see the New Dresden rescue vehicle turn onto Main Street and head away. Ralph felt pain in his stomach, and visualized his brother spread out in that blue and white vehicle.

"Oh, what to do now?" He asked himself.

Ralph laughed out loud remembering the two girls that he and his brother used to date. Four of us in a pickup truck, he said to himself. Louise was her name. What was that other girl's name, my brother's date? Can't remember…it's been so long. Ben should have known better, being three years older.

Typing class…yup, that's where I got to know Louise. That's why I took typing. It's sure paid off lately, he thought. I sure like the pleased look on Tom Hastings' face when I rattle those keys.

2

FRIDAY MORNING, THE DAY AFTER THE TRAIN ACCI-
DENT, Tom checked his e-mail. He looked out the window and saw
a vehicle pull into his driveway. His fingers, which were busy on the
keyboard, stopped and lowered to his lap when he noticed the police
car. The train accident…that's why the car is here, he thought. I told
only one other person about what I saw…Floyd, the barber.

The man who got out of the driver's side appeared big. He wore
a pair of sunglasses that covered almost half of his face. By the
looks of the uniform, it had to be someone from the sheriff's office,
Tom thought. The man stood by the car for a moment and looked
around. When the officer came down the sidewalk, he waddled. The
expanded bulk of shirt above his belt suggested he was a person who
ate too much and did not get enough physical exercise.

Tom waited for the doorbell to ring before getting off his chair
to open the door.

"Hello, Sir. I'm sorry to bother you. I'm Sheriff Peterson of Big
Lakes County. Are you Tom Hastings?"

Tom noticed the sheriff firm up his jaw as he tilted it upward
slightly.

"Yes, I sure am. What can I do for you?"

"According to some people I talked to in New Dresden yesterday,
you were the closest witness to the train accident. Is that right?"

"Well, that's possible. There were some other people around. I
did hear someone say something to me right after the train hit the
pickup."

"That was probably the guy that gave me your name. Could you
tell it to me like you saw it happen?"

"Well, okay. I'll give it a try. When I heard the horn and the sound of the train approaching, I looked at the intersection. The two gates had just come down—red lights were flashing. Then, I noticed the pickup truck. It was on the tracks and wasn't moving."

"Did you see anyone in the pickup?"

"Well, not exactly—not right in the truck."

"What do you mean by that?"

"I saw someone open the driver's side door and jump out onto the road just before the train hit."

"You're sure of that?"

"Yeah, the person sort of disappeared—the train hit moments later."

"Tell me about this person that you claim to have seen. Was it a young person? A man or a woman?"

"Well, it looked like someone young, mainly because of the jump—someone agile. I would guess, a young man."

"Is it possible you could have imagined that someone jumped? From the pickup, I mean."

Tom's stance firmed. His eyes narrowed and horizontal furrows formed above the eyebrows. "Ah, sheriff, I don't think so—someone did jump from that pickup truck."

"Well, okay, Mr. Hastings. I'll tell you this. No one else saw anyone jump from the pickup, not even the two engineers. They had a perfect view—better than yours."

Tom inhaled deeply and wished the sheriff would go away. The deputy who accompanied the sheriff stood next to Tom's garage. He had sauntered over there and peeked inside the shop.

"Thanks, Mr. Hastings," the sheriff said as he cleared his throat. "Nice place you've got here."

The sheriff waddled back to his car and Tom saw him say something to the deputy. The two officers lingered by the front bumper for a few moments and broke out laughing. Tom felt irritated and slighted as he saw them get into the car. Maybe I did imagine the person jump, Tom thought, scratching the side of his head as the sheriff's car disappeared around a bank of trees.

MAIN STREET IN NEW DRESDEN lost its bustle in September. The tourist season was over except for a few stragglers. There was only one out-of-state car parked on Main Street, near the grocery store…it had North Dakota plates. The man who sat behind the steering wheel patiently waited for his wife, who had just emerged from Stillman's Super Market.

Even though there were several open parking places up and down Main Street, a UPS van double-parked directly across from the post office. Double parking in New Dresden was as common as black flies in July. A laundry van blocked a red pickup, which had parked in front of the hardware store. A gray sedan blocked the alley between the liquor store and the post office. The driver had gone into the post office and left the motor running.

The train accident had happened the previous day. The awkward appearance of the metallic debris next to the railroad tracks drew a glance from most people driving in and out of town. Pedestrians on Main Street gathered in small clusters to chat and send wary glances toward the track. The mood of the townspeople had definitely been affected. There didn't appear to be the usual *good morning* and *nice-day-out* expressions.

Instead, Tom heard subdued voices saying, *poor old Ben—never knew what hit 'em. Ralph's all alone now—*

The racks of flowers and plants next to the hardware store had dwindled to one. Tom saw *half-price* written on a cardboard box as he drove by.

"I hear you were the closest one to the accident yesterday," Jerry said when Tom entered the counter room in the post office.

"Geez, Jerry, that's something I hope never to see again. Ben never had a chance."

Jerry touched the back of his head. He did that habitually after recovering from a blow received at the hands of a local outlaw four years earlier. Jerry came very close to being victim number four at the hands of a lunatic renegade, former CIA agent, who had killed people in order to remain anonymous and hidden from the FBI during the days of *Blue Darkness.*

"Wonder why he didn't get out of the pickup?" Jerry asked.

"Maybe he had a heart attack," the postmaster added.

Tom's forehead furrowed as he visualized the pickup door opening and a body leaping out of harms way, just before the sickening crunch. If the sheriff doesn't believe me, why should I talk about it? Tom asked himself.

3

TOM HASTINGS HAD MOVED BACK TO CENTRAL MINNESOTA and his log home that he had sold almost three years ago. The five-year repurchase option on his property in the sales contract proved to be a good decision for him. After living in Minneapolis for the past two years, he felt happy to be back in the country.

The memory of the murder of his neighbor and friend Maynard Cushing had diminished. Every time Tom drove up the township road and made the left turn, he glanced at the house in which Maynard had lived. He thought about the nice view looking out the Maynard's office window…the field and trees beyond. Tom wondered what happened to the computer that he had helped Maynard master. Someone else lived there now, but it will always be Maynard's house, he thought.

Life in the city for a couple of years and a month vacation in Florida proved to generate more trauma than he could possible fathom.

A serial killer had besieged an apartment high-rise in Minneapolis where he lived at the time. After surviving terrorizing experiences in the high-rise, Tom rented a condo in Florida and spent a month in the sun. While there, he got caught up in the middle of a group of desperate people, some willing to kill to gain possession of a valuable gem.

The daily visits that Tom made to New Dresden are delightful, he said to himself. On the day of the train accident, I glanced at a treed area while rounding a curve before entering the city limits. I touched the brake pedal lightly hopefully to avoid a speeding ticket.

The speed limit changed from forty miles per hour to thirty while driving on the curve, bushes and trees partially hiding the sign…not giving the motorist any warning. That section of the highway was often patrolled by sheriff deputies and state patrolmen.

Tom remembered the speeding ticket he had gotten. He saw forty-four on his speedometer. Tom noticed the sheriff's car near the tracks and knew it was *too late*. Even though it happened almost five years ago, he always remembered to slow down when driving on *Purgatory Curve* and approaching the small town.

TOM ARRIVED IN NEW DRESDEN and squeezed into a parallel open space on Main Street. He walked across, picked up his mail and visited with Jerry, the postmaster. Looking across the street, he saw a man with a brown flattop cap sitting on a bench. Tom didn't know his name, but the man sat there often. The gray-tweed jacket, which the man wore, is something from the past, he thought.

Tom entered the supermarket and smiled, seeing Ellie behind the counter. She's been the head checkout clerk at Stillman's Super Market for years, he thought.

"Good Morning, Tom," She said.

After picking up a newspaper from a rack, he laid it down on the counter along with seventy-five cents. "What's new today?" Tom asked Ellie.

"The same as usual—nothing ever happens around here."

Tom stared at her.

"Well, except for train accidents," Ellie added, her chin tilting sideways.

Ellie hadn't changed any, he thought. She still has that big smile and a pleasant, soft voice…efficient and always willing to help shoppers.

"Have you been in the new pub?" Ellie asked.

"Yes and I like it a lot including the new location. The building that housed the old pub needed to be torn down anyhow," Tom answered. "Building a new one on the corner across from the hardware store was a great decision."

"Have you met the new owners?" Ellie asked.

"You mean Billy and Sue."

"Yes, they've done a great job," Ellie said.

Tom grabbed the newspaper and headed across the street to deposit a check he had received in the mail. He admired the handicapped access station in the foyer of the bank. The *Borders Café* ramp and other handicap facilities in New Dresden are evidence of human compassion, which the community demonstrates so well, he thought.

A friendly, smiling face from a bank employee greeted Tom as he slid his endorsed check on the varnished surface of the teller window. "Thank you," the teller responded.

Leaving the bank, Tom headed across the street to the sidewalk leading to the hardware store. He noticed Kyle Fredrickson standing in the doorway of his office, the door partially open. Kyle had been brokering real estate in this community for almost ten years. Tom had good memories of Kyle handling his property transaction. He gave Kyle a lot of credit for doing a great job on his original property-selling contract.

Tom slowly walked down the main aisle of the hardware store, boards creaking with each step. Matt Nelson still owned the store. The magic of a captivating inventory improves with each passing year, Tom thought.

He talked to Matt about satellite Internet access as the clerk rang up his five-pound bag of screws, which Tom planned on using to attach plywood to his garage walls. Sipping from a Styrofoam cup of deluxe coffee, he listened as Matt talked up a new Internet broadband service. After cracking a few peanut shells and paying for his purchase, Tom walked out onto the sidewalk.

There had been some changes up and down Main Street since Tom Hastings had moved back from Minneapolis. *Fred's Vacuum Shop* had been replaced with *Bev's Embroidery*. *Adam's Realty* had changed hands and got renamed *King Realty*. Sabrina King had purchased the business almost a year ago. The previous owner, Linda Barr, had been a frustrated lady because her competitor Kyle Fredrickson landed most of the sales. Sabrina and Kyle often joined forces to orchestrate the purchase and sale of a lot of property, Tom had heard.

Listening to people talking at the supermarket, Tom learned that the body shop around the corner from the bank had change owner-ship. Kelly Brown had purchased and expanded the business shortly after Tom had moved. He currently employed four people, including a young local man by the name of Bruce Sanford.

Four years is a long time, Tom thought. I'm back home where I belong. All the traumatic experiences that happened during the last five years are history. Tom continued to play tennis and go for long walks almost every day. He remained in good physical condition, but his loneliness frustrated him.

STEVE STEIGER BRAKED HIS SEMI-TRUCK and brought it to a noisy stop at the stop sign next to *Stillman's Super Market*. He had been driving for *Master Truck Lines* for over twenty years. His firm supplied products mainly for service station convenience stores. He had just dropped some of his load at *Nabor's*, a block away.

Nabor's had been in business for close to thirteen years in New Dresden. Competition in the service station and convenience store business remained intense. Besides the *Nabor's* station, there are three other competitors in the area. *Quality Supply* at the main inter-section across the street from the bank, *Buzz's Stop and Shop* north of the tracks and *Hundart's* just out of the city limits to the south. Steve delivered products to all four businesses.

Steve's mother Edna expected him home for dinner. They lived together in a small house on the western edge of New Dresden. Steve grew up, never knowing his father's identity. The biggest concern in Steve's mind remained his mother's health. She had been diagnosed with breast cancer six months ago.

Steve's mother had an appointment at the clinic in Big Lakes on Monday. He had scheduled his routes that day so he could ac-company her. A black puff of diesel exhaust spurted upward from the dual pipes above the cab as Steve crossed the intersection and headed for the street that would lead him home.

Kelly Brown waved as the semi slowly passed by his auto body shop. Steve and Kelly were classmates in high school. Steve was the tight end on the football team. Kelly played tackle. Steve had been a groomsman at Kelly's wedding. Steve smiled while thinking of Kelly's two sons. I'll walk over to the shop for coffee tomorrow, he thought. I really like those two boys of his...hopefully they'll be there.

After he stepped down from the cab, he could see his mother in the window. Steve frowned when remembering his mother's usual greeting. She would always tell him that his truck sounded different than others...*I can hear it from miles away.*

His mother waved. Steve slammed the truck door shut, picked up his suitcase and headed for the front door. Pausing, he allowed a kiss on the cheek before entering. "Oh, Steve, it's so good to see you again. How was your run?"

"Just fine and how are you feeling?"

"Not so good lately, Steve. I'm afraid of my appointment on Monday—of what they'll tell me."

"Oh, Mom, you'll beat this rap easily. Nothing to worry about," Steve said. He turned his head. I'll be forty-eight later this year, he thought. I can't imagine living here alone, he said to himself.

4

MARY ANN'S RESTAURANT ON THE EAST SHORE of Borders Lake continued to be a favorite hangout for Tom Hastings. One of the reasons he liked it so well is because of its location...so close to home. Harold Kraft and his wife Mary Ann had repurchased it while Tom lived in Minneapolis. Tom had liked the interim owners, but he appreciated Mary Ann and Harold even more. The restaurant and bar had recently been redecorated and looked attractive to him.

On Saturday evening Tom sat on his favorite high stool near the *Mary Ann's* bar watching television. He had both elbows planted on the small round table. The threat of a strike by the big league baseball players had ended, and the Minnesota Twins led the division, likely headed for the playoffs. Harold came by to toss a couple of logs into the fireplace. He stopped by Tom's table.

"Harold, I'm glad to see you and Mary Ann back. This place has never been the same without you. How's the new house?"

"Thanks, Tom. We're glad to be back. Mary Ann really likes it—especially the kitchen. Who's ahead?"

"The Twins."

"Good, they're going to win the division. Not only that, but we're going to be watching them in the World Series in October. See you later."

TOM SAW PETE AND LISA SMILIE enter the room and take a couple of stools at the bar. He saw Pete nudge Lisa's shoulder after glancing around and spotting him. Tom gestured for them to join him. Pete and Lisa owned the property next to Tom's roadway… their house accessed by a short roadway off the township road.

"There wasn't much left of Ben Talbot's pickup truck, was there?" Pete said after he sat down on one of the three high chairs at Tom's table.

"No, Pete, there sure wasn't. Hi, Lisa, how are your turkeys doing?" Tom asked.

"So far, four survivors—if I could get rid of that nasty gray owl, we would have more of them."

"Pete, did you know Ben Talbot very well?" Tom asked.

"No, but I went to school with his nephew."

"Who's that?"

"Reggie Logan. I hear he's back in the area. Not much good I can say about him."

"I've been over to their farm several times. I've never heard either Ben or Ralph mention a nephew," Tom said.

"That's because Reggie Logan is not one that they would be proud to mention," Pete added firmly, a snide look on his face.

Lisa took a sip of her drink and said, "If you see a slick red sports car go by, that's probably who it is."

"Where does the nephew—Reggie Logan—live?" Tom asked.

"Not sure—farther away the better," Pete said. "That no-good-for-nothing bugger beat up little Albie Pierson—left him for dead. If those bird watchers hadn't come by—who knows? Tom, how come you spent time at the Talbot farm? Have they gotten you into a tractor?"

"No, but I help 'em with their computer. They bought one a few months ago and called me to help set it up. One thing led to another and the next thing you know, they put their bookkeeping on it."

Tom hadn't heard of Reggie Logan before. He asked, "When was this Albie Pierson incident? Was it during high school days?"

"Yup, Reggie was a senior and Albie a freshman. Reggie beat him into a bloody pulp. Albie almost died. The Pierson's sued Theresa Logan. It didn't do any good—one person's word against another. Reggie could do no wrong—that's the way his mother saw it. The rest of us thought different. Never could figure out why the sheriff didn't push the matter."

"Why don't you tell Tom about Marty?" Lisa prodded.

"Then, there was Marty. He enters the picture and eventually marries Reggie's mother. Reggie did all he could do to get rid of him and finally succeeded. Poor Marty got caught stealing from the Talbot bank account—an unauthorized transfer of twenty thousand dollars. Marty denied that he signed the mailed transfer request. No one believed him. His wife divorced him and sent him on his way. I bet Reggie had something to do with the signature on that transfer. One of the bank employees had testified the signature was indeed that of Marty Bishop. It amazed me that a handwriting expert hadn't been called in. His attorney was asleep at the switch.

"Theresa sent Reggie to college. Oh, he went to college all right—never graduated. It took him only one year to run through his education money.

"Come on Lisa, let's go home. I've been talking too much—too much beer. Good seeing you, Tom."

PETE AND LISA SMILIE LIVED in a house surrounded by twenty five acres of land, most of it wooded. Their western boundary adjoined Tom Hastings's roadway. When they bought the property seven years ago, the house and outbuildings needed extensive repairs. Working together, they got rid of a ton of junk and remodeled the house. Except for the living room carpet, the project appeared finished. Tom remembered sitting on their new couch in front of the fireplace…comfortable and cozy, he thought.

Lisa was born and raised in Italy. She and Pete had met in Naples when he was in the army. They fell in love and Pete talked her into moving to America. She struggled with adjusting to country living during the first few months. Pete's love and support helped her overcome missing her family. Her new life became a rich and happy experience. She worked in a factory in Big Lakes, the county seat fifteen miles northwest of New Dresden.

Pete worked at *Lakes Electrical,* a high-tech business a few miles north of Big Lakes. He had earned his way up to management…even had his own office.

Pete had shopped for real estate for almost a year before finding the perfect place for his new bride. His love of country living had drawn him and Lisa to their current property, which they purchased through one of the realties in New Dresden. Pete's big passion is wildlife, Tom thought. He stores bags of corn in the garage to feed wild turkeys and deer.

Yesterday, Tom noticed Pete stopping at *Quality Supply* with his truck. He watched Ted roll out two large bags on a dolly—probably corn, Tom thought. Pete picked up both bags, one under each arm, and tossed them into the box. Wow, that guy is really strong. He's got to be at least six-two and two hundred pounds or more of muscle.

Tom respected Pete for saving his life when he had been stalked and threatened by a killer on his own property about four years ago. Pete had used outstanding surveillance and his deer rifle to drive away a renegade CIA agent, who had the drop on Tom and planned on shooting him. Within an hour, sheriff deputies had captured Robert Ranforth. It ended weeks of *blue darkness*…days of tension and fear.

Tom thought about their mutual neighbor Maynard Cushing,

who had been murdered by Ranforth earlier. The exiled CIA agent had lived anonymously in the community for years. Pete had affected the course of history in the New Dresden area. Ranforth is no more…life in prison…maybe not enough.

TOM WATCHED PETE AND LISA LEAVE *MARY ANN'S*. He remained at his table and thought about the negative remarks Pete had made about Reggie Logan. Tom's mind returned to the picture of a person leaping from the pickup truck. *Whoever was behind the wheel jumped out just seconds before the train hit.* The sheriff didn't believe me but he's wrong…absolutely wrong! Tom said to himself.

A loud voice interrupted Tom's thoughts. "Hey, Tom, come on over and join us. Don't be so stuck-up."

Glancing toward the table where the sound came from, he recognized a couple of friends who he had met at *Bayside* restaurant in Big Lakes…Darrin Landis and his wife Brenda. She currently managed the Bayside, a place that Tom visited often. Tom hesitated since he had planned to leave *Mary Ann's* shortly, but the invitation became compelling and he joined them.

"What 'cha doin' over there by yourself anyhow?" Darrin asked.

Tom had noticed a third person at their table, a woman. He grabbed his jacket that hung on the back of the chair and accepted the offer.

"Tom, you know my wife, Brenda. I want you to meet Jolene Hunt. She was a classmate of Brenda's—they grew up together—old buddies. Jolene lives near here on Lake Trevor. Ever heard of it?"

"Yeah, I know where it's at—just a little west of Borders Lake. I've been there. Glad to meet you Jolene."

After Jolene and Tom shock hands, Bill added, "Have some appetizers, Tom. We have some more coming—need another drink?"

"Ah, okay. How long have you lived on Lake Trevor, Jolene?" Tom asked.

"I bought the property just over a year ago."

Jolene is an attractive woman, Tom thought. She has long blond hair and a slim figure. Tom felt a warm glow inside when she smiled and touched his arm momentarily. The warmth lingered and he liked the feeling of excitement that found its way into the pit of his stomach.

"Tom, did you know Ben Talbot, the man who was killed in the train accident?" Jolene asked.

"Yes, I did. I've spent a few evenings at the farm helping Ben and his brother with their computer."

"I feel so bad. We're sort of related. I loved Ben," Jolene added.

"Related, the word around here is that the two brothers had only one living relative, their nephew Reggie."

"I would like to share the details with you, Tom, but it's too much in the past and too private."

Tom stared at the woman. "I understand. I've got something bothering me, too. It has to do with Ben Talbot and the train accident."

"Problem, what do you mean?"

"I was standing on the sidewalk in front of the hardware store when the train approached. Ben's pickup sat dead still on the tracks. I saw someone jump out just before the train hit. Whoever I saw disappeared on the other side of the train."

"I'm shocked! This is the first I've heard that—somebody else in the pickup. I wonder if the sheriff knows about that?" Jolene asked, her face masked with concern.

"Yeah, he does. Actually the sheriff came out to my place the very next day. He said he heard that I was the only witness. I remember telling him distinctly that I saw someone jump out. He didn't believe me. Maybe he thought my eyes are bad…being a senior citizen."

"The sheriff knew and he totally ignored what you said!" Jolene exclaimed as she rolled the glass in her palms.

"Well, folks, I've got to go. Thanks for the drink, Darrin—and the eats. Nice meeting you, Jolene."

TOM PICKED UP HIS TAB and left the table. He sliced into a narrow open spot at the bar next to a couple of young men. Laying his tab on the bar surface, he brought up his wallet.

The head of a dark-featured, curly haired young man at the bar turned. He looked at Tom with his dark, piercing eyes. Tom noticed a shiny, silver earring in his left ear and a tattoo on his left wrist. Tom nodded to him while waiting for the credit card to process.

Tom became uncomfortable as the young man continued to stare at him.

Tom said, "How are you doing?"

"I always do great—don't you ever forget that."

Tom didn't respond while he signed his credit card slip, feeling glad that the person had turned away. Sure sounds like a big jerk, Tom thought.

After Tom left the restaurant, he drove his pickup onto the state highway and headed for home. He thought about Brenda's classmate and how attractive she appeared. Tom wondered how she connected to the late Ben Talbot.

5

MUSIC THAT HAD SPILLED OVER from Our Savior's Lutheran Church could be heard as far away as the bank and grocery store. The funeral for Ben Talbot had begun mid-morning on Monday in New Dresden. Because of limited seating, Tom was one of several who sat on folding chairs in the church basement all-purpose room.

After the service ended, people in the lower level room waited until the church emptied before leaving. By that time the pallbearers had placed the casket in the hearse…the relatives and close friends waited in their vehicles.

A county sheriff's car escorted the steadily lengthening procession up Main Street. It crossed the railroad tracks and moved beyond the city limits, around the big curve, and onto the county highway, heading for the cemetery only two miles away. The hearse carrying Ben Talbot's body followed the sheriff's car, which continued on past the cemetery as the hearse turned onto the asphalt roadway that led to the wrought-I gate. Tom became part of the procession with his pickup...next to last in line.

TOM PARKED HIS VEHICLE and walked with others across a freshly mowed grassy area and onto the roadway. After entering the cemetery, he paused near the stone that marked the place where his wife, Becky, had been buried. Bitter thoughts of the hijackers returned. They had caused the plane to crash that killed all the passengers including his wife seven years earlier.

It's been a long time living alone, he thought. The women that he had dated since his wife's death couldn't adjust to country living. There's no way in God's heaven that I'll ever move from here again, he thought.

He joined the mourners who had gathered in a tight cluster around the gravesite. Ralph, brother of the deceased, stared straight ahead...his eye's glued to the casket...his facial expression remained stoic, not changing for a moment. Tom recognized the young man standing next to Ralph. He's the same guy I saw at *Mary Ann's* on Saturday evening, he said to himself. The earring is unmistakable. He has to the nephew that Pete had talked about. And then his eyes focused on a woman. She stood off to one side. It's the same one I met at Mary Ann's that same night.

The reverend had finished with his prayers and comments at the graveside. He tucked a black book under his arm and headed toward the wrought-I gate. Tom wandered back to his wife's grave and became absorbed in memories of a beautiful past. Loud voices interrupted his privacy and that of several others.

"I know that you did it. Why don't you admit it?" said a woman, pointing her finger.

Tom turned to look. The woman, who he had met at Mary Ann's, confronted the dark-haired young man. You would think that she would wait until they were at least out of the cemetery, he thought. First time I've ever seen a shouting match at a funeral.

"What the hell are you talking about? Leave me alone. God, Uncle Ben is not even in the ground yet," the young man responded, his face flushed. The palm of one of his hands shielded him from his accuser.

Others coming from the gravesite stared and showed expressions of disgust. A noisy pickup truck, lacking a muffler, momentarily drowned out the loud exchange between Jolene and the young man.

Tom noticed an older man standing outside the wrought iron fence, near the main gate to the cemetery. He had long gray hair that was tied into a ponytail. Tom looked at the long fingers that grasped the rail...unusually long, Tom thought. The man appeared to be interested in the loud and aggressive conversation between the dark-haired young man and Jolene Hunt.

6

JOLENE HUNT THREW HER PURSE down on a chair as she walked into her kitchen. She felt upset and knew that Reggie Logan had been spoiled rotten since getting out of diapers. Her relationship to Ben Talbot had been private. She was not about to divulge her secret that Ben Talbot had been her father. Even Ben's brother, Ralph, didn't know the truth.

Heck, I didn't even know myself until about ten years ago, she thought. If my mother hadn't died, I may have never known. Oh, how angry I was, but didn't have the heart to scold my mother. She had suffered enough and was dying. My anger took a back seat on that day while watching the tears stream down her cheek.

Fort Woods is where my mother met Ben Talbot. He was a corporal in the army...going overseas, my mother had told me. It was too much for her to bear. *"I did something wrong and you were the result,"* She had told Jolene. How can I ever forget those words? Jolene asked herself.

I knew that eventually I would have to meet my father. The regrets I have for not contacting him…almost too huge for me to bear. Too late now, she thought, while inhaling deeply. He was alive and healthy when I first saw him at the grocery store in New Dresden.

She felt that her sudden interest in the death of Ben Talbot is going to be scrutinized, she said to herself. Even if I announce publicly that Ben is my father, hardly anyone is going to believe me. I'm mortified by the thought that Reggie Logan will eventually inherit everything.

Jolene tightened her lips together and sighed. On to more pleasant thoughts, she said to herself. I liked the man who I met at Mary Ann's last Saturday. Tom Hastings is his name…he told me about seeing someone jump from the pickup, just before the train hit, she said to herself. If he actually did…*no reason he should lie about that*—then, my father's death may not have been an accident. Jolene stood at the window and looked out over the water. *Reggie Logan… he killed his own uncle! He's a criminal…I demand justice!*

Jolene worked as an abstract specialist at *Midwest Title Company* in Pine Lakes. She had about a fifteen minute drive to work each day…much shorter than the commute in Kansas City that she had put up with for ten years.

After attending the funeral in New Dresden on Monday, she went back to work on Tuesday morning. Later that afternoon, she sat at her desk tapping a pen on a notepad. I'm not concentrating on my work, she thought.

Leaving her desk she walked down the hall to the doorway of her boss, Craig. After knocking on his door lightly, she entered.

"Craig, I've been dealing with a personal problem lately and need some time. Could I have tomorrow off?"

"Sure, I guess that would be okay. Is there anything that I can do to help?"

"No thanks, Craig, but I appreciate you asking."

After studying his concerned expression for a moment, she returned to her desk and placed a call to the county attorney's office in Big Lakes. Jack McCarthy, the head prosecutor, agreed to meet with her.

THE COURTHOUSE IN BIG LAKE COUNTY is a handsome building, Jolene thought. The three-story masonry structure towered over an attractive landscape. The extra wide sidewalk that connected the street to the public entry doors is well manicured compared to the one parallel with the street. Six sitting benches are placed in strategic areas allowing visitors comfort and privacy. Jolene looked at one of the maintenance men on his knees picking up debris from underneath one of the benches as she walked up the sidewalk. She smiled, noticing him peek at her while passing.

Two massive front doors opened into a large vestibule with an open stairway. Marble steps complimented the large tiled squares that made up the floor. Choosing the stairway over an elevator, Jolene walked to the second floor where the courtroom is located. Before proceeding, a security woman, sitting at a table, asked Jolene to show her identification. After the woman returned Jolene's ID, a uniformed deputy smiled and allowed her to pass.

According to the marquis in the vestibule, the county attorney's office is near the end of the corridor, Jolene thought. She stopped in front of a frosted door with black lettering: *Big Lakes County Attorney.*

She entered and closed the door behind her. A woman dressed in red and white smiled from behind a desk. "May I help you?"

"Yes, I have an appointment with Mr. McCarthy."

The woman looked down at a paper. "Are you Jolene Hunt?"

"Yes, I am."

"Mr. McCarthy will be with you shortly. Please have a seat."

Jolene looked around the room and noticed the high ceilings. A black fan suspended from above rotated slowly, not making a sound. The door behind the receptionist opened and a young man peeked around the edge of the door.

He looked at her and asked, "Are you Jolene?"

"Yes, I am," she responded.

"Please come in," he said and extended a hand. "Hello, I'm Jack McCarthy."

The young man escorted her to a chair near his desk. He walked around and sat in a black, high-back office chair.

"What can I do for you, ah—? Is it Miss or Mrs.?"

Jolene smiled. "Miss, thank you." She cleared her throat. "Have you heard about the train accident in New Dresden, Mr. McCarthy?"

"Yes, I sure have. I understand a New Dresden farmer was killed. Tragic—his pickup lodged on the crossing—must have had a heart attack. That's what the sheriff and medical examiner said."

She shifted in her chair and leaned forward slightly. "That's exactly the reason I'm here. I met this man—a gentleman who was a witness. He told me there was a second person in the pickup truck. This man saw someone jump out of the pickup truck just before the train hit."

Jolene noticed McCarthy furrow his forehead and raise his eyebrows. He is staring at me, she thought. I wonder if the bitterness and anger are showing in my eyes.

"Who is this person that told you that, Miss Hunt?" McCarthy asked.

"His name is Tom Hastings. He was nearest the accident when it happened. He lives on a lake near New Dresden, on Borders Lake, I think."

"When and where did this witness tell you that story?"

"Ah, it was last Saturday at *Mary Ann's* restaurant."

"*Mary Ann's*, that's a good restaurant. I take my wife there for dinner often. How well do you know this witness—the one you mentioned, Tom Hastings?"

"I just met him that evening."

"I see. Are you related to the deceased, Miss Hunt?"

"Well, yes and no."

"What do you mean by, yes and no?"

Jolene held her breath for a moment. She looked up at the ceiling and fidgeted with her hands. "Oh well. This is going to come out sooner or later. Ben Talbot was my paternal father. That fact has been a well-kept secret, known by only a handful of people. My mother and most others, who were aware of my secret, have passed away. Mr. McCarthy, I trust that my relationship to Ben Talbot will remain confidential."

McCarthy's lips tightened. "Did Hastings say who it was that jumped from the pickup at the last second?"

"No, but I have a pretty good idea who it was."

"Who?"

"Ben Talbot's nephew, Reggie Logan."

"That's a serious statement, Miss Hunt, especially if Hastings didn't recognize the person who jumped—and there appears to be some disagreement that someone actually did."

Jolene answered abruptly, "I believe Hastings. He was closest to the scene. Besides, why would he lie about seeing someone?"

"Miss Hunt, there's going to be a hearing that will decide how Ben Talbot died. Other than your statement this morning, there's no reason to suspect Talbot's death was caused by anything else—other than an accident. The sheriff didn't mention anything about Hastings. Our medical examiner didn't mention any complications regarding the cause of death. God, there wasn't much left—oh, sorry." The attorney hung his head.

Jolene nodded her head. "That's okay, Mr. McCarthy, I understand." She moved forward slightly in her chair. "Tom Hastings told me that the sheriff came to see him the day after the accident. He told the sheriff what he saw—the person jump from the pickup. He also said the sheriff didn't believe him. Why don't you talk to him—Hastings?" Jolene asked.

"Hmm, maybe I will. Thanks for coming in, Miss Hunt. I'll look into this matter—I'll discuss it with Mr. Hastings and the sheriff."

"Thanks, Mr. McCarthy."

STEVE STEIGER FELT STUNNED. He had taken his mother to her medical appointment yesterday. After her examination, the doctor called them into his office. He had bad news. The cancer in his mother's body had spread and she had less than six months to live.

Steve originally handled the diagnosis with much more difficulty than did his mother. The news had come only the previous day, but his mind continued to fill with tragic thoughts of his mother dying. He heard her humming in the kitchen while preparing breakfast.

My suitcase is packed and I'm scheduled to pick up a load in Fargo later in the day, he said to himself. My biggest concern is leaving his mother alone. "I don't like the idea of leaving you alone, Mom," he said earlier in the morning.

"Oh, don't worry about me, Steve. I'll be just fine. Martha will keep an eye on me," she had replied, smiling.

He began imagining living alone in the house. Steve had never known any other home. He had never been interested in women, mainly because his mother discouraged him when he first began dating. "They're out for only one thing—money," she had told him over and over again.

When he looked in the mirror, he realized he wasn't any *Clark Gable,* but not all that bad. The thick reddish hair that spread into a smart looking beard was attractive. Steve took a lot of pride in keeping his beard trimmed, not like some of the guys he worked with. My handsome six-foot frame is slim and doesn't have any defects, he thought.

Steve's number one hobby was reading, mainly books about the old west. His bedroom had two walls of shelves, all filled with paperbacks. Once a year, he would go over his collection and select a bunch that he would donate to a Big Lakes charity. Steve would often lie in bed imagining himself on a white stallion, galloping along at top speed, guns-a-blazing. Time to grow up, he thought. The only white stallion around here right now is my truck.

Steve, over his mother's objections, had bought a satellite dish and he subscribed to a country western network. The nights he spent at home were mainly in his room watching cowboy westerns. He scolded himself for looking forward to having a television downstairs in the living room. His mother was against having a television in the house.

Over his mother's objections, he would leave her occasionally and spend the evening at *William's Pub.* Steve established a friendship with the new owner, Billy Hartman, who had purchased the bar and grill from Hector Mathison. Steve's most recent excursion to the pub resulted in downing four beers. Before he had left the bar, he fantasized dating the bar waitress. She has a nice build, he thought. I wonder if she has a boyfriend. The smile he had gotten from her each time she brought over a beer turned him on. On one occasion he placed his fingers over her hand–she didn't pull it back.

7

THE VISITING TEAM'S DUGOUT on the baseball field in New Dresden had been tipped over, exposing a mass of twisted 2-by-4's. Good thing the season is over, Tom thought, approaching the railroad tracks in his pickup truck. He glanced at the speedometer on Thursday morning, making sure it read under forty. He smiled seeing a sheriff's car parked on the side of the road near the tracks. *Purgatory Curve* will not punish me today, he thought.

The speed limit changed abruptly from forty to thirty miles per hour when rounding the curve. Because of a heavy stand of trees, the sign doesn't become visible until it is sometimes too late to slow down. It all depends on how fast one goes in the forty-zone, he said to himself.

After fishing out his mail from a box in the post office, Tom headed to *Stillman's Super Market*.

"Hi, Tom," Ellie said.

He laid down a newspaper and a dollar. She handed him a quarter in change and they swapped weather information.

"Going to get cold," she said.

Crossing the street, Tom headed for *Borders Café*. Pushing the door open, he saw Henry sitting at his usual spot…two years haven't changed my friend Henry, he said to himself.

"That was quite the wind we had last night," Henry said.

Tom ran a thumbnail across the dip just under his lower lip. "Yeah, I noticed one of the dugouts at the ball diamond is tipped over."

"Worse than that, the steeple blew off the church and left a gaping hole. Didn't you see the blue plastic up there?" Henry asked.

"No, I didn't. Which church was that?"

"Our Saviors Lutheran—it's the one you can see from the grocery store."

Henry's smile turned to a frown. "Word around town is that you saw someone jump out of Ben Talbot's pickup truck—just before the train hit."

"Word sure gets around, doesn't it? I mentioned it to only one person the day of the accident," Tom said.

Henry smiled and said, "Not too many secrets around here."

"I suppose you were in for a haircut and heard it at the barber shop. Floyd Pella was the only one I told that day, except for the sheriff the next day," Tom said.

Henry smiled. "Well no. Actually, I heard it at the hardware store."

"Being gone the last couple of years, I must have missed a ton of news."

Henry laughed. "Nothing really big happened until you got back. You must be the town jinx."

After discussing some of the news from the front page of the daily newspaper, Henry got up and headed for the checkout counter.

"Heading back for your usual nap, Henry?" Tom asked.

Henry smiled and said, "It's all part of the job."

Tom drove toward his home and neared the cemetery when a red car came up close behind him. It sharply veered and begin to pass. After coming abreast, it slowed and Tom recognized the young man, who drove the car. He had seen him at the bar at Mary Ann's and at the funeral. Instead of passing, the car shifted closer to the midline.

"Damn! Get over!" Tom exclaimed loudly.

Instead, the car moved dangerously close. Tom's pickup was on the shoulder and he began to brake—the truck lurched as the right front tire negotiated the unpaved shoulder of the road. The red car sped ahead, leaving Tom fighting to keep the pickup from going into the ditch. After a series of sways, his truck settled back onto the road. What the heck was that all about? He said to himself angrily, while watching the speeding car disappear over the hill.

Reporting this incident would be a waste of time, Tom thought. I didn't even get the license number. Even if I did, would the driver have his keys taken away? Would the driver go to jail? My brother from Washington would've reported this, Tom thought. He calls the police if a car radio is too loud.

When Tom got home, his answering machine beeped. The message came from Jack McCarthy, the county attorney of Big Lake's County. Tom still felt angry and upset about the incident on the highway. Tom returned the call. A representative from the county attorney's office requested a meeting with Mr. McCarthy.

After hanging up the phone, Tom muttered, "Here I go again—the devil is following me around."

TOM'S BOOTS CLATTERED ON THE MARBLE STEPS at Big Lakes County courthouse as he made his way up to the second floor. Tom responded to the county attorney's request and agreed to meet on Friday. He wore his black boots that he normally reserved for special occasions such as funerals and weddings. Tom felt that the upcoming courthouse meeting qualified.

After passing through security on the second floor, he moved down the corridor and entered Jack McCarthy's office. The attorney stood next to the receptionist desk.

"You must be Tom Hastings."

"Yes, I am. Did you call me in to ask about the train-pickup collision?"

"Yes, exactly that, would you come in and take a seat? Right over there would be fine," McCarthy pointed. "This shouldn't take too much of your time.

"I received information that you witnessed the train-pickup truck accident in New Dresden. Is that correct?"

"Yes, it is."

"Would you describe what you saw exactly the way you saw it?"

"I had just come out of the hardware store and heard the train's horn."

"What direction was the train coming from?"

"From the southeast—well, I think that's what direction it was. Main Street in New Dresden is confusing regarding direction. Have you ever looked at that big wooden map?"

Jack McCarthy laughed and said, "Continue, Mr. Hastings. What happened next?"

"I saw a pickup trapped between the flashing gates. And then suddenly the train wheels screeched God-awful. Just before the train hit the pickup, I saw the door open and someone jump out."

"Which door?"

"The driver's side."

"Did you recognize who it was?"

"No, I didn't, but it was someone agile—a young man, I thought."

"So, after the collision, the train traveled a distance before stopping. That would mean whoever you saw would be out of sight all that time, while the train slowed. Is that correct?"

"Yes, Mr. McCarthy."

"Thank you very much, Mr. Hastings. If I need your testimony, would you be willing to attend a hearing?"

"Yes, I would. When will it be held?"

"Approximately a week from today. I'll let you know as soon as it's put on the docket."

"Okay."

"Have a good day."

Tom left the courthouse and headed for the bookstore. His friends Susan and Joe had moved their store to the other side of Main Street. The woman behind the counter greeted Tom when he entered.

"Hi, Tom, we've got the book you ordered."

"Great, Trisha. I was hoping it was in. Where are Joe and Susan?"

"They're out to lunch, and should be back in a few minutes."

"I'll wait."

Tom browsed around for a few minutes and made another selection…a mystery novel. It was a story about a series of murders that took place in the lake country. Title: *Sleep Six*.

"Hi, Tom," said a voice from behind him.

Susan and Joe had arrived. Tom got the big hug from Susan and the usual firm handshake from Joe. The marks from Velcro straps of a golf glove were still evident on the back of Joe's hand.

"So, how many holes did you get in this morning, Joe?" Tom asked.

"Shh—" Joe whispered. "I've been raking the leaves in the yard," he said.

"Yeah, lots of leaves this year, Joe," Tom responded, chuckling. "Did you guys hear about the train accident?"

"Wasn't that awful?" Trisha said.

"Poor Ben Talbot," Susan remarked. "He must have had a heart attack, and stopped the pickup on the tracks without knowing where he was."

"I'm not so sure, Susan. There was someone else in the pickup. I was a witness."

"What's all that? Someone else! There were two people killed?" Trisha asked seriously.

Tom rubbed his chin with two fingers. "No, there was only one person killed. The other person jumped clear."

"Hmm—that's the first time I've heard that one," Joe said.

"You'll hear more. I'm testifying at an official hearing regarding the death."

"Hearing, huh—when's that gonna be?" Joe asked.

"Next week—gotta go, see you guys later," Tom said. He paid for his purchases and left.

8

TOM HASTINGS HAD NEVER ATTENDED A DEATH HEARING before. He appreciated the informality compared to his experience with being a witness in a civil trial, and a jury member at a criminal trial.

Two weeks had passed since the accident. Medical Examiner Dr.

Grady Bar presided at the hearing and asked Tom the same questions as the county attorney had done earlier. As Tom answered, he looked into the anxious eyes of his previous questioner Jack McCarthy, sitting at the opposite end of the table.

Dr. Bar said, "Thank you very much, Mr. Hastings. I would like you to remain while—I—ah—question the two engineers."

Tom's heart skipped a beat…his face flushed…the two trainmen's firm facial expressions meant only one thing to Tom…especially with one of them shaking their heads. They aren't going to agree with me, he said to himself.

"Now, Mr. Manning, would you give me your full name and what you do for a living?"

"I'm Sully Manning. I'm a locomotive engineer employed by Canadian National Railway."

"Were you driving the freight train that struck a pickup truck in New Dresden on Thursday, September 16 of this year?"

"Yes, I was."

"Would you tell the panel what you saw?"

"After rounding a curve and approaching New Dresden, I saw a pickup truck on the tracks between the gates. It appeared stalled—just sat there."

"What did you do then?"

"I yelled at Brian. He pushed the brake lever with all he had. Didn't do much good. We were too close—couldn't stop in time. It was terrible—never hit anyone before." Sully dropped his chin and put a hand over his face.

"Did you see anyone in or around the pickup?"

"Nope. No one."

"What direction was the truck heading? Was it coming into town or going out?"

"It was heading out of town, toward the ball diamond."

"Thank you very much, Mr. Manning."

The next witness, Brian Retzlaff the conductor agreed with everything that the engineer had said. Tom sat in stoic silence while listening to the answers. Glancing at the panelists, it looked obvious to him that they believed the trainmen. Tom's eyes locked on one of them, a woman. Her expression full of doubt…none of them believed me, Tom thought disgustingly.

After Doctor Bar finished, he nodded at the county attorney. Attorney General McCarthy looked at Tom. "Mr. Hastings, could you have been mistaken seeing someone—ah—jump out of the pickup truck?"

Tom stuck to his guns and insisted that he saw a person jump from the truck. His feelings turned to mild anger when noticing the grins on the faces of the engineer and conductor.

"Thank you very much for coming, Mr. Hastings. You're excused," the doctor announced.

Tom felt dejected when prodding down the marble stairway. During his return drive from Big Lakes, Tom begin to doubt himself. Maybe, *I didn't see someone jump.*

9

JOLENE HUNT SAT AT HER DESK overlooking Main Street in Pine Lakes. The county hearing regarding her father's death happened yesterday. She felt devastated after hearing about the results. I'm going to have a hard time working on abstracts today, she thought. How could they…all those intelligent people…not believe Tom Hastings? Instead they came up with a disturbing conclusion… *the death of Ben Talbot was caused by the impact of the freight train– accidental.*

Looking out the window, she saw Tom Hastings drive by in his pickup. Jolene set down the document that she reviewed and got up off of her chair. I wonder if he is also affected by the decision, she thought. Tom may feel dejected, too. No one believed him at the hearing except me.

She watched as he stopped his pickup in a parking lot at the dental office of *Dr. Styles, Family Dentistry.* As Jolene watched him enter the dental office, she felt the need to talk to him. Quickly she scrawled a note. *Please meet me at the Locomotive at noon. I'm buy-*

ing. She signed it and left her office. "I'll be right back, Terry," she said to the woman behind the front desk.

TOM ENTERED THE DENTIST'S RECEPTION ROOM and felt pleasantly surprised by the fresh smell…not usual in a dental office because of all the medications they used.

"Mr. Hastings, you're on time. I'll tell Beth that you're here."

He smiled at Jody, the receptionist. She returned his smile and continued punching the keyboard at an amazing speed, Tom thought. The door opened and a woman entered pulling on the arm of a young boy.

"No. I'm not going in there," the boy shrieked.

"Ah, it's not going to hurt. You can't go another night with that toothache."

"I don't care. I'm not going in there."

Jody's fingers came to a stop. Her head turned toward the new-comers, a frown on her face. Tom expected the next hour to be noisy. He gazed above the newspaper and remembered the first toothache that he had experienced during grade school days. It wasn't fun… the dental assistant wiping the tears away from my cheeks.

One of the dental hygienists entered the waiting room. "Right this way, Mr. Hastings," she said. She beckoned with her fingers and Tom followed her into a room and took a seat on a dental chair. She took his glasses and chained on a bib.

In the next ten minutes, he experienced the scratching sounds of a dental instrument working the root walls of his incisors, cupids, bicuspids and molars. Later came the gritty feeling of a gray powder that she had retrieved from a mini paper cup. The rotating rubber tool slurped over his enamel, returning for a refill, over and over.

"Close your lips," she said after placing a plastic tube into his mouth.

The tube gurgled as it emptied the debris from his mouth. He took a deep breath and reopened his mouth. A few minutes later Dr. Styles entered.

"How does everything feel?" he asked.

"Gritty," Tom answered.

Dr. Styles sat on his stool, laughed and picked up a mirror with one hand and a sharp looking instrument with the other. He proceeded to peck around all the teeth. "How do things look to you?" he asked Beth.

"Fine—always fine with him—his teeth appear to be in great shape."

"Okay, Tom. I agree. Beth is right. Things look good."

It always feels so fresh to have my teeth cleaned, Tom thought after paying his bill and leaving the dental office. He unlocked his pickup and got inside. After inserting the key in the ignition, he noticed a piece of paper stuck under the windshield wiper. Stepping outside, he jerked the note off the windshield. After reading it, he smiled and muttered, "An attractive woman is going to buy me lunch—yes!"

After parking his truck on Main Street, he walked toward the restaurant. He enjoyed visiting and shopping in Pine Lakes. There are an amazing number of small shops and businesses for a town of only about four thousand, he thought. Pausing across the street from a furniture store, he looked down at the brick-faced sidewalk…nice touch. Tom made a mental note to check out the lawn chairs that are displayed outside.

Continuing toward the *Locomotive,* he stopped for a red light before crossing the street. Pine Lakes is large enough for two sets of traffic lights. When the light turned green, Tom crossed the street and entered the restaurant. He didn't spot Jolene.

"Only one?" the hostess asked.

"No. I'm meeting someone," Tom answered and continued to look down the line of booths. He saw a wave…Jolene. She sat in a booth at the other end of the room. Tom took a seat across from her.

"Hi, Tom. I see you got my note."

"Sure did, what's up?" asked Tom smiling and happy that he fell into a pleasant situation.

The waitress arrived and asked, "Are you ready to order?"

"You first, Jolene," Tom said.

After they ordered, Jolene said, "First of all, it's nice to see you again. I'm upset with the results of the hearing on the cause of Ben Talbot's death. I read the results in the newspaper this morning. You testified, didn't you?"

"Yes, I did and the conclusion didn't help my ego very much."

"They didn't believe you, did they?"

Tom inhaled deeply. "No, they didn't and it was mainly because neither of the two train men saw anyone jump."

"How many of them were there—the train drivers?"

"There were two, an engineer and a conductor. Apparently, it was their word against mine."

"Tom, I called the county attorney, McCarthy, this morning. I am going to contest the hearing result."

"Contest it! Why? Ben Talbot wasn't a relative, was he?"

Jolene's eyes looked down at the table. "I'm his daughter!"

Tom narrowed his eyes and tightened his finger on the porcelain ear of the coffee cup, just short of his mouth. "You were his daughter!" he exclaimed. "I heard that Reggie Logan was the only living relative."

"Look, Tom. Would you spare me any questions? Just believe me. I believe you."

Tom stared at his new friend and thought, what the heck am I getting into here? He looked out the window and noticed the brick surfaced sidewalk had the usual bustle of people walking to-and-fro.

"I'm not going to leave this alone, Tom. I think that little guttersnipe of a Reggie Logan killed my father. I would appreciate it if you would stick by your story. Sooner or later, someone is going to believe you."

"Well, Jolene. I'll stick to my story, but the crash is probably a done deal."

Jolene picked up the slip. "I've got to get back to work. Thanks for coming over. It's my treat today."

They walked out onto the sidewalk and shook hands. The handshake lasted longer than usual, Tom thought as he looked into her eyes. He pulled on her arm and forced a hug. Geez, she makes me feel warm all over, he said to himself as he watched her cross the street.

Tom walked toward his pickup and saw a young man standing on the sidewalk. What's he doing resting his hand on the hood of my pickup? Tom asked himself.

Tom stopped and said, "Yes?"

"So, what are you and that bitch plotting? Huh!"

"Look, you—Reggie or whoever you are. I didn't like what you did to me on the highway the other day. Another move like that and you'll be hearing from the sheriff."

"What move? What highway?"

"So, Jolene is right. You are a guttersnipe."

Tom pushed Reggie's arm off the hood and walked around to the driver's side. He opened the door and paused. His adversary had a smug looking smile on his face. I'd sure like to plunk my fist into that snoot, Tom thought, but instead I best get into my pickup and get out of here.

10

THE DAYS OF SEPTEMBER IN MINNESOTA brought about the expected changes in the landscape. Some of the maple tree leaves had begun to turn bright red. Virginia creeper vines that lined the Hastings's greenway to the west had changed from a dark green to a deep, dark red.

The greenway, about the size of two football fields, is a grassy mowed area west of the tennis court. It's bordered by a large stand of trees on the south and three rows of young spruce and pine trees to the north. A small open, cultivated field marks the western boundary

Tom went for a walk that Friday afternoon. He saw a flock of ducks pass overhead. He watched as they set their wings and glide downward toward the water...the spring hatch is getting conditioned for the eventual flight south.

Turning north, he headed up the trail that led into the woods. The memory of moose visiting his land three years ago remained fresh in his mind. He continually scanned the trails for a sign of their tracks. It appears as if the moose have gone for good, Tom thought.

Not so with Prancer my favorite deer, Tom said to himself while staring at huge deer tracks in the soft soil…he's still here. Tom remembered how Prancer had objected to the moose invading his land. The big deer would courageously stand out in the open field and just stare at me. I knew that Prancer was sending me a message. *This is my territory. Get rid of the moose.* No one's ever believed my moose-deer story, and I can't blame them, but it's true.

On the return walk to the house, he passed the tennis court. Stopping, he reflected on all the court activity during the summer months. Tom was hoping for a few warmer days…he wasn't quite ready to take the net down, not just yet.

After returning to the house, he made a phone call. "Hello, may I speak to Jolene Hunt?"

"Sure, just a moment please."

"Hi. This is Jolene."

"Jolene. This is Tom Hastings. Would you like to go out for dinner this evening?" Tom asked nervously, his voice crackling.

"What a nice surprise. I certainly would. Do you know where I live?"

"Lake Trevor, isn't it? Tom asked smiling.

Jolene laughed. "Yes, west of county highway 14. My address is 5203 West Trevor Drive—any idea where that is?"

"I'll find it. How would 7:00 be?"

"Perfect. I'll see you then."

Tom hung up the phone, sat there and wondered if his decision had been the right thing. That woman is surrounded by controversy, he thought. She and Reggie Logan are enemies. I may get myself caught right in the middle…the young punk is harassing me already. Oh well, a good Chardonnay will fix that.

RALPH TALBOT CONTINUED TO FEEL DEPRESSED. For the first time in his life, he and his brother would not bring in the corn together. Ralph visited New Dresden that morning and saw Edgar Sandvik drive by in his beat-up Dodge pickup. Ralph smiled receiving the usual stiff salute that Edgar was well-known for. Ralph felt good and walked up the sidewalk to where the Edgar had parked.

He saw Edgar exit the truck and with quick, jerky strides enter Stillman's Super Market. Ralph followed him into the store.

He didn't see Ellie at her usual spot, the main checkout counter. Instead she worked on inventory in the first aisle.

"Hi, Ralph. How's it going today?" she asked and returned to her station to take care of the rapidly advancing Edgar Sandvik.

"Slow down, Edgar," Ellie said. "There's not a fire, you know."

Edgar pulled his billfold out of his back pocket and asked, "How much?"

"Edgar, I need to talk to you," Ralph interrupted.

"What about? I'm busy. Can't you see?"

"Ah, get real, Edgar. Come on outside when you're finished. I'll be by your pickup."

Edgar grabbed the paper bag and headed out the door. He saw Ralph leaning against his truck.

"Careful, Ralph. Don't scratch it," Edgar said and burst out laughing.

"Edgar, I need some help with the corn this fall. Would you be interested?"

"Yeah, I'll help out—your brother being gone and all that. When are you starting?"

"Next Monday, I think."

"I'll be there at 7:00 in the morning, sharp."

Ralph felt pleased that Edgar would help him, even though the fidgety one couldn't drive a truck straight. Ralph also intended to ask Ned Stockwell to help. When Ralph returned home, he spent time entering invoices on the computer. Setting on the desk were two copies of a will that he had drawn up on behalf of he and his brother. He had created the will by himself using computer software. He intended to surprise his mentor Tom Hastings...show him that his tutoring had succeeded.

MARTY BISHOP'S REPUTATION HAD BEEN RUINED. My step-nephew and the sheriff railroaded me, he thought bitterly. They got me convicted on a theft charge…a felony. At least I didn't have to spend any time in jail. I've always wondered why the prosecutor recommended mercy to the judge.

He had been totally frustrated with a witness, who testified and insisted the signature on the money transfer was his. No jail, but the conviction depleted all his savings to pay the twenty thousand dollars to the bank and a fifty thousand dollar fine.

Marty sipped on a cup of coffee in his small apartment in New Dresden. The smoke from the cigarette that he laid down in an ashtray spiraled upward. Some of the coffee splashed out onto the floor when he rose from the chair heading to the pot for a refill.

He had agreed to divorce Theresa because he couldn't stand her son, Reggie. Marty and Theresa kept putting off signing the papers and they actually never did finalize. Later, Marty had decided to go after Ben and Ralph, to get paid the quarter-million dollars that the court had wrongfully assessed him. It was their bank account that he had been accused of stealing from.

They laughed in my face when I approached them on the matter, he thought bitterly. They wouldn't even consider a compromise. "Find another sucker," Ralph had said and doubled-up with laughter.

The anger Marty felt didn't go away. He didn't steal a nickel and nobody believed him. His felony conviction had followed him to Kansas. He finally had to settle for a job with a road construction contractor. After being bored to death for five years and working as a highway flagman, he quit his job. Packing his belongings together, he had returned to New Dresden, Minnesota.

Marty insisted on clearing his name and gain compensation for his loss. His first visit to a lawyer in the New Dresden bank building didn't go very well. The lawyer told Marty that his premise for a lawsuit would be a hard sell. "You would have to prove that the signature on the money transfer wasn't yours. "You would have to get the witness to admit that she had lied–that may be next to impossible, especially since she had moved away."

It was the money transfer document that got me convicted, Marty thought. I wonder what the sheriff had against me. He had said that I threatened and abused Reggie Logan. So I pushed the brat around a little, what's the big deal. *"Bishop hit Reggie Logan with his palm—in the face—drew blood,"* the sheriff had testified.

An aggravating case of arthritis had settled into Marty's left elbow. He felt thankful that he could us Medicare to help defray the expenses of his clinic visits. The costs of the daily medications that he needed accumulated on his credit cards–they were close to being maxed. His tenure as an executive with a manufacturing company in Big Lakes did provide enough retirement money to pay rent and keep a vehicle running…and that's about all, he thought.

My only hope may be with that bully of a sheriff, he thought. Perhaps it's time to mend that fence and build a new one. This time I'll be in it.

He tucked his billfold into a shabby gray coat, which kept him warm in September. I'll need a warmer coat when winter comes. He pulled the brim of the gray hat down over his eyes, headed down the steps and out the front door.

BIG PINE CASINO APPEARED CROWDED. Marty Bishop walked up and down the gaming aisles slowly. The brim of his gray hat, pulled low over his eyes. The guy should be here, he thought.

Marty had walked several of the aisles and searched for a certain person. In a far corner of the massive casino room, he saw a group of individuals gathered at a short row of colorful machines. *There he is.* Marty had recognized the puffy ruddy cheeks that welled up from underneath the brim of a white cowboy hat.

He approached and stood behind the big man for a few minutes listening to the garbled utterance of a mixed bag of curse words. Marty lit a cigarette, not knowing whether smoking was allowed. The man's stomach bulged over his belt buckle. It's gotten a lot bigger, Marty thought.

The big man turned his head. Their eyes locked. "Well, well—if it isn't the Marty man. Heard you moved back he-ah."

Marty stood and stared. "TA, I'm willing to let bygones be bygones. If you've got some time, I'd like to talk to ya'."

"Sure. Time for a break anyhow. Tell you what. You scoot over to the bar over there. I'll join you in a minute," said the big man, pointing.

Marty nodded, took a deep drag of a cigarette and looked around. "Just think, people. You elected this monster. You're a bunch of idiots," he whispered to himself.

11

TOM BECAME CONCERNED THAT HIS DINNER DATE would feel uncomfortable going out in a pickup. Driving slowly in a wooded area west of the county highway, he found the sign that read, "West Trevor Lake Drive." After following it for about a mile and seeing an address marker of 5203, he turned onto an asphalt driveway.

Jolene answered the doorbell and appeared ready to go. She had on a black dress and gold jewelry. In heels, she's almost as tall as I am, Tom thought.

 You look super sharp," said Tom nervously.

She laughed when Tom opened the passenger side door to his pickup.

"How am I going to get up there, in this?" she asked.

"A little push and you're in."

"Where are you taking me?" she asked.

"To Mary Ann's," Tom answered.

"Oh great, that's where we met, isn't it?"

"Yup, it is," Tom said.

After helping his date out of the truck, Tom escorted her to the entry foyer of the restaurant.

"Hello again!" exclaimed Mary Ann. She had a stack of menus in her arms.

"A table for two—non-smoking," Tom said.

"Right this way, folks."

Mary Ann appeared all smiles. Her husband Harold had over-come previous challenges and they both appeared to be happy with the restaurant. Harold waved from the bar area when Tom glanced in his direction. After seating her customers, Mary Ann said, "Jackie will be with you shortly."

"What looks good to you?" Tom asked his date.

"It all looks good. I'm starved," Jolene said with a wide smile.

"I'm in a good mood today and feel like ordering a bottle of wine. Will you help me drink it?" Tom asked.

"I'll do my share."

"Well, things have quieted down the past week, in and around New Dresden. What about Pine Lakes?"

"Tom, I'm going to continue to try to expose Reggie Logan. The guttersnipe continues to hang around where I work. I think its harassment. Some days, he parks across the street, gets out of his car and leans against it, continually staring toward my office window."

Tom frowned and his regret deepened at not being believed at the hearing. "That's absurd! Perhaps you should report him to the sheriff."

"From what I've heard so far, the sheriff is a family friend of the Logans. He was close to Reggie's mother. Just how close, I don't know. I need to find out more about that. Have you heard any-thing?"

"No, I don't know much about the Logan's," Tom said.

"I heard the sheriff had a lot to do with Theresa getting divorced in the first place. Then, he had something to do with her new hus-band, leaving town, after she died. Marty is his name…Marty Bish-op."

"Theresa. So that's what her name is, the former wife of Marty Bishop. What does this Marty Bishop look like?" Tom asked.

"Long gray hair with a pony tail, I hear."

"Whoa—that's the guy I may have seen at the cemetery. He was watching you and Reggie Logan slug it out."

"I didn't notice him—too busy taking care of the guttersnipe. Would you believe that one of Logan's eyes was wet at the funeral, as if he'd shed a tear," Jolene said angrily.

"How about changing the subject?" Tom asked. "Jolene, the Internet is predicting fifty degrees tomorrow. Would you like to play some tennis? I have a court at my place."

"Well, I haven't played in some time but I surely would like to try. I could sure use the diversion."

"If you like, bring your swimsuit—a hot tub awaits you."

"That sounds grand. I can't wait."

Tom pushed the brake in his pickup after the headlights shone on two deer in a ditch not far from Jolene's house. The vehicle swayed slightly, and Jolene grabbed his right arm. He felt the squeeze, which made him feel warm everywhere inside. He smiled, but wasn't sure what the feeling meant.

After parking in her driveway, he exited his pickup and walked around the other side. Tom opened the door, and assisted her out.

"Good night, Tom. I had a wonderful time," Jolene said.

"So did I," he responded and hugged her tight.

She stayed in the embrace for a moment, and backed away. Looking up into his eyes, she turned to open the door. Tom stood and watched as Jolene entered her house and did not look back.

TOM SPOTTED A DEPUTY SHERIFF CAR as he rounded *Purgatory Curve* on Saturday morning. The overhead lights flashed and he saw a small red car parked in front of the deputy's. Tom expected to see Reggie Logan in the driver's seat. Tom shook his head...it's not the menace in the car. The driver appeared taller than Reggie and wore a gray hat...a gray ponytail extended from under the hat. Same guy that Jolene and I talked to last night, Tom thought.

Tom slowed the pickup to thirty and crossed the railroad tracks. After parking next to King Realty, he entered the mailroom and noticed two men looking out the window. I've never seen those two guys before, he thought. That's sure a swanky leather jacket one of them is wearing.

The two men stopped talking after Tom had entered, and he wondered why. When Tom opened the door to leave, one of them turned toward him...their eyes locked for a moment. The man quickly looked away.

Tom entered Stillman's and saw another stranger standing next to the front window, also looking out. Tom grabbed a basket, tossed in a couple of newspapers and moved up an aisle. When he approached the checkout counter, the stranger looking out the window hadn't left. One of John Stillman's daughters ran the main clerking counter. Ellie didn't work on Saturdays.

"Thanks. Have a nice day, Mr. Hastings," the young woman said.

Tom picked up the bag and looked out the window, beyond the stranger. The two men, who he had seen in the post office had crossed the street and walked toward the bank. The man wearing the leather jacket raised an arm and he looked back at the checkout girl. She frowned and shrugged her shoulders.

Tom walked outside and headed up the sidewalk toward the hardware store. He saw the red car, which the deputy sheriff had stopped earlier, parked next to *Borders Café*. The man with the gray ponytail stood next to it, facing the two men, who Tom had seen in the Post Office. They stood in front of the bank. Tom looked toward the grocery store and watched as the stranger, who he had seen earlier in front of the window, cross the street.

After reaching the sidewalk on the other side, the man from the grocery store headed toward the ponytail man. They both got into the red car.

At the same time, the two men in front of the bank had gotten into a different car. They pulled out onto Main Street, hesitated at the stop sign and took a right. The red car followed.

Tom pulled his pickup into the parking lot at *Banyon's Lumber.*

"What can we do for ya' today, Tom?" Chuck asked.

"I need six sheets of 3/8s plywood—both sides rough is okay."

After backing his pickup close to the opening of the storage shed, Tom opened his end-gate and helped Chuck load the plywood. Tom liked the smell of fresh lumber. Building things is so positive, he thought. It's going up rather than down. Forward ever, backward never…his high school class motto.

Chuck's brother Perry sat in his office talking on the phone when Tom signed the invoice. Tom paused and looked at the framed photographs on the walls. There must be ten bagged geese lined up in front of their shotguns, he thought.

When Tom crossed the tracks heading out of town, he noticed the deputy sheriff's car maintained its position, still looking for speeders. He made sure his speedometer read under forty as he approached *Purgatory Curve.* Groceries and refreshments are expensive enough without adding the additional cost of a speeding ticket, he thought.

Tom looked forward to Jolene's visit. He spent a couple of hours dusting and doing general cleaning. No doubt, she would think of his home as a bachelor pad...he didn't want to turn her off and expected her at 4:00.

Jolene's Toyota pulled into Tom's driveway on time. She stepped out onto the driveway dressed in sweats and a tennis racquet in hand. "Hi, Tom, I'm ready," she said confidently.

"Yeah, I can see that. Okay, let's head out to the court." The last Saturday in September has turned out beautiful, Tom thought. The sky is blue and there isn't any wind.

Tom and Jolene played tennis for an hour. After they returned to the house, Tom snapped the caps off of a couple of beers and they sat on the deck.

"What's the latest on you and the county attorney, Jolene?"

"There's nothing new since we talked last—well, not exactly—"

Tom elevated his chin slightly and turned toward her, waiting... expecting more.

"I talked to a friend of mine yesterday. She works in New Dresden. She said that she had heard the Ben Talbot death was no accident. I'm not alone—others are talking."

"Are they also talking about a speedy red car?" Tom asked.

Jolene laughed lightly. "No, not really—most of the talk is about the pickup, and your version of what happened before the crash."

"Speaking of red cars, a deputy sheriff stopped one for speeding earlier today. It was the gray-haired, ponytail guy," Tom.

"Marty Bishop, so he drives a red car, too."

"Well, there could be another person with a gray ponytail, but it looked like the same man I saw at the cemetery—the day of Ben's funeral."

"As I had told you before, I didn't see him. I was too busy fighting with the guttersnipe," Jolene replied sharply.

"Jolene, almost every time I go into New Dresden, something happens—well, not always, but just today, I saw strangers, just hanging around—standing and watching."

She laughed. "Strange characters—there's plenty of them around New Dresden, for sure."

"Oh, I just remembered. One of them got into a red car—looked like the one that the speeder drove—Marty Bishop, perhaps."

"Hmm, maybe they're going to rob the bank," Jolene said jokingly.

The hot tub, steaks on the grill and the wine…the evening went well.

"It's getting late, Tom. I need to get home," Jolene said quietly while stretched out on the sectional in Tom's den.

Tom wished that she would stay longer. "Jolene, I understand."

Tom walked her up the sidewalk toward her car. She opened the door with one hand and extended the other. Tom grasped it and pulled her close. She remained still for a moment and then pulled back. "Tom, I really like you. I enjoy being with you, but you're going to have to give me some more time."

"What do you mean by that?" Tom asked.

"As you know, I moved here not long ago. The main reason that I moved was because of a failed relationship. I got hurt very badly. I need space, at least for now. "

"Geez, Jolene. I can understand that. I have no problem just remaining your friend," Tom said, almost believing it himself.

"Good night, Tom."

Jolene turned the key and backed the Toyota out of the driveway. Tom watched and experienced the usual sinking feeling as the car disappeared up the driveway around a bank of trees.

TORFIN PETERSON HAD JUST GOTTEN OUT OF BED. He sat on the edge of the mattress and placed a palm against his forehead where a throbbing headache had emerged. I know my career is about to end, he thought grimly. Sooner or later, the state guys are going to get involved in the Talbot case and they'll find out the truth. Meanwhile, I've got to hold on for just a bit longer…perhaps only for a month.

He thought about a former high school classmate from Missouri who he had been e-mailing. She said that I can come down anytime I want. Yeah, she lives in the country…the boondocks. They'll never find me there.

Heading for the bathroom, his left knee buckled. I've got to lose some weight, he thought. When I get a hold of all that money and move to Missouri, I'll join a fitness center.

After getting dressed, he sat down by the kitchen table with a cup of coffee. It's Sunday morning and I'm sure glad I have the day off, he said to himself. Glaring at the sheet of paper in front of him, he winced at the total at the bottom of the page…one hundred seventy-five thousand dollars. That's only part of the amount that I owe, he thought.

I wonder if the five hundred thousand from the Talbot estate is going to be enough. If not, it was a lucky stroke that Marty Bishop came around with his proposal. I should get at least another fifty from that job. Staring out the window, he felt a nagging throb in his right temple.

He placed his left hand on his forehead and scratched the bare area just below his receding hairline. Was that eleven o'clock? Or was it one o'clock that I told Marty? One, I hope. That's when the timer releases the lock.

What if they get caught? He thought and gasped. *What if Marty talks?* It shouldn't happen…it will not! Tomorrow morning all my deputies will be miles away. I made sure of that when making out the schedule.

12

JONATHON WILLS LIVED IN THE COUNTRY, two miles south of New Dresden. After using a piece of toast to wipe the last of the eggs from his plate, he wailed "thanks," to his wife and drove into town in his four-door Dodge sedan. He parked in the alley, next to the post office in spite of several available parking places on Monday mid-morning in New Dresden. As usual, he left his car running. I'll be right out, he thought.

When Jonathon exited the post office, he focused on his mail, sifting through a stack of envelopes. Arriving at the alley with his head still down, he walked toward his car. He looked up...no car. Did I park somewhere else? He asked himself. Jonathon looked up and down Main Street. My God, my car's been stolen!

Moments later, he smiled and nodded his head. Someone is playing a practical joke on me. Looking across the street, he expected Kyle Fredrickson to be watching from a window...doubling up with laughter. It was either Kyle or the barber Floyd, or both.

I'll show 'em. Pretending to ignore that his car was missing, Jonathon continued on to Stillman's. Inside, he got permission from Ellie to use the phone. He smiled after hanging up. My wife is coming to get me and the jokesters will not have the satisfaction of seeing me frustrated.

Standing in the foyer of the grocery store in his gray bib overalls, he kept glancing at the door of *Fredrickson Realty*. Bob stood there with the door partially open. Jonathon expected the gleeful Floyd to show up at any moment. He's probably got someone in the chair, Jonathon thought.

MATT NELSON HAD BEEN IN THE BANK MAKING A DE-
POSIT. He chatted with one of the tellers who prepared his receipt.
After leaving the bank, he walked up the sidewalk. Somewhere
along the way, he usually slipped between two parked vehicles and
jaywalked across the street to his store.

Abreast of *King Realty,* he stopped and looked back. The car
parked in front of the bank looked out of place…an awkward angle.
Isn't that Jonathon's car? He asked himself. The front part of the
Dodge is beyond the stop sign and partially into the intersection. I
wonder what's going on with Jonathon. He never parks over there.

Matt saw two men get out of Jonathon's car. They walked up
onto the sidewalk and stopped. After glancing around the street,
they entered the bank. Two more men got out of the car. They also
hesitated on the sidewalk before entering. What the heck's going
on? Matt asked himself. He glanced through the window of *King
Realty.* Sabrina looked up from her desk and waved.

Jonathon's Dodge is running…not unusual, he thought. Jonathon
is probably in the bank. Matt shrugged his shoulders and continued
up the sidewalk. Before crossing the street, he looked back again.
Jonathon never parks over there. What were those men doing in his
car? There's something goofy going on.

He turned around and slowly walked back toward the bank, confused. Getting on his tiptoes, he peeked through the bank window.
The glare from outdoor light made it difficult to see clearly. Then,
he saw it…a hand holding something solid. What is in that hand? He
asked himself. Is it a gun?

Matt trotted up the street. When he came abreast of *King Realty*
again, the owner, Sabrina had just come out the door.

"Hey, Matt. Take it easy. Where's the fire?"

"Sabrina, something's happening at the bank. I'm not really sure,
but there may be someone in there with a gun."

"A gun!"

"Well, maybe not. Jonathon Wills is in there and he could be
playing a game." Matt laughed nervously. "You know Jonathon—he
really pulls some fast ones."

JONATHON WILLS HAD RETURNED TO TOWN as a passenger in his wife's sport utility vehicle. She halted at the stop sign next to the grocery store. "Look, there it is!" Jonathon exclaimed. "Here is where I get even with those jokesters. Hold it. I'm getting out."

Jonathon quickly opened the passenger door. He exited and pranced across the street. Pulling the driver's side door open, he got into the Dodge and wondered why it was running. Doesn't matter, he thought. I've got those guys and laughed out loud. "Kyle and Floyd are going to eat crow," he muttered, while shifting into drive. He grabbed the steering wheel with his long brawny fingers and drove off. After circling the block, he honked as he drove by the barbershop.

His large hazel eyes glowed as he glanced to his right, and saw the empty space next to the bank. Jonathon's high-pitched voice exclaimed, "Whoopee!" as he came to a stop at the intersection. He laid his oversized thumb on the horn again while passing by the lumberyard.

MATT AND SABRINA HAD BEEN WATCHING as the Dodge drove away from the bank.

"Ah, that explains it. There's Jonathon now," Matt said, smiling.

"Yeah, but he didn't come out of the bank. That's his wife's vehicle parked by Stillman's," said Sabrina. He came from there.

The noise from Jonathon's horn added to Matt's amusement. He laughed again. "Well, I might have suspected—Jonathon and some of his buddies are playing games."

Suddenly a booming, loud noise reverberated off the outside walls of the buildings along Main Street.

"What was that?" Sabrina asked nervously.

Matt shrugged his shoulders. "Dunno, probably Jonathon and another one of his tricks. The clown probably figured out how to get the Dodge to backfire."

Matt became startled by another loud, snapping-popping noise. "Holy heavens, Sabrina, that's a gunshot. You better get back into your office. This could be for real."

Matt watched Sabrina safely go through her door, then he quickly stepped behind a van and peered over the top, anxiously staring at the bank.

ELLIE AT THE GROCERY STORE had heard the car honk. She had just closed the cash register drawer. Looking out, she saw Dorothy Sandberg open the bank door and step out onto the sidewalk. Ellie amused herself while watching her trying to pull on a pair of gloves. Probably got them for Christmas...a little small, Ellie thought.

Ellie saw Dorothy grab her cane that had been tucked between her arm and coat. The red and white matches her classy red hat, she thought. Cautiously Dorothy ambled toward the curb. Suddenly, Ellie saw two men come dashing out of the bank. One of them waved a pistol in the air, and the other carried a shotgun. Ellie became momentarily paralyzed. *Those are real guns!*

She flattened her palms against the counter top and got up on her tip-toes. And then she saw Dorothy point her cane at the man with the shotgun. I've got to get hold of myself, she said to herself. *This is for real out there.* Ellie's composure returned. She turned and yelled, "John, there's some men in front of the bank. They've got guns!"

Ellie felt her heart beating fast while hearing her boss's footsteps approaching. John Stillman moved past the checkout station and stopped in front of the window, his hands on hips and mouth agape. She saw him quickly move into the entryway and lock the two outside doors. He quickly returned inside and pointed at Ellie. "Get down behind the counter, Ellie. They're robbing the bank!"

TOM HASTINGS HAD JUST FILLED HIS PICKUP WITH GAS at *Nabor's Service Station,* a block away from the supermarket. He walked into the station and used a credit card to pay. After signing the slip, he returned to his truck.

Pausing at the stop sign, he took a left just beyond *Bev's Embroidery* shop and entered *Banyon's* lumberyard.

"Sure quiet around here this time of year," Tom said to Chuck while waiting to sign the invoice. He had requested six two-by-fours.

The young worker out in the yard had finished loading the lumber into Tom's truck box and said, "All set, thanks."

Tom turned his truck around and headed back toward the street. He stopped and observed a cluster of used farm tractors waiting their turn at the *Ford Equipment Company*…one of them had a *For Sale* sign fastened to the radiator. Nice looking tractor, he thought.

Tom parked the truck at the stop sign next to *Stillman's Super Market.* He reached for the latch to open the door when suddenly his windshield shattered. What the heck! The noise…what is that? Tom sat in shocked amazement and stared at the fragments of glass that he saw on his lap and the seat next to him.

Looking up and attempting to see between the multitudes of cracks in the windshield, he could make out two men on the sidewalk in front of the bank. They walked in circles…one of them waving a pistol, the other a shotgun. Tom ducked low, deadly afraid and not daring to drive off. Peeking over the edge, he saw a woman with a red hat waving her cane at the man with the shotgun.

MATT NELSON REMAINED CROUCHED BEHIND THE VAN. He saw two men in front of the bank waving their guns. Matt's fear and curiosity prevented him from rushing across the street to his store. He looked across the street and saw his son and daughter come out the door, each carrying a case of pop. Earlier in the day, Matt had instructed them to fill the pop machines. They are obeying my instructions well, he thought…however!

Matt cupped his hands over his mouth and yelled, "Call the sheriff, Erik, they're robbing the bank!" Erik and Jessica turned toward him, appearing totally confused.

Matt yelled again. "The bank—they're robbing the bank! Get

back inside! Call the sheriff!"

ERIK SAID, "Holy crap, Jess. The bank—Dad says someone is robbing it!"

"Oh, yeah—sure. Tell me another one," said Jessica sarcastically.

"Ka-pow! Ka-pow!" The loud noise of two gunshots reached
their ears. They looked at each other and ran.

Erik pushed his sister ahead of him through the doorway. Closing the door, he yelled, "The bank—someone's robbing it. Dad's
trapped across the street."

He headed toward the gun department, knocking down two dis-
plays as he sped by. Erik grabbed a rifle off a rack. "Where are the
shells, Jess? Hurry!"

Jessica grabbed a box off a shelf. She flipped open the top and a
bunch of shells fell to the floor. She handed her brother the box and
got down on one knee.

Erik slid four shells into the magazine. "That should be enough."
Pausing, he stuck a few more in his pocket and headed for the door.
He could see his dad across the street, stooped down behind the van.
Erik looked back and saw Jessica and two clerks following him. He
turned and yelled, "Stay back, there could be some shooting."

Opening the door slightly, he anxiously looked toward the bank
and then into the store. "They're still there, Jess. I've got to get out
there and protect Dad."

He dashed out the door and across the sidewalk, taking up a position behind an all-terrain vehicle mounted on a trailer. Erik stayed
low and racked a shell into the chamber. He aimed hastily and pulled
the trigger. Racking another shell, he peeked over the top of the all-
terrain vehicle and watched. Moments later, he fired again and saw
one of the robbers drop something. Erik fired once more and the
robber disappeared behind the corner of the bank.

TOM WATCHED TWO MORE MASKED MEN come out of the bank. There are now four of 'em on the sidewalk, he said to himself. A van coming from the west slowed and stopped at the intersection. One of the robbers waved his pistol in the air and approached the van. Its wheels squealed as it sped away. Tom ducked when the robber aimed his pistol at the van and fired.

Tom heard two more shots in quick succession. They are louder and sound like a deer rifle, he thought. One of the armed men pointed his gun toward the other end of the street and fired.

The robber with the shotgun had gotten down in front of the hood of a pickup. Two others, who carried bags, crouched low on the sidewalk. One of them got up and sprinted toward the corner of the bank. Another rifle shot rang out and the bag flew out of his hands. He left the bag lay and dashed around the corner. The robber, who carried the second bag followed and safely got out of sight of the shooter.

13

FLOYD PELLA HAD JUST SPREAD LATHER on the face of Ralph Talbot. His client asked, "What's that kid doing with that rifle?"

Floyd walked over to the window and gasped when he heard the explosion after young Nelson pulled the trigger. "What the hell is going on?" Floyd muttered. "What the heck!" he exclaimed.

Ralph got up off the chair, his face still covered with lather and stood beside the barber.

"Ralph, someone is shooting out there. See Jerry, behind the window at the post office. He just ducked."

Floyd felt Ralph's hand on his shoulder. "Something strange is going on in this town. First, your brother in the pickup, and now there's a shootout on Main Street."

AT *BANYON'S LUMBER,* Chuck walked toward the front door, heading for his office when he heard a gunshot. He looked toward Main Street and saw some men waving guns. He dashed inside. "Hey, Perry, take a look out the window, toward the bank," Chuck yelled.

Perry dashed over. "Holy smokes, there's a robbery going on over there."

They crouched low after hearing more gunshots. Looking out, they saw one of the robbers attempt to hijack a van. Another robber spun around and dropped the bag he had been carrying.

"Someone is shooting at 'em!" Chuck exclaimed.

"Gad, wish I had my deer rifle here," his brother murmured.

"Look, Perry, one of the robbers is trying to pick up a bag from the sidewalk."

Chuck and Perry both ducked when hearing another shot. They saw the robber dash around the corner of the bank and stop. The other robbers trotted up the sidewalk toward *Kelly's Auto Body Shop.*

"Look, he's trying it again," Perry said as he and his brother watched a second attempt by one of the robbers to recover the bag. Perry jerked back from the window when he heard another shot.

"He's giving up and running after the other three," Chuck said.

"Uh-oh, Kelly better lock his door. They're going to try to steal one of his vehicles, I bet," Perry said as he watched the robbers approach *Kelly's Auto Body.*

BRUCE SANFORD HAD JUST FINISHED HELPING HIS BOSS Kelly Brown paint a 1975 Thunderbird. I better get this mess cleaned up, he thought. And then he heard a loud blast.

"Did you hear that?" Kelly asked.

"Hear what?"

"Sounded like a shot. Whoa, there's another one," Kelly said.

Bruce had just picked up three paint cans. His eyes widened. "Yeah, I heard 'em. Those are gunshots."

Kelly had dashed to the window that overlooked their front lot.

"Holy Jesus, Kelly, there's some guys coming up the sidewalk and they've got guns—four of 'em."

"Bruce, get the shotgun from my office—hurry. I'll get the rifle."

Bruce sprinted to the office. He emerged moments later carrying a double-barreled shotgun and a handful of shells. He yelled, "Hey, Kelly, they're trying to rip off one of our cars!"

Hearing Kelly's footsteps and the sound of a bolt-action…a sound unmistakable to a deer hunter, Bruce turned and looked into Kelly's eyes…wide open and excited. This is scary as hell, Bruce thought. Holding his breath, he saw his boss open the front door slightly and poke the barrel out. Kelly aimed it high and pulled the trigger.

The deafening crash reverberated off the steel walls. Bruce peeked out the window and saw three of the armed men duck behind a vehicle. The fourth emerged from behind an open door of a car. Jesus, I bet that he's trying to hot-wire it, he thought. Bruce watched as the man got down on all fours and crawled around to the back of the car.

"Quit messing with my cars," Kelly yelled and fired another shot over their heads.

Bruce saw the armed men move away from the lot and break into a run. He joined Kelly in the doorway and saw all four of them in a shallow ditch, heading out of town.

TROOPER TODD BUCHOLTZ of the Minnesota State Patrol had just finished issuing a ticket. The woman had snapped her seatbelt on after he had pulled up behind her car…too late. The trooper knew that it wasn't on when their vehicles had met. He had been patrolling a state highway within fifteen miles of New Dresden.

He looked forward to spending the weekend with his wife and two sons. They had moved from Iowa three years ago. He had been a state patrolman in that state for nine years before moving to Minnesota. They lived at a lake-country home a few miles out of New Dresden.

His receiver crackled. "Darrin at dispatch. Are you close to New

Dresden, twenty-nine ten?"

"Yup, not too far away—why, what gives?" the patrolman asked.

"There's a bank robbery in progress in New Dresden!" the dispatcher exclaimed.

"Holy smokes! Details, please?"

"At least four of them, all armed. How far away are you?"

"About ten minutes. How about backup? Is anybody else close?" Todd asked.

"Check your scanner. Mitch shouldn't be too far," the dispatcher responded calmly.

Todd flipped the scanner switch to tune in all the units in Big Lake's County. Leaving it on, he pressed the trunk lid button. Outside, he grabbed the M-16 rifle from the trunk and propped it on the passenger seat, barrel to the floor. Two county deputies and another state patrolman had responded on the scanner.

One of the deputies estimated about thirty minutes, the other thirty-five. Mitch, his highway patrol buddy, could make it in about twenty minutes.

"Darrin, put the helicopter on alert in Duluth. If they're not immediately available, try St. Paul. It sounds like we're going to need one," Todd said.

"Be careful, Todd," the trooper heard Darrin say, as he pressed the *Yelp* siren button.

The siren on his car screamed, and the red and blue lights on top flashed. Todd pushed the gas pedal to the floor and headed for New Dresden.

He had previously met the owner of the New Dresden bank at a safety training session in Big Lakes in April. What's his name? Todd asked himself as he turned off the state highway and onto the county road that led to New Dresden.

He smiled when seeing a pickup ahead pull off to the side of the road. Good boy, he thought. I remember that banker. Lavelle is his name. Arne Lavelle....

Uh-oh, there's a tractor ahead...it's pulling a manure spreader... ugly and crawling, taking up most of the road. Damn, he doesn't hear the siren, Todd thought. I can't get around him...the ditch is too steep. Pushing the brake pedal, he slowed and came up behind the spreader and pressed the *Phaser* siren button. The siren's pitch changed, and the guy in the tractor cab jerked his head around. The tractor moved aside to the shoulder.

After getting by the spreader, Todd continued at full speed toward New Dresden, slowing only for curves. He knew that stretch of highway and estimated another four minutes.

He thought about his wife and two sons. Sherri would often worry about the dangers that existed for a state patrolman. She had learned how to accept it, but at times she would bring it up. "Maybe you should do something else, Todd," she had said.

Damn, another vehicle ahead…a van really going slow. I can't risk going around it on these curves. The van did move over to the shoulder, but not until Todd had taken a little more rubber off the tires.

Todd knew that the hill ahead was the last one…soon as I get to the top, New Dresden will come into view, he said to himself. And then he saw them… his heart jumped into his throat. There they are! Jesus, four of 'em…if they open fire, I'm gone. Todd jerked the steering wheel to the right with both hands. He held his breath as his car hit the ditch. Bouncing off clumps of dirt and small rocks, one of the wheels hit something hard. The top of his head hit the roof and he paid a price for not wearing his hat. Slightly stunned, the trooper knew he had to move fast when his car came to a stop.

Grabbing the door handle with his left hand, the door swung open. His other hand had released the seat belt. Grabbing the rifle, he flung himself down on the grass. Peaking over the top of the road, he spotted a barrel, probably the shotgun, he thought. Todd remembered what the dispatcher had said. *They're all armed—four of them.*

One of the suspects appeared from behind a cluster of tall golden-rod weeds. Todd found himself staring into the muzzle of a shotgun. He ducked and heard the buckshot hitting the side of his car. Two quick pistol-shots followed. He slid his hand down to his holster, unsnapped the strap and pulled out his Beretta, a .40- caliber automatic. He racked the slide and laid it on the grass.

Raising his head to get another look, he heard, "Crack! Crack!"

Todd's head ducked instantly. That last bullet may have nicked my hair, he said to himself. Without raising his head, he grabbed the automatic, and raised it above the edge of the road. He pointed it toward the suspects and pulled the trigger five times.

Peeking over the road, he saw no one and assumed that the bank robbers had all ducked down. Grabbing the M-16, he aimed it toward where they had last appeared and waited.

Any minute, backup should arrive, he thought anxiously. During the lull in the shooting, he could hear the faint sound of a siren… music to my ears. He could hear garbled voices coming from his opened car door. The backups are talking. Flicking the switch on the belt transmitter, he lowered his head and said, "I'm pinned down, just northwest of town. There're four of 'em, all armed—across the road in the ditch."

The trooper peaked over the shoulder of the road. "Uh-oh, there go two of 'em," he spoke calmly into the transmitter. "They've broken toward the woods."

Todd raised the M-16 and fired at one of the fleeing suspects. The robber dropped to the ground. Todd heard a bullet whistle overhead and ducked. Much too close, he thought. Still on his stomach, he swung the rifle and fired at the other suspect. Todd saw him waver and disappear behind a tree. Facing the transmitter, he added, "I think I've hit a second one."

Todd checked with his transmitter, making sure of his switch. "One of 'em is down! One ran into the woods! Two of 'em are still in the ditch!"

Where are those backup guys? He thought anxiously. Damn, maybe they don't hear me.

Spotting movement off to his left, he raised his body a little. The last two suspects had sneaked along the ditch toward the hill. He swung the rifle in their direction, but they had run across the ditch and disappeared into the woods.

An enormous sense of relief came over the trooper. I'm not hit and the robbers are gone, he said to himself. Back in his car, he used the eyes in back of his head to watch the ditch and the woods. Todd put his lips up to the microphone. "Darrin! Darrin! Are you there?"

"Jesus! Todd—uh—you're okay. Hell of a lot of noise came

from your transmitter, but I couldn't make out what you were saying. You really had me worried for a minute. Backup should be arriving any minute."

"Have you contacted the bank?" the trooper asked.

"Yeah, a Wendy Sanderson answered. She was hiding under her desk—not sure if the robbers had all gone. I told her to get back under the desk and stay there until help came."

"Be sure to call the medics, but have them go into town first."

"It's a done deal, Todd. They're on our frequency and listening."

"If my car still works, I'll head over to the bank and wait for backup."

"Ten-four," the dispatcher responded.

Todd spun his car back onto the highway, and glanced at the fallen robber. That guy isn't going anywhere, the trooper said to himself. My priority right now is the people in the bank.

THROUGH THE MAZE OF CRACKS IN HIS WINDSHIELD, Tom had continued to watch the action in front of the bank. Ducking occasionally when danger dictated, he saw three of them working their way toward *Kelly's Auto Body Shop.* The fourth robber had made attempts to recover something from the sidewalk and remained at the corner of the bank. Like the others, he had a bandana tied over his face. When he gave up and left, Tom noticed his long and gray hair.

The robbers mingled for a few moments, and one of them attempted to stop a van coming into town from the west. Tom glared with amazement as the van gained speed and bolted through the intersection, heading toward Nabor's. He silently cheered the woman driver and muttered, "The driver got away from the robbers. Good for her."

All four robbers had disappeared from Tom's view when they entered Kelly's lot. Moments later, he had heard a rifle shot...another shot. Then he saw the robbers run from Kelly's lot and head up the ditch toward the hill.

The robbers had gotten beyond the city limits and trudged along the shoulder of the road. He noticed one of the robbers had paused and dropped behind, holding an object to his ear. Is that a cell phone? Tom asked himself.

And then Tom saw a police car come over the hill just west of town. The overhead lights flashed and the siren screamed. Geez, the robbers and the police car are going to meet head on! Tom said to himself and held his breath. The front end of the police car dipped severely and it came to a skidding stop.

He saw the robbers lie down and the police car head toward the ditch. Looks like a state patrol car, Tom thought as he saw the vehicle stop in the ditch across from the robbers. After witnessing a spectacular exchange of gunfire, he saw two of the robbers get up and run for the trees. Tom heard rapid-firing rifle shots. One of them fell!

Tom heard more shots come from both ditches of the highway. The two remaining robbers crouched low in the bottom of the ditch and began sneaking northwestward. They made a run for the woods and disappeared.

14

MAIN STREET BECAME DEATHLY STILL after the four robbers had gone. The shooting up the road had ceased, and not a single person had yet moved onto the street. The silence got interrupted by the sound of sirens in the distance.

Tom watched the trooper in the ditch get back into his car. Hearing the roar of the engine, he saw chunks of grass and dirt spew from the spinning tires as it successfully returned to the highway surface.

Moments later, the trooper's car pulled up across from the bank. Tom saw the trooper push open the car door. Carrying a rifle, the trooper quickly ran around the car and crouched, keeping his vehicle between himself and the bank.

Tom gasped when seeing two of the robbers emerge from the woods, near the top of the hill. They ran onto the road and got into a car that appeared out of nowhere. Tom could hear the squeal of the tires as it made a hurried U-turn and headed away. Was that a red car? Tom asked himself.

Tom could hear a vehicle speeding into town from the north. A siren blared and he heard a thumping sound as it bounced when hitting the railroad crossing. The state patrol car pulled up next to Stillman's, directly across from the bank, and a trooper got out. He also carried a rifle. The two troopers raced across the street and stopped by the door of the bank.

Another state patrol car, siren blaring like the other, came from the other direction and rounded the corner next to Nabor's. It went right through the stop sign next to Tom's pickup and angled across Main Street, stopping directly in front of the bank where the other two officers waited.

Tom watched as the three troopers, weapons drawn, entered the bank. It seemed like hours…actually, only minutes had passed since the original siren. He could see John Stillman standing by the door, peeking through the window. Tranquility had returned to Main Street. Tom saw an occasional head bobbing behind the windows at *Borders Café.*

He also spotted movement behind the glass door at Quality Supply. The door remained closed, but someone wearing a red shirt stood behind the glass.

Two of the officers emerged from the bank. A tremendous feeling of relief flooded the mind of Tom Hastings. He wondered how many others, including John Stillman and Ellie in the supermarket, shared his feelings.

An ambulance had appeared at the top of the hill to the northwest. It continued on into town and stopped when a trooper walked into the middle of the road and raised his arm. Moments later, two trooper cars and the ambulance headed up the road near where one of the robbers had fallen.

One of the troopers hurried across Main Street toward Tom's pickup. Fragments of glass clattered to the pavement when Tom opened the door and stepped out.

"Everything okay in there. Are you hurt?" the trooper asked.

"I think I'm okay—got some scratches and nicks from the glass. Uh-oh, never noticed this before."

"What's that? Blood—you're hurt!" the trooper exclaimed.

"Don't feel a thing, but looks like a cut in my shoulder."

"Here, let's take a look at that."

Tom removed his shirt. The trooper added, "You're gonna need medical attention, but it doesn't look serious. Stay right here. I'll see to it that you get some help. More medics' are on their way."

Another siren! The wailing sound came from the north, a deputy sheriff's car. Speeding down Main Street, it stopped in front of the bank. The occupant, a uniformed deputy, got out and hurried across the street to join the trooper standing by Tom's pickup.

They talked briefly and the deputy headed into Stillman's. The trooper had gone across the street to *Quality Supply.* Minutes later, Tom saw him hurry to the lumberyard. After leaving Stillman's, the deputy worked his way up the sidewalk on Main Street, checking on people along the way.

PEOPLE IN THE BUILDINGS REMAINED INSIDE. Finally John Stillman emerged from his store to talk with the deputy. Arne Lavelle, manager of the bank, came out of *Borders Café* and joined them. He had been visiting with a friend and sipping coffee when the shooting started.

Matt Nelson had hurried across the street where his son, Erik, stood with the butt of his rifle planted on the sidewalk. They waited for the deputy to check them out. "Nobody hurt over here," Matt said.

Soon people moved out onto the sidewalks. Another sheriff's car arrived and had parked next to Tom's pickup. A deputy got out and asked, "Are you okay?"

"Yeah, just some bruises and a cut. I'm waiting for the medics. Hey! There are two troopers up the road over there. That's where the robbers went into the woods."

"Yeah, I know. We're waiting for the helicopter—should be here in a few minutes."

"Ah, deputy—there's something you guys should know."

"What's that?"

"I saw two of the robbers come back out of the woods—up near the top of the hill, further up from where the troopers are standing. They got into a car. It did a U-turn right on the hill and disappeared."

"How many robbers did you see?"

"Four of 'em—the first trooper hit one over by the trees where the ambulance is parked."

"Thanks for the info about the car. Two of the suspects got in, you say?"

"Yeah—I think the car was red."

"Thanks," the deputy said as he got into his car. The tires squealed as the deputy sheriff's car sped toward the ambulance.

TOM HASTINGS HAD GOTTEN A RIDE TO THE HOSPITAL in Big Lakes with a deputy sheriff. He chose not to ride in an ambulance. "Not that big a deal," he had said when questioned about the cut in the shoulder.

After Tom's wound was treated, the deputy drove him back to New Dresden. "Thanks for the ride," said Tom. "Why don't you drop me off by my pickup, over there by Stillman's?"

"Mr. Hastings, see that car parked in front of the bank?"

"Yes I do."

"That's likely the FBI here already. They'll be doing the investigating. You're a primary witness. I'm sure they'll want to look at your pickup, too."

"Am I supposed to hang around here, or can I go home?"

"Why don't you go over to your pickup and I'll check it out?"

"Okay," Tom answered and strolled across Main Street.

John Stillman came out of the store. "Tom, did you get patched up?"

"Yup, I'm as good as new. Not so with my pickup, though."

"I see that. Does it run?" John asked.

"Dunno—haven't tried it yet—can't touch it until the cops check it out. Uh-oh, here they come now."

A man and a woman approached from across the street. There's something familiar about those two, Tom thought.

"Hello, sir. We're with the FBI. I'm Agent Bill Brown and this is Agent Susan Crenshaw. Are you hurt?"

"Yeah, I got cut up a little, but I'm all patched up."

"Is this your truck?"

"Yes it is."

"Could I have you name, address and phone number, please? We'll need to ask you some questions. You were parked here during the robbery, right?"

"Yup, I sure was. I'm Tom Hastings."

After the agent wrote down his name, address and phone number, he looked up, "Hastings—oh yeah—we've talked before. Remember, about four years ago—the Maynard Cushing case."

"Sure, I remember now. You two came to my house. You stayed over at the resort."

"Look, Mr. Hastings, we've got some work to do here, including checking out your truck. Why don't you go on home? I'll ask one of the deputies to give you a lift. We'll give you a call later. Okay?"

TOM'S PHONE RANG TWO HOURS LATER. Two FBI agents called to announce their arrival. A few minutes later, history got repeated. He watched as Agents Brown and Crenshaw walked down his sidewalk.

He smiled remembering his suspicions and awareness the first time around. The agents came previously to investigate the murder of his neighbor Maynard Cushing.

Tom opened the door and said, "Come on in. It's good to see you two again. Remember the last time?"

Agent Brown smiled. "Sure do."

"We're not going to take much of your time," Agent Crenshaw said.

Tom explained what he had seen after his windshield got shot. He finished by saying, "I was scared as hell."

"I can understand that, Mr. Hastings," said Crenshaw, smiling. "Did you recognize any of the robbers? Was there anything about them that caused you to be curious?"

"Well, there is one thing. One of them had long gray hair. I think it was gray—but—"

"But what, Mr. Hastings?"

"The mannerism of the robber, with the long gray hair, looked strikingly similar to someone, who I've seen around here before."

The two agents anxiously stared at Tom. Crenshaw placed her pen against the notepad and asked. "Who would that be, Mr. Hastings?"

"A man by the name of Marty Bishop, I think. I don't really know him, but only know who he is."

"Marty Bishop—do you know if he lives around here?"

"Well, from what someone has told me, he moved here recently from Kansas. He's related to the Talbot's. Ralph is the one you would want to talk to. He and his brother run this hog farm—well, not anymore. Ralph's brother is dead—train accident a couple of weeks ago."

"Thanks so much, Mr. Hastings," Agent Crenshaw said.

"You've been most helpful," Agent Brown added. "Oh, we're done with your pickup truck. If you wish, hop in and we'll give you a ride into New Dresden."

ACTIVITY UP AND DOWN MAIN STREET in New Dresden changed for days following the bank robbery. No one was injured in the bank except for Lois Haugen, a teller, who hit her head on the corner of a cabinet counter when getting up from the floor.

Dorothy, who accosted the robbers with her cane, demanded and got a new one, compliments of the bank.

Arne Lavelle was often seen visiting with people on the sidewalk discussing the ins-and-outs of what had happened.

There were two other tellers on duty when the robbers had entered. Obeying the intruders, the tellers opened the cash drawers. The robbers grabbed out the bills and dropped them into two canvas bags. Three other employees remained at their desks and had gotten down on the floor as instructed.

The safe was time-locked and could not be open until 1:00 p.m. Manager Arne Lavelle told people that he had watched some of the action from the window at *Borders Café*. He had seen young Erik Nelson shooting at the robbers with a deer rifle after taking up a position behind a parked flatbed trailer, loaded with an all terrain vehicle.

One of the bullets from Erik Nelson's rifle had hit one of the moneybags, knocking it from a robber's grasp. The exterior of the canvas bag had been splattered with blood when the officers recovered it from the sidewalk.

The bag contained about half the money that had been stolen from the cash drawers. Except for a blackened bullet hole through a stack of twenties, the bills had not been damaged.

The robbers had taken the second bag. According to Arne Lavelle, about ten thousand dollars was missing. Arne had been elated learning that no one at his bank had gotten shot.

The latest news at the *Borders Café* verified that only two of the robbers had been captured, but neither one cooperated. One of them is still in serious condition at the hospital in Big Lakes. The whereabouts of the other two robbers is unknown. Stories at *Borders Café* varied…the robbers were seen in different towns, at bus stations, shopping malls, airport terminals and other places.

One of the bullets from Erik Nelson's rifle had penetrated a stack of feed bags stored on a cart at the *Quality Supply* store. One of the bags had exploded strewing the contents across the ground. No vehicles were at the gas pumps during the robbery. The woman at the checkout counter in the convenience store had witnessed the entire episode.

Newspaper reporters from Fargo parked their van at *Quality Supply* after the robbery. They used the checkout lady's interview to produce a half-page article in the *Fargo Forum* the very next day. Her picture appeared on the front page showing her standing on the loading dock pointing to a bullet hole in a partially empty feed bag.

Jerry, the postmaster, had been telling people about the strange scene across the street. "It looked like a picture of *Santa Claus and Snow White*—Floyd's white beard, next to Ralph's lathered face."

Tom showed up for lunch with his friend Henry at the *Borders Café.*

"How's your shoulder?" Henry asked.

"It feels fine in spite of the itchy stitches. I feel pretty lucky considering a shotgun blast went through my windshield."

"I hear you'll need a new one," Henry said.

"Yup, and it looks like the insurance company is going to pay for a new seat, too. The police pretty much wrecked the darn thing digging out the pellets lodged in the backrest."

15

RALPH TALBOT HAD BEEN GLAD that Edgar agreed to help bring in the corn, even though he knew Edgar wasn't very good at driving the truck. Ralph's brother Ben had been the best at positioning the truck alongside the moving combine. The two brothers had agreed that dumping on-the-run is preferable…saved a lot of time… the auger ran too slow.

They had successfully mounted a corn head attachment to their combine, which they normally used to harvest oats. Finding a good, used, thirty-inch head wasn't easy. If it wasn't for Dana over at *Ford Equipment Company,* we would've never found one, Ralph said to himself.

Edgar's erratic driving caused some of the kernels to spill onto the ground, Ralph thought, and cringed. The darn truck wanders too much when he's behind the wheel. Some day, Mister Salute is going to take out the transmission, too.

Edgar had arrived in the field with the truck and came up behind the combine. Ralph watched nervously as the truck edged closer and closer. Because of Edgar's erratic driving, Ralph needed to pay a lot of attention to the spout, making sure it aimed at the open part of the truck box. Oh that crazy nut, Ralph thought, as Edgar had a difficult time maintaining constant speed.

Ralph frowned when the truck left a little too early dumping a considerable amount of corn on the ground. He didn't wave back at Edgar, who gave him the traditional salute while heading back to the farm. After the hopper had filled again, Ralph pulled away from the rows and parked next to one of the two empty wagons, which would eventually be pulled to the corn bins with a tractor.

The truck should be back by the time the hopper fills again, he thought. Ralph anxiously looked over his shoulder. The hopper is almost full. Where the devil is that Edgar? Ralph had to stop the machine…the hopper is full. He pushed the lever to disengage the power-take-off. Waiting anxiously, he sighed. Aha, there's the truck, at last.

As he watched it approach, he pulled the lever to engage the power-take-off. Something's different, he thought. The truck is moving along steady and smooth. Edgar doesn't drive like that.

Ralph smiled after the hopper got dumped on that run without any spillage. As the truck turned and moved aside to park and wait for another hopper full, he saw the driver…it's not Edgar. Oh, probably Ned or Reggie, he thought.

It usually took three hoppers to fill the truck. Ralph returned to where he had left off. After the third dump, Ralph stretched his neck to see who drove the truck. The lenses of his glasses had fogged with dust and debris and he failed. Doesn't matter, he thought. Whoever's driving is doing a heck of a good job.

After dumping the hopper load into a partially filled wagon, Ralph returned to where he had left off. A couple of rounds later he had filled the wagon and could see the truck approaching for another load. Ralph stopped the tractor and got down to check the combine.

Hmm, it's coming faster than usual, he thought. Ralph stood on the ground, expecting to talk to the truck driver. Holy smokes, it's speeding up. He continued to stand next to the combine, fully confident that the truck would slow and stop. It kept coming. "What! Hey—"

TOM HAD SLOWED AND APPROACHED the railroad tracks when he noticed a Minnesota State Patrol car parked on the side of the street. The patrolman stood next to the open window of a purple jeep. He bent over slightly and peered into the open window. Hey, that's Todd Bucholtz, Tom thought. He remembered the patrolman who was the first officer to arrive during the bank robbery. The trooper also accompanied the posse that had pursued the bank robbers into the woods.

The woman sitting behind the wheel reached out with her hand and grasped a piece of paper…must be a ticket, Tom thought… another victim of *Purgatory Curve.* Tom smiled and waved as he passed.

He entered Stillman's and watched Ellie tear off yesterday's sheet from the calendar hanging by the door. The new page had a big black 8 in the middle.

"Good morning, Tom. Every time I look out that window, I shudder—the bank robbers, waving their guns and shooting—I was scared as the dickens. Ah-hah, looks like your windshield has been replaced."

"Yup, the pickup is good as new—a new windshield, and a new seat coming up. It's just what I've always wanted."

Ellie exclaimed and pointed. "The slug that hit your pickup could have come through that window and right in here!"

Tom looked at Ellie and smiled wide. "See ya' later," he said and left Stillman's. Just before opening the door of his pickup truck, the town siren sounded. He looked at his watch. It's only 11:14, he said to himself. Why is the siren blaring? The siren routinely went off three times a day, but at specific times…the next one isn't due until 12:00 noon. Tom saw someone running across Main Street toward the fire hall.

About two minutes later, the fire truck roared up Main Street and crossed the railroad tracks heading northeast. A second siren sounded. The blue and white rescue vehicle rounded the corner by Stillman's and followed the fire truck.

TOM HEADED FOR HOME AND WONDERED WHERE THE FIRE IS…probably another one of those brush fires, he thought. While driving down his roadway, he saw Prancer. The deer stood in a patch of tall grass that lined the roadway. Prancer lifted its head when the pickup approached. Tom stopped and watched the deer through his new windshield. He noticed the generous numbers of gray hairs in the hide. The deer raised its tail and bounded into the woods.

After parking the pickup, Tom could hear additional sirens on the state highway. He hesitated while walking across the driveway to his house. The sound gradually dissipated and stopped. Not that far away, he thought. Something must have happened on the state highway. Tom continued on into his house.

He worked at his computer a couple of hours and then the phone rang. "Tom, this is Jolene."

"Hi, what's up, Jolene? Your phone call is a welcome surprise."

"Tom. My father's brother has been killed!"

"Ralph—killed! How? When?"

"It happened on the farm, just before lunch hour. He was harvesting corn and must have fallen, so someone had said."

"So, that's what those sirens were all about—just after 11:00 this morning in New Dresden—also, later on the highway."

"Tell you what, Tom. Let's go out for dinner. I'll buy. I need to talk to someone and you're a good listener. Otherwise, I'll just pace around and be frustrated."

"Well okay. What time did you want me to pick you up?"

"How's 7:00?"

"Fine, I'll see you then."

16

ON FRIDAY EVENINGS AT *MARY ANN'S,* the dinner traffic is heavy compared to weekdays, Tom thought.

"Hi, Tom, whose your friend?" Mary Ann asked when they entered. "You two were here a couple of weeks ago, right?"

"Mary Ann, this is Jolene Hunt."

"I'm happy to meet you, Jolene. Where do you live?"

"I have a cottage on Trevor Lake."

"Oh, I know where that is. A few miles beyond the western shore of Borders, right?"

Jolene smiled. "Yes, I'm happy to meet you, too, Mary Ann."

"Let's see a table for two—non-smoking—by the window."

As they followed Mary Ann into the dining room, Tom noticed Reggie Logan sitting at the bar. Tom sat down across from Jolene and said, "Jolene, don't look now, but your favorite person is here. He's sitting over at the bar—Reggie Logan."

Jolene lowered the menu. "Yeah, I hear he hangs around here a lot, and that doesn't surprise me. Well, I'm not going to let him spoil my evening. He can go to hell as far as I'm concerned."

Tom looked deep into her eyes. He saw bitterness and resentment. She's not going to dismiss the death of Ben and Ralph Talbot without a battle, he thought. The sheriff is going to have his hands full. I hope she pushes the issue to the hilt. I did see a person jump from the pickup truck…no way anyone can tell me otherwise, he thought. I wonder if Reggie Logan is still going to be at the bar by the time we finish with dinner.

"Did you hear who was at the farm when Ralph got killed?" Tom asked.

"I heard that the sporty red car was there for sure," Jolene said. "Anyone else?"

"Ah, Edgar—something or other. Then, there was someone else—a neighbor—don't know the name."

"So, Jolene, what do you plan on doing? Complaining to the sheriff isn't going to do much good, is it?"

"I'm not sure. I am considering hiring a private investigator. It's just too big a coincidence that the Talbot brothers both get killed while Reggie Logan is around."

"Do you suppose there will be another hearing?" Tom asked.

"Well, there better be. But then, you can't rely on the sheriff. I told you earlier how he was connected to Reggie's mother."

"Yeah, I remember you mentioning something."

"You know, Tom. I'm really shook up. This means that Reggie Logan is in line to inherit everything. Ralph automatically inherited my father's share of the estate. I'd rather have it all go to charity than to that guttersnipe."

Tom touched his mouth with a fist. "Geez, I'm so sorry that you're so upset."

"If you actually did see Reggie Logan jump from the pickup truck, just before the train crash, then my father's death wasn't an accident."

"Oh, I did, Jolene—I swear on a bible. I did see someone." Tom placed a hand over his heart.

After they had finished dinner and left the booth, Jolene walked to the check-out counter. She reached in her purse and brought out her wallet. Tom stood nearby. He saw Reggie still sitting at the bar, next to the young man he had seen him with about a month ago. "What do you think, Jolene? Should we have an after-dinner drink?"

"Why not?" She replied firmly.

They took one of the high tables a short distance from the bar. After they got seated, Reggie Logan turned. Staring at the couple, he said loudly, "Well, the dreamers are here. Can I buy you two a drink?"

Jolene's face flushed. Her lips quivered as she replied. "No thanks. I don't drink with animals."

Reggie's expression changed to a cross between a sneer and a smile. "You better watch your step, lady. I'm not sure what you're up to, but whatever it is, it won't do you any good." He turned on the stool and patted his friend on the back. "You hear that, Chad? You are now drinking with an animal."

Tom sat quietly while listening to the bitter exchange between Reggie and Jolene. He looked at her face and noticed her jaw set firmly and her eyes flashing. Reggie Logan, you better watch your step or this woman is going to devastate you, he thought.

Tom and Jolene had finished their after-dinner drinks and left the restaurant. Tom drove his pickup down the state highway and headed back toward Lake Trevor when a red car passed traveling at a high rate of speed. The brake lights came on and the red car slowed. Tom caught up to it and braked. "Geez, looks like we have some kind of game going on."

"Now what is that guttersnipe up to?" Jolene asked sharply.

Tom looked at the speedometer…down to forty-five. He flicked the left turn signal. As he pulled abreast, the car accelerated. A mile down the road, it slowed again.

"I've got the license number. I'm going to report this," said Jolene angrily.

The red car played the game five more times before Tom turned the pickup onto the county highway.

"Tom. I mean it. I'm calling the state patrol tonight."

"I hope you do, Jolene."

17

WEDNESDAY DIDN'T COME SOON ENOUGH FOR TOM. He needed to talk to Henry at Border's. After buying the paper at Stillman's, he spread it out on a table in a far corner at the café. At exactly 11:15, he anxiously watched as Henry crossed Main Street. After visiting with someone on the sidewalk for a few minutes, Henry entered.

"Have a seat, Henry. What's new today?" Tom Asked.

"Well you know what's new. You must know all about Ralph Talbot getting killed."

"Yeah, I heard he got crushed by a truck."

"That's what I heard, too. Matt Nelson told me that Ralph was dead by the time he and Cliff Monroe got there. Cliff drove out in the rescue vehicle."

"What happened? Was he trying to fix something, or what?" Tom asked.

"Talking to Matt, he said it was unusual. One of the wheels on the combine was dented inward, and the tire was flat, too. He said it would have taken more than a sledge hammer to make a dent like that."

"Does that mean the wheel got hit when Ralph did?"

Henry leaned forward slightly in his chair. "It does sound that way."

"Hmm—what did the sheriff say? Or didn't the sheriff come out?" Tom asked.

"Oh, he did get out there, I hear. The sheriff said he's a hundred percent sure it was an accident."

"Was there anyone who thought it might not have been an accident?"

Henry smiled. He looked up at Tom. "There are rumors—nothing that I can say for sure. Some people are talking that both Talbot's dying so close in time—too much of a coincidence—and there is so much money."

"Money! What's that all about?" Tom asked.

"Again, rumors—only rumors. I've heard it said in here that they had over seven hundred thousand dollars in certificates of deposit at the bank."

Henry stopped talking. He watched a woman who had come into the restaurant.

"Who's that, Henry?" Tom asked.

"Oh, that's Wendy Sanderson. She works at the bank–in the back. She would know how much money the Talbot's have in their account."

"Wow, the certificates plus the land and equipment. The estate is probably worth close to two million dollars!" Tom exclaimed.

"That's where the problem comes in—the estate settlement. You may have heard about Ben and Ralph's nephew. He's been hanging around and he's the only living relative—well, sort of."

"Yeah, I know who you're talking about. Is he the one who drives a red sports-like car?"

"That's him. He drives it mighty fast, too, I hear."

"I've seen it out on the county highway. I think he may have tried to run me off the road."

Henry frowned. "That doesn't surprise me. He has a reputation for doing things like that."

Tom took a deep breath. "Well, that Reggie weasel had better not pull that again. My friend is supposed to call the state patrol to complain about it—too soon to hear anything back yet."

"There's another rumor that's going to make some noise."

"Yeah, what would that be?" Tom asked.

"Theresa Logan's second husband was at Ben's funeral, I heard."

"Does he have long gray hair tied into a pony tail?"

"Yes, I believe he does."

"I saw him there. But, what claim could he possibly have if he's divorced?"

The rumor is that the divorce officially never went through."

"When did Theresa Logan die?" Tom asked.

"About six years ago."

"How about her first husband, when did he die?"

"About five years before that."

"Well, Henry. I've got to go. See you later."

Henry's news will be of huge interest to Jolene, Tom thought. Slowing down while approaching his turnoff, he looked left and saw the silos. They are surrounded by rows of outdated machinery. Byron Schultz, my neighbor, retired from farming over five years ago.

BYRON'S WIFE EVA STILL WORKS PART-TIME in the public school system in Pine Lakes, Tom thought. I can still taste her cookies. Tom turned left up their roadway.

Eva answered the door. "Come on in, Tom. It's nice to have you back. You're just in time for you-know-what."

"Yes, Eva. You have me all figured out. Hi, Byron, I see you look as healthy as ever."

Byron is a lean, tall man with a full head of dark hair, Tom said to himself. He was born and raised on this farm. Dairy cattle have been his entire life.

Eva set the platter of vanilla cookies on the table. "There you are, Tom. Your favorites, aren't they?"

"Any of your cookies are my favorites," Tom answered, barely beating Byron's fingers to the plate.

Byron reached for his second. "Are you still working with computers? We're thinking about getting one," Byron said.

"Yes, I am. You knew the Talbot's, didn't you? I set one up for them a few months ago."

"We're just shocked at what happened to them," Eva said, and brought her fingers up to her eyes.

"Those two men were so careful. It just doesn't fit. Neither drank. They were experts with machinery. I used to deer hunt with them—they always played it extra safe," Byron said.

"I thought that you knew them pretty well. That's one reason I stopped—to listen to what you two think may have happened."

Eva pushed the platter in Tom's direction. "Have another."

"Sure will. Thanks. They're great. Was there anything wrong with Ben's health?" Tom asked.

"Gosh no—they were both able as fifty-year-olds," By said. "Their hearts were good and strong. When I went in for my physical a couple of months ago, Ben was there for his, too. The doctor bragged about his numbers—blood pressure and all that."

"Do you think it's a possibility that their deaths weren't accidental?" Tom asked.

Eva's face turned serious. "I don't see—no, there's no way anyone would want to harm either one of them."

Byron put his hand on his wife's arm. "We've heard some bad things about that nephew—Logan—Reggie Logan is his name."

Tom swallowed and took a deep breath. "Thanks for the cookies,

Eva."

"Please stop again," she said.

The couple hasn't changed at all, Tom thought as he walked out to his pickup.

A cluster of oak leaves swayed in the wind and drifted gently down to the asphalt driveway as Tom drove up from his roadway. Geez, I wonder if I should relay Henry's information about the dented wheel and the Talbot cash to Jolene? Tom said to himself. Reporting it to the sheriff sure isn't going to do any good. Jolene will likely force the issue, and fight the county's decision about the death of her dad...especially after her dad's brother dies a few days later. I wonder if she reported the license number of that car that harassed us the other night.

18

TOM CALLED JOLENE. "Hi. Could I buy you lunch today? I'm going into Pine Lakes later this morning."

"Sure. I'd like that," she replied.

"I'll meet you at the *Locomotive* at noon."

Main Street in Pine Lakes paralleled two sets of railroad tracks. One of the main intersections had a set of traffic lights...the heart of the business district. The *Locomotive* restaurant occupied one of the corners at that intersection. The business where Jolene works is only half a block away, he thought. Tom parked the pickup and took a booth in the restaurant that overlooked Main Street.

At two minutes past 12:00, he watched Jolene pass by three pedestrians while crossing the street. She walked with her head lowered and moved at a brisk pace. Jolene disappeared from view as she proceeded around the corner of the building. Her entrance into the restaurant brought a smile to Tom's face. She returned his smile and headed for his booth.

"Tom, I'm anxious to hear your news," Jolene said as she dropped onto the seat across from him.

"Relax, Jolene. Would you like some coffee?"

"No thanks. I'll order some tea."

Tom smiled and began relating the conversation he had had with Henry. Jolene leaned forward with her stomach pressing against the edge of the table. Jolene's eyes enlarged and she interrupted when hearing the words: *dented wheel.*

She placed both of her palms on the table. "Was it on the combine or the tractor?"

"The combine—that's what Henry had said. He used the words: *flat as a pancake.*"

"So, if the wheel dent was fresh, how did it happen? Did something crash into it? Was it another vehicle, perhaps a truck?" Jolene asked.

"According to Henry, a hired hand, Edgar, drove the truck that day. There was also a second tractor in the field. They used it to pull the wagons back to the farm after they got filled with corn."

"Tom, the whole farm deal sounds like foul play, just like the train crash. Did the sheriff do the investigation?"

Tom smirked. "Yeah, I heard the sheriff did show up. According to what someone said at the hardware store, it took the sheriff only five minutes to decide that it was an accident."

Jolene's chin tilted up slightly. "I don't trust the sheriff. His relationship to Reggie Logan puzzles me. I need to learn more."

"I know nothing about that, Jolene," Tom said, shaking his head slowly.

"I don't know for certain either, but I'm going to find out. I wonder if Jack McCarthy would be interested in knowing what caused the dent in the wheel."

"Hmm…maybe a truck bumped into it," Tom said, his eyes opening wider.

"Tom! I need to know if the truck has a fresh dent—or maybe some kind of a mark on the bumper. I wonder what color the combine harvester is."

"I really don't know."

"Do you know Wendy Sanderson?" Jolene asked.

"No, I don't, but I know who she is. Works at the bank, doesn't she?"

"Yes, she and her husband Tim live on my lake. She's the controller at the bank."

"What does her husband do?"

"He works for the railroad–in administration, in Fargo."

Tom nodded and looked at Jolene. Her expression looks wild–she's plotting something, he thought.

"Tom! Would you be interested in an adventure? I would like to visit the farm—at night, when no one is around. I wonder if anyone is staying at the house."

"Whoa! So what you're really asking me is to trespass on the Talbot farm?"

"Well, sort of, how about tomorrow? I'm thinking between 10:00 or 11:00 at night."

Tom looked down at the table. I don't feel comfortable with Jolene's request, he said to himself. "Let me think about it, Jolene—sounds risky as heck."

"Maybe so, but if the sheriff isn't going to do anything about it, someone has to. I feel that it's my duty."

"Yours perhaps, but not exactly mine. Tell you what. I'll think about it and let you know." Tom feared that he didn't have the heart to turn her down even though he didn't think much of her idea.

"If you don't come, Tom, I'm going it alone."

Tom frowned as Jolene re-crossed the street and entered the door of *Midwest Title Company.* He paid the bill and headed for his pickup. Geez, he thought. What's this lady getting me into?

19

TOM LOOKED UP AT THE MOON ON FRIDAY NIGHT. It's a quarter-full and keeps popping in and out of a high bank of clouds, he thought. Tom stood on his deck, sipping a bottle of beer. He glanced toward the driveway expecting to see a set of headlights emerge. He had agreed to join Jolene in the adventure of investigating the combine wheel and truck bumper.

His stomach knotted as the headlights appeared. Tom wore a baseball cap and jacket…a flashlight tucked in his pocket. After seeing the brake lights come on, he exited the house and walked across the driveway. Jolene got out of her Toyota four-wheeler and stood by the door. She smiled when Tom approached.

"This is the night. Are you still game?"

"Not really, but I hate to see you go there alone."

Jolene shook her head. "Look, Hastings, I can do this alone—you know that, don't you?"

"Do you have a flashlight?" Tom asked.

"I sure do, how about you?"

"Yup, I wonder if I should take my gun."

"Now why would we need a gun?" Jolene asked showing fear for the first time. "This is not an assault. It's an investigation. Besides, a gun could work against us if we get caught."

"Get caught! Caught at what? We're only driving in to have a look at a piece of machinery," Tom exclaimed.

Jolene smiled wide. "Ah, don't worry. We'll do just fine."

Two small deer crossed Tom's roadway just before the Toyota drove onto the township road.

Jolene turned her Toyota onto the county highway, and they drove in silence. A couple of miles later, she headed up the state highway. Three minutes later, she slowed. "Is that the mailbox?"

"Yup, that's it."

Jolene turned the Toyota onto the farm road. "I don't see any *No-Trespassing* signs saying that we shouldn't be doing this," she said.

The headlights flashed across the front of the house as Jolene slowed her Toyota. The yard light in the middle of the farmstead illuminated a large gray metal building on the western edge. Four pieces of farm machinery had been parked near the building. Looking north, Tom saw the shadows of a tall bank of trees pretty much blanketing a low-slung wooden hog barn. Jolene drove the Toyota to the gray metal building and shut off the lights and motor.

After getting out she flicked on her flashlight and said, "I think I see what I'm looking for."

The beam illuminated a red combine. "Look, Tom. There's the wheel, the tire's been removed, and there's the big dent." Jolene knelt beside the wheel and touched the surface.

"This sure looks fresh. Something real powerful hit this machine," She said.

Jolene shone her flashlight on metal beyond the wheel. "Is that blood, Tom?

"Where?"

"There on that metal panel."

"Oh, maybe it is. Hard to tell when the metal is red to begin with. Looks like someone blocked up the wheel to get the tire off."

"I wonder where the truck is." Tom said.

"It's probably in the shed."

Jolene brought out a small camera from her pocket. She proceeded to take a series of photographs. "Come on, Tom. Let's see if we can get into the building."

The small door on the south end of the building opened when she pulled. Jolene entered and shone her flashlight across the room. "There it is, Tom—the truck."

"Tom! Look at this—a scratch and a streak of red." Jolene took another series of photographs.

"Jolene! I hear a vehicle!"

20

SHERIFF TORFIN ALLAN PETERSON opened the refrigerator door and grabbed a bottle of beer. After popping the top, he thought about the Hunt woman and her friend Hastings. Damn that woman. Fighting her wouldn't be nearly as bad for me if she hadn't hooked up with Hastings, the train accident expert.

They're both a pain for me and I can't afford to have the likes of them getting in my way. He lifted the bottle, took two deep swallows and wiped the fuzz off his lips. This is my county. If they continue to nose around, it's going to cost 'em, big-time.

After his last swig from the bottle, the phone rang. He had been watching a sitcom rerun following the news. "Damn that phone," the sheriff muttered. He didn't want to miss the sitcom. Its tonic for me…takes my mind off my problems, he said to himself.

The bank had called again earlier that day. That Smith guy from the bank is a bag of cheese, he thought. So I'm three months over-due…big deal. I'll hit it big at the casino one of these days and stuff the cash down his throat. He flung the empty beer bottle against the wall.

"What's that, Reggie? Trespassers at the Talbot farm? You stay put! I'll be there in ten minutes. Don't do anything stupid."

A measure of excitement galloped through his mind. It could be Hunt and Hastings prowling around the farm…wouldn't surprise me one bit, he thought. This could be a major opportunity.

My reputation in this county is going to go down the tube, unless I find some way to come up with the money and get rid of those two pesky flies. "This could be my big chance to do just that," he said out loud.

Marty appears to have bungled the bank job, he said to himself. The dummy made a miscalculation. He thought I had said eleven o'clock. *No, damn it, it was one o'clock.* That's when the safe opened. Marty would be in jail if I hadn't picked him up on the highway, he thought aggravated.

The sheriff's sneer changed to a smile thinking about the helpless people of New Dresden. They're dependent on me…just the way I want it.

Hatless, he squeezed into the front seat of his car, his bushy gray hair brushing against the top rail of the doorframe. He extended his lower lip and wet the bulging hairs of his droopy mustache as his car backed out onto the street.

JOLENE AND TOM SWITCHED OFF THEIR FLASHLIGHTS. The rafters supporting the metal roof creaked when a gust of wind swirled against the building.

"I don't hear a thing," Jolene said.

Tom grabbed her arm. "I sure did, seconds earlier. We could be in trouble, Jolene," he whispered.

"Let's not panic. Come on, let's take a look outside," she said calmly.

They stepped out the door. "See. There's no one here. You must have heard a vehicle that passed by on the highway," Jolene added.

Tom took a deep breath, feeling his heart rate increase. "I don't think so. Let's get the heck out of here."

"Oh, come on, Detective Hastings. I need some more pictures."

Reluctantly, Tom followed Jolene back into the shed.

Jolene continued to clicked the camera. "Okay, Tom. I've got what I need. Let's go."

Tom got in the passenger seat and nervously watched Jolene turn the key. She turned around and headed for the road. They almost got to the mailbox when suddenly he saw flashing lights. And then he heard the drone of a fading siren. He saw Jolene stomp on the brakes.

"Damn, we've got company," she said while removing her seatbelt and reaching into the back seat.

Tom saw her remove the camera from the back seat and place it into the glove compartment.

A big man got out of a police car. He didn't wear a hat or uniform, but he had a badge pinned to his shirt. Tom saw the holster and gun attached to his belt that supported a large belly. The officer flicked on a flashlight and approached the Toyota. The side of Jolene's head lit up from the beam.

The sheriff's face beamed, Tom thought. His eyes danced with excitement. "What are ya' doin' here?" he asked firmly.

"Just looking around," Jolene said. "No law against that," She added.

The sheriff crouched and noticed Tom in the passenger seat. "You stay put, sir. Lady, step out, please."

"You're driver's license, ma'am."

Jolene got out of the vehicle and dug out her license from her purse.

"Don't you know that this is private property?"

"Ah, officer—it was all my idea. I felt it necessary to look at the combine harvester that killed Ralph Talbot. He was my uncle, you know."

"You're trespassing. Who's your passenger?"

"Tom Hastings. He's a friend of mine."

"Hastings, huh, you're trespassing, too, mister. Oh, yeah, Hastings! I've been to your house—nice place. "So what the hell are you doin' here?" the sheriff yelled.

Tom felt his blood begin to boil. "I just went along for the ride, sheriff."

"You two stay put. I'm making a call."

The sheriff returned to his car and got inside. He was on the phone for a few minutes before returning to the Toyota. "I'll have to ask both of you two to get into my car. We're going to wait for the tow truck. After that, I'm taking you both to Big Lakes."

"Tow truck! What the heck for! We didn't do anything—just got curious. Besides, there weren't any 'No Trespassing' signs," said Jolene, pointing her finger.

"Don't get smart with me, lady. You're in enough trouble as it is."

After guiding Tom and Jolene into his car, the sheriff walked over to the Toyota and sat on the passenger seat. He grabbed the keys from the ignition and opened the glove compartment. Reaching in, he brought out Jolene's camera.

21

JOLENE AND TOM GOT A FREE RIDE to the Big Lakes sheriff's office. They were led to a small room where an officer asked for their identification. He laid the IDs next to a keyboard and keyed in the information. Jolene sat down by the small counter while Tom continued to stand. Jolene's face flushed. "Officer, I want my license back and I want to make a call."

"You'll have to talk to the sheriff," he responded.

Tom noticed Jolene's face had reddened with anger. Her fists clenched as she got up off the chair and marched toward the sheriff.

"Sheriff, what are you charging me with?"

"Illegal trespass," he answered. "You have the right to—"

"I insist on calling an attorney!"

"Sure, go ahead. There's the phone."

Tom watched as she jerked the receiver off the hook. "I need a phone book," she said angrily.

The officer behind the desk reached in a drawer and pulled one out. Jolene walked over and jerked it out of his hand.

"Watch it, lady, or you'll be spending some time with us," the officer growled.

Tom put his face into his hands. He wished he were home, safe and sound in bed. Watching Jolene punch numbers on a phone, he tried to think of the name of an attorney.

After Jolene finished on the phone, she returned to her seat next to Tom. "That lunatic—he's determined to make it tough on me. My attorney will be here within half an hour."

Jolene and Tom remained sitting until Attorney Patrick Levitt came through the door.

Jolene rose and approached her attorney. They talked for a couple of minutes. Mr. Levitt approached the officer at the counter. "What are you holding my client, Jolene Hunt, for?"

"We're not holding your client. She can leave anytime she wishes."

"How about her friend, can he leave, too?"

"Yes, he can. There aren't any charges."

The attorney turned and met the glare of his client.

Jolene looks furious, Tom thought.

"What the heck is that sheriff pulling? Putting us though all this and—no charges!" Jolene exclaimed.

"Ah, Jolene—you best hold it down. Let's go while the getting is good. Hastings, you're with my client, aren't you?" Levitt asked.

"I guess I am. Not that I want to be at the moment," muttered Tom as he looked at Jolene and saw the anticipated frown.

"Okay, let's get out of here, you two," the attorney responded.

As they walked toward the door, the sheriff waved and interceded. He cleared his throat and pointed his finger at Jolene. His hand shook and he said, "Miss Hunt, I advise you to stay away from the Talbot farm and keep your nose out of the Talbot affairs—the accidents. Do ya' hear me?"

Jolene put both hands on her waist and said rapidly, "Sheriff Peterson, I have a vested interest in what happened to Ben Talbot. I'm not going to allow you to intimidate me. I plan on going over your head on this matter. There may have been a crime committed that you are intentionally ignoring. The voters of this county will be interested."

The sheriff smirked and stormed out of the room.

Out on the sidewalk, Patrick Levitt stopped his client. "Jolene, you have the right to say anything you want. However, please be careful not to accuse anyone of anything. And don't do anything illegal."

"Thanks for coming so soon, Patrick. I really appreciate it, Jolene said contritely."

"Hey, we don't have a vehicle!" Tom exclaimed.

The desk officer showed up jingling a set of keys. "Your keys ma'am—you may pick up your vehicle at *Lake's Towing,* after you pay their fee," he said and smiled.

"Fee! You guys have all the nerve," Jolene trumpeted as she jerked the keys out of the officer's fingers.

The officer shook his head and headed back inside.

"Patrick, would you mind? We need a ride," Jolene said.

When Patrick Levitt dropped off his two passengers at Lake's Towing, Tom noticed that the Toyota had a broad shallow dent in the back door on the passenger side.

"Damn-it, Tom. My camera is missing. Bet that stupid sheriff took it—remind me to make a note and call Patrick."

22

JOLENE DROVE HER TOYOTA ONTO TOM'S DRIVEWAY. "I feel embarrassed, Tom. It's not your battle."

"No, it's not my battle, but the sheriff seems to be deliberately ignoring evidence—that's troublesome to me. I'm concerned that he may have a relationship with Reggie Logan."

"Yeah, I have the same feeling. Did you say Reggie Logan's mother and father are both dead?" Jolene asked.

"Yeah, Theresa died about six years ago. Reggie's dad about five or six years before that, so I've heard," Tom said.

"I wonder if there's anyone around living around here that would remember Reggie's parents."

"If there isn't, then perhaps a library may have some information."

"The library! Yes, that's a great idea, Tom. I bet Reggie's mother and dad would have had their obituaries in an outdated newspaper. The library has copies of them. Oh, Tom. The court house: *Register of Deeds.* There has to be some information about the Logan's somewhere."

"Since you have so much to do, I can help. I'll ask Henry. He may know of someone that lives around here—that would be familiar with the Logan's background."

"Thanks so much for coming along, Tom."

"You're welcome, Jolene. Oh, there's one more thing. You're not going to like this, but there's a dent in your car—the back door on the passenger side."

"What!" Jolene jumped out of her Toyota. She walked around back and squatted down by the back car door. "Jesus—man—this wasn't there when I first picked you up."

"Yeah, it looks pretty recent," Tom said after exiting the vehicle.

Jolene looked up at the sky. "Now, I'm really mad. That guttersnipe isn't going to get away with this. You can count on that. I've gotta go, Tom. Thanks again."

Tom extended his hand. Jolene took it, and gave Tom a deep clenching hug. They parted and Jolene got back into her car and drove off.

JOLENE WALKED INTO THE OFFICE of county attorney, Jack McCarthy, and took a seat. A couple of minutes later, a man entered. Jolene begin to rise...he lifted his hand. "Please remain seated."

"Miss Hunt, what brings you here today? I bet it's about the Talbots and Reggie Logan."

"Mr. McCarthy, I believe that Sheriff Peterson of Big Lakes County is deliberately ignoring evidence."

"Whoa, wait a minute," the county attorney responded, appearing stunned. "You better have proof."

"First of all, he ignored what Tom Hastings had told him—that someone jumped from the pickup before the train hit. Secondly, he ignored the evidence of the dented wheel and the red stain on the truck bumper."

"Miss Hunt, The county medical examiner interviewed the engineer and the conductor. They said no one jumped from the pickup. Your friend, Mr. Hastings, must have been mistaken. What's this about a dented wheel and a red stain on the truck? What truck?"

"Mr. McCarthy, are you aware that one of the combine harvester wheels where Ralph Talbot died was damaged? The dent is fresh and caused the tire to go flat. Someone driving the truck crashed the front bumper into the wheel. The crash may have caused the death of Ralph Talbot. It could have been deliberate.

"And, the son-of-a-gun stole my camera."

"The hearing is day after tomorrow, Miss Hunt. Are you willing to testify?"

"Yes, I will testify. It's my duty," Jolene responded firmly.

"I'll inquire with the sheriff as to the whereabouts of your camera. You know, Miss Hunt, even if you can convince the medical examiner that the truck hit the combine, that won't prove that someone did it intentionally."

"But if it was an accident, why didn't the hired hands volunteer the information on that day?"

The county attorney raised a finger to make a point but said nothing.

"Well, how about if the people that were on the farm that day were to be questioned?" Jolene continued.

"They will be, Miss Hunt—they will be. Now if you'll excuse me, I have some work to do."

"Oh, and there's one more thing. See this—it's the license number of a car that harassed Tom and I on the road the other night."

"Miss Hunt, that needs to be reported to either the state patrol or the sheriff's department."

I know that, she thought. There're just too many things on my mind.

23

"YOU'RE NEXT." Floyd muttered to Tom Hastings.

Main Street has lots of parking spaces open, Tom thought on a mid-morning in the middle of October. He had found a spot right next to the barbershop.

Nick Smith had gotten up from the barber chair. "Good to have you back, Tom," he said.

"Thanks, Nick. How are things out on the point?"

"Quiet—a lot more quiet than around here. Two big accidents, I hear—not to mention the big bank robbery."

Floyd piped in, "I hear some people don't think they were accidents."

"What's that all about, Floyd?" Nick asked.

"To begin with, Tom here—he claims someone jumped from

the pickup just before the train hit. That throws a lot of suspicion on the first Talbot death. And then, the Hunt woman says a truck hit the combine and had something to do with Ralph Talbot getting killed."

Nick looked at Tom. "What about it, Tom?"

"The people at the death hearing didn't believe me. You'll have to talk to Miss Hunt about the other deal—the damaged combine harvester," Tom said.

"I hear you were there in the machinery building with the lady," Floyd said, stepping back from his customer, holding a pair of scissors in one hand and a power clipper in the other.

Tom frowned. "Floyd, I'd rather not talk about it anymore. Okay!"

Nick Smith shook his head and left the barbershop. Tom remained quiet until Floyd finished. "Here's ten, Floyd. Keep the change."

"Tom, I believe you—about someone jumping from the pickup. I think there's something real shaky going on. Everyone knows what that nephew is like. He's out for the money. You just wait—if he gets his hands on it, he'll be out of here like a rocket."

"Floyd, do you know anything about the sheriff being a friend of the Logan's?"

"No, I don't, but I bet I know who would know?"

"Who would that be?"

"Martha Cramer. She lives on the western outskirts of town."

The door opened and Ned Stockwell entered. His blocky physique filled the doorway and he bumped the doorframe when entering. A triangular flat piece of plaster fell from the ceiling. It clattered to the floor a few inches from Ned's toe. He struggled in getting the door closed. "Hey, Floyd! You're bombing me."

Ned's wife owned and managed *Bev's Embroidery* shop across from the Ford Equipment Company business. Ned did odd jobs around town and at some of the lake cabins.

"You've got to be more careful coming through the door, Ned," Floyd said, laughing.

"Hey, have you heard the latest?" Ned asked.

"No, what's that?"

"Marty Bishop is back in town."

"Yeah, we all know that. He showed up at Ben's funeral."

"Yes, but he's still a brother-in-law to Ben and Ralph. The divorce never went through."

Floyd shook the apron and chunks of hair fell to the floor. He stood holding the apron. "Well, come on, Ned. Are you here to talk or to get a haircut?"

NED STOCKWELL HAD SIGNED THE PAPER just below the line while the ink from his wife's signature dried. They had accepted a lease on a building that formerly housed a vacuum cleaner shop. It surprised Ned that they needed his signature on the lease, but not on the equipment loan at the bank.

His wife, Bev, had told him that the bank didn't need his signature on the loan. "I am buying forty-six thousand dollars worth of equipment and supplies," she had said. Bev had quit her job in Big Lakes after deciding to go into business for herself. She gave up a guaranteed salary and put their financial security on the line, or at least Ned thought so. Then, she traded her car for a red Grand Prix at *Bates Motors* in Big Lakes. Ned wondered how she was going to make the payments.

The money that Ned earned doing odd jobs fell off dramatically during the winter months. He accepted several types of work but snow removal wasn't one of them. Ned hated snow.

Ned had gotten a college football scholarship after graduating from high school. He had been the greatest fullback in his high school's history, scoring fifty-two touchdowns in a four-year period. "No-neck Ned," his teammates called him.

In the first quarter of his college freshman year, Ned and his buddies got drunk in their dormitory. That resulted in several of the players getting suspended, including Ned. Returning to his home in disgrace, his father chastised him. His mother had been sympathetic, especially when eyeing the space where his front tooth was knocked out during football practice. She offered to dip into her savings to replace it. Ned felt self-conscious about the space in his mouth but didn't have the good sense to accept his mother's offer.

When his father died of lung cancer, Ned's life changed. His self-worth improved and he took a new job with a local plumbing firm. One evening, he had joined his co-workers for beers at *William's Pub* and met Beverly Sandgren. They got married a year later. His mother wanted a grandchild, but Ned and Bev couldn't have children.

When his mother died, Ned became depressed and hung around the pub most every evening. A couple of beers per evening grew in numbers to seven or eight. Eventually, he lost his job and almost his marriage. Ned went into alcohol treatment and regularly attended Alcoholics Anonymous. His personality changed and he seldom smiled. Instead, he became argumentative and cynical.

Spending evenings at home with his wife, he became aware that she avoided discussing financial matters. Ned wondered where she got the money to pay off the mortgage. His curiosity got satisfied one day when he overheard a conversation. Bev had called someone *Dad*. As far as Ned knew, his wife had always been an orphan.

Ned did some snooping and discovered his wife did have a real father. It had taken him three hours to find the key to Beverly's lock…the small drawer in her vanity. He became flabbergasted when learning that her dad was Ralph Talbot…she had a copy of her birth certificate. Since losing the plumbing job, Ned's odd job list included working for the Talbot brothers. He had helped them with the corn harvest for years, never once realizing that Ralph was his father-in-law.

Ned knew the two bachelor brothers had lots of money. He felt upbeat thinking that his wife is a living relative…Uh-oh, perhaps some inheritance. Ned wondered how much the two brothers were worth…likely over a million, he thought.

24

JOLENE HAD JUST HUNG UP THE PHONE. She sat at her desk at work and looked out the window. Tom Hastings had called and told her about Martha Cramer. Jolene had prepared a document outlining the reasons why the two accidents could have been murders. The hearing had been scheduled for tomorrow…not much time. She needed to visit the Cramer lady today…immediately after work.

The pavement ended part way down Spangler Avenue, and the surface changed to gravel. There are only three houses on the avenue, all on the same side, she said to herself. The first two are white and the farthest one is green. According to information I got from Tom, Martha lived in the green one.

Jolene touched her brake, stopping her Toyota in front of the house. She got out and looked across the other side of the avenue, noticing a tight stand of ash trees. They stood tall and naked…leaves long gone. Beyond the stand of trees, she saw a swamp, surrounded by tall brown grasses and dark topped rushes. She watched two ducks circle and land in the middle.

The single garage attached to Martha Cramer's house obviously is not being used, she thought after noticing brown weeds projected through the multitudes of cracks in the concrete driveway.

Jolene climbed the three wooden steps and stood on the small, railed landing. She pushed the button next to the doorframe and waited. Moments later, she caught a glimpse of a face in the bay window. Jolene elevated a fisted thumb into the air, relieved that Martha is home–time is of essence, she thought.

The door knob turned and the door swung open. Martha Cramer stood in the doorway and stared at her visitor. She wore metal-rimmed glasses, her white hair tied into a bun. The enlarged knuckles of her left hand clutched a cane.

Jolene assisted by pulling open the storm door. "Yes. Can I help you?" Martha asked.

"Martha Cramer? My name is Jolene Hunt. I would like to talk with you. I'm interested in community history. People tell me you have a fantastic memory."

Martha smiled. "Welcome to my humble home. What you say your name is?"

"Jolene Hunt—Jolene Hunt."

"Come on in, Jolene, and have a seat. Can I get you some tea?"

"Yes, I would like some. Here, let me help you."

The old wooden cabinets reminded Jolene of her mother's house…the white pearl knobs. "You sit, Jolene, and I'll be with you shortly."

Jolene noticed that the living room had several framed pictures on the wall and the shelves, filled with nick-knacks, used up all the available spaces. The potbelly stove in the corner is radiating a moderate amount of heat, she thought. Minutes later, Jolene rose and helped Martha with a tray loaded with a steaming pot and two cups.

"Where do you live, Jo—ah?"

"Jolene—my name is Jolene."

"Oh yes—memory isn't too good, you know."

"On Trevor Lake. Do you know where that is?"

"Sure do. My husband and I had a cottage there once. He's dead, you know."

"Martha, do you remember a Theresa Logan?"

"Oh, yes. I remember her well. She died of cancer, poor thing. She had two husbands."

"Do you remember her son, Reggie?"

"I do, but I wish I didn't."

"Why, Martha?"

"He's a bad one, that Reggie. His dad isn't much better."

"You mean Mr. Logan."

"No, not Alvin—his dad is Torfin Peterson."

"Torfin Peterson! Who's that?"

"The sheriff—his first name is Torfin. They had quite a thing going you know—Torfin and Theresa."

Her words stunned Jolene. "How do you know all that?"

"I was their housekeeper. They didn't think I noticed—but I did. That Torfin was there late at night—too many times."

25

THE MEDICAL EXAMINER CALLED THE HEARING to order. He turned to the county attorney, Jack McCarthy, and asked. "Are you ready?"

"I am, Doctor."

Dr. Bar, the medical examiner for Big Lakes County, described what he witnessed after arriving at the farm. "The emergency rescue vehicle and a fire truck from New Dresden were parked next to the tractor. The body of Ralph Talbot was lying on the ground next to a combine. The victim's skull was fractured and there was considerable internal bleeding in the brain. He likely died instantly.

"There was also a huge bruise above the knees and in the thigh area. Likely some of the upper leg bones were fractured. The victim must have been adjusting or fixing something on the combine and fell. He had to have hit his head hard."

Matt Nelson, the fire chief of New Dresden, was called as the first witness. He confidently took a seat in the witness chair.

"Mr. Nelson, would you tell County Attorney McCarthy what you found after arriving at the scene out in the cornfield?" the chairman said.

Matt explained that the victim was lying on the ground, already dead. "The tractor engine was idling…the power-take-off to the combine harvester was not turning."

"As I understand, you were the first person to respond to the emergency call. Is that correct?"

"Yes, that's true."

"Who called about the accident, Mr. Nelson?" the county attorney asked.

"Don't know."

Edgar Sandvik became the next witness.

"Mr. Sandvik. Would you have a seat please?" Edgar appeared confused and hesitated.

"Please, up here, Mr. Sandvik."

Edgar stood up and trotted to the witness chair. He explained about being asked by Ralph to help with the corn harvest. County Attorney McCarthy asked, "Mr. Sandvik, did you do all the hauling of the corn the day that Ralph died?"

"Naw, I did the truck hauling most of the time…then sometimes the tractor, but not all of it."

"Who else participated in the hauling on that day?"

"Ah…who else?" Edgar said, appearing confused.

"Yes. If you didn't do all the hauling, someone else must have been helping you."

"Ah—Oh, Ned—he helped out."

"Ned? Is there a last name?"

"Stockwell. He helped us that day."

"Anyone else?"

"Well, I'm not sure, but Reggie may have taken a load."

"Reggie—Reggie who?"

"Ah—Reggie Logan, the nephew—Theresa's boy."

"Did Reggie drive the truck or the tractor?"

"Don't know."

"Mr. Sandvik. You told me earlier that you were the one that found Ralph lying on the ground."

"Yeah, I sure did."

"What did you do?"

"I got out of the truck and went over to him—Ralph."

"Yes, and what did you find. What did you see?"

"His head was sort of caved in. He wasn't breathing."

"What did you do next?"

"I headed hell bent for leather back to the farm. Reggie was there and he called for help."

After Dr. Bar dismissed him, Edgar smiled and saluted the doctor, and then he turned his head and saluted the people sitting at the table.

Ned Stockwell, who had just arrived at the courthouse, got called next. He looked nervous and worried...his fingers in constant motion, sliding on each other and occasionally clasping. After clearing his throat, he told the medical examiner and county attorney that he mostly drove the tractor and unloaded the wagons into the bin.

When asked if he drove the truck, he replied, "Once or twice."

Reggie Logan's turn came. He took the stand, confidently looked around the room and smiled. His smile intensified while looking at Jolene and Tom who were close to the door. He testified that he volunteered to drive the truck twice and give Edgar a break. "My uncle was up in the cab when I took the load back to the farm."

Jolene nudged Tom. "Yeah, I'll bet Ralph was up in the cab," she whispered. "That dent in the wheel came from the truck and Reggie was driving it, I bet."

Reggie Logan smiled widely after getting dismissed from the witness chair. The sheriff got called next. The clumping noise of the sheriff's boots disrupted the quiet atmosphere of the room as he thumped his way up to the witness chair. The boot noises ended and the witness chair creaked as the sheriff took his seat. Sheriff Peterson smiled and nodded toward the officials behind the long table.

After the first question, the sheriff looked up at the ceiling, his smile disappearing as he grabbed the arm of the chair with his hand. He told the investigators that he didn't see anything unusual. "Ralph must have slipped and fallen—hit his head—split it open."

"When did you arrive on the scene?" McCarthy asked.

"Just before the ambulance took him away."

"Ah, Sheriff, did you notice the wheels of the combine? Was one of them dented—the closest one to the victim?"

"Yeah, I did, but that probably happened long before."

"What makes you think that?" McCarthy asked.

"Well, if you ever saw Edgar Sandvik drive a truck, you would know why things get dented. He's not the smoothest."

"Sheriff, I went out to the farm the other day and the dent in the wheel appeared to be quite fresh."

"So the wheel was dented—no big deal. It happens on farms all the time," the sheriff said.

"You're sure that the wheel did not get dented on that day—at the time of the accident?"

The sheriff frowned and his lips came together tightly. His right hand gripped the chair arm. "Well, you damn right I am. Are you accusing me of making it up?"

"No not at all, Sheriff. I just want the truth."

The county attorney returned to his chair. He reached down and picked up a paper. "Sheriff Peterson, would you tell us about an incident that happened on the Talbot farm after the alleged accident—it has to do with two trespassers?"

"Yup, I got a call that evening about a strange vehicle parked in the farmstead."

"Who was it that called?"

"Reggie Logan."

"After you got to the farm, what did you find?"

"I stopped a Toyota sport utility vehicle on the roadway as it tried to leave the farm."

"Who was in the vehicle?"

The sheriff pointed toward the door. "Those two over there—the man and woman—next to the door."

"You mean Jolene Hunt and Tom Hastings."

"Yup—it was them."

"I understand that Miss Hunt took some photos. Did you take the camera from her?"

"Yes sir, I confiscated it. What they were doing was illegal, you know."

"Do you have the camera?"

"Yes."

"Where is it?"

"It's in our vault. We're sending it back to the lady."

"Did you take out the film?"

"Yeah, I did. We had it developed and none of the pictures turned out."

"Will Miss Hunt get the bad pictures and the negatives back?"

"Ah—guess not. Someone threw 'em away. They weren't readable anyhow."

"Sheriff, I think you should make an effort to find the pictures and negatives, and return them to Miss Hunt."

"Yeah, I'll check into it."

"Thanks very much, Sheriff. I know you're a busy man."

The sheriff pushed his chair back and stomped away from the table. He didn't look back and headed out the door.

The medical examiner stood and announced that the hearing had ended. He said the decision on the cause of death would be announced in a few days. After thanking everyone for coming, he sat down.

Jolene stood, her face contorted with disbelief. Over! How could this hearing be over? I wasn't called, she said to herself angrily. Other than the court reporter, examiner and county attorney, the rest of the people in the room got up and headed for the door.

She approached Jack McCarthy. "Mr. McCarthy, why didn't you call on me? Earlier you indicated that I would be questioned about what I saw at the farm."

"Miss Hunt, I didn't call on you because your search was illegal. While your observations could be used at a death hearing, it would not be allowable in court. Even in this hearing, your story would have been suspect, considering the circumstances."

"Mr. McCarthy! We both know what the hearing result is going to be. The sheriff got his way. Did you know that he is the paternal father of Reggie Logan?"

McCarthy glared at Jolene. "Miss Hunt, I cannot base my decision on rumors—small town talk."

Jolene turned and stormed out of the room, followed by a confused Tom Hastings.

Tom followed her down the marble steps and out the front door. When they got to their vehicle, Tom said, "Did you notice the man on the bench?"

"Notice who?"

"The pock-marked face man with the gray ponytail, Marty Bishop. He watched us leave."

JACK MCCARTHY SAT AT HIS DESK. His assistant, Mark, stood

in front of the window, which overlooked the parking lot down below. "Touchy—very touchy situation," Jack told his assistant.

"I can't believe that Sheriff Peterson is the father of Reggie Logan," Mark said.

"Rumors—just rumors, but, if it's true—then perhaps Miss Hunt
is onto something."

"Darn it, we checked the truck bumper—nothing," the assistant
remarked.

"Yeah, but that was a few days after the accident. And the bumper did look freshly polished. Someone buffed that bumper. The
wheel on the combine had been replaced, including a spanking new
rubber tire. I did see the dented one during an initial visit. There was
no sign of the old wheel, nor did anyone claim to have replaced it.

"Mark, I'm going to recommend to Dr. Bar that we delay the
result. We need to continue to investigate Ralph Talbot's death."

"Torfin Peterson isn't going to be happy."

"To hell with Peterson," McCarthy said.

26

JOLENE FOUND IT DIFFICULT TO CONCENTRATE on the day
after the hearing. She sat at her desk watching vehicles go through
the traffic signal. Another *accident,* she thought. That's going to be
their conclusion. My only consolation was noticing the facial expression of the county attorney after the meeting ended. *Jack Mc-
Carthy was obviously not satisfied with the hearing,* she thought
hopefully.

Jolene felt convinced that Reggie Logan murdered her father
and Uncle Ralph. Since there wasn't a will, the next event would
be the settlement of the estate. She punched in the county attorney's
number.

"Miss Hunt, the settlement of the estate is going to take place at
the family attorney's office. I will not be involved."

"Mr. McCarthy, I am not interested in any of the money. I only want justice," Jolene said.

"I share some of your uncertainty about the conclusions of the sheriff and medical examiner. Your strongest alternative would be to engage an attorney and file a wrongful death lawsuit. However, based on the evidence so far, I doubt you would win.

"Another suggestion for you would be to hire a private investigator—that is, if you wish to pursue this case," McCarthy said.

"Yes. I have seriously been thinking about that. Do you recommend anyone special?"

"Sorry, Miss Hunt, but I can't do that—check the yellow pages."

Jolene rang the number of her attorney, Patrick Levitt. They agreed to meet at his office on 4:00 p.m. Friday afternoon.

Jolene had high expectations, but became disappointed with her attorney's advice. Her former classmate and now her attorney Patrick Levitt wasn't very enthusiastic about initiating a lawsuit based on existing evidence. He also had mentioned that there weren't any private investigators located in the area.

She drove home, feeling depressed. After arriving, she sat on the couch with a glass of wine. Picking up the phone she punched in Tom Hastings number. "Hey, how about meeting me at Mary Ann's. I need someone to talk to. I'm depressed."

"Sorry to hear that. I'll try to help. How about 7:00?"

"Sure."

FALLING ORANGE OAK LEAVES showered Tom's pickup as he left his driveway and headed up the roadway. The fall colors are at their high mark for the season, he thought. He had been out in the woods cutting and splitting firewood all afternoon. He welcomed the call from Jolene even if she focused on the deaths of the Talbot brothers.

While passing by the Talbot farm, he noticed three cars parked in the driveway. One of them is red, he said to himself. I assume it belongs to Reggie Logan.

Mary Ann's parking lot had lots of empty spaces. Heck, it's a Friday, but the summer tourists are pretty much gone for the season, he thought. Tom parked his pickup and headed inside. "Has my friend arrived yet?" he asked Mary Ann.

"Well now, what friend would that be?"

"The tall blonde woman, you've met her before."

"Oh, yes, I have. But, I haven't seen her come in yet."

"Do you need a table for dinner?"

"Not right now. I'll wait at the bar. When Jolene shows up, would you send her over?"

"Oh sure, Tom."

Tom took a high table in the bar area and sat in a position to be able to watch the door. He felt tension when seeing two men sitting in a booth. One of them had gray hair pulled back into a ponytail... his face pock-marked.

When Jolene made her entry, she spotted Tom immediately and headed for his table. Tom stood and held out his hand, assisting Jolene onto a high stool.

"Anything big happening at the title company?" Tom asked.

"Reggie Logan has stopped harassing me as much, but I still see him hanging around once in awhile."

"He's probably feeling confident that your snooping isn't getting anywhere," Tom said.

"Snooping! Tom, I'm not snooping."

"Ah—sorry—didn't mean it that way. Yet that night at the farm may be considered snooping."

"Damn it, Tom. If I don't investigate, who's goin' to—the sheriff? What a joke he is—and that goes for the rest of 'em in that courthouse."

Tom put a hand on her arm. "Steady, young lady—steady."

"Tom! I'm going to test your memory. When you saw the person jump out of the pickup truck, were there any vehicles waiting on the other side of the track?"

Tom removed his hand and Jolene lightly punched his shoulder with her fist. "Think, Tom, think!"

"No, there were not. But, wait a minute—there was at least one vehicle approaching. I just vaguely remember seeing something white, coming down the road," Tom said, scratching his forehead with a finger.

"Was it a car, or what?"

"Don't know, because I focused on the pickup."

"I talked to my attorney today. Remember him? He's the one who bailed us out from the sheriff's office that night."

"I sure do remember. It was quite the evening."

"I was hoping that Levitt could steer me to a private investigator, but he didn't know of any. As a matter of fact, he got doggoned negative. Seeking the truth didn't seem to turn him on. I wonder what would happen if I put an inquiry in the *Big Lakes Tribune and Pine Lakes Enterprise*?"

"What sort of inquiry?"

"To search for someone, who may have been driving a white vehicle approaching the track, when the train hit the pickup?"

"Well, that certainly would be a long shot. It could have been someone from out of town. But then, it wouldn't hurt to try," Tom said.

Jolene frowned as she stared at the windowed wall. "That's exactly what I'm going to do. Don't look now, but Marty Bishop is sitting at a booth against the wall, under a window. Whoops, they're getting up to leave."

Tom watched the two men put on their jackets. "Jolene, there's something weird here—the bank robbery that I witnessed. Marty Bishop's gray hair—his stance and mannerism resembles one of them—the bank robbers."

"Tom, didn't you tell all that to the FBI?"

"Yes, I sure did. I'm surprised that he's still around. But then, we saw him at the courthouse the other day, didn't we?"

"The other day—it was only yesterday, Tom," Jolene responded and laughed. "You're losing it, Tom."

Tom continued to watch the two men as they left the restaurant. Shaking his head, he said, "I could be wrong—gut feeling tells me it was him. Oh well. Perhaps it's a coincidence—still—you would think the FBI would have checked him out."

"I bet they did. They're probably watching him like a hawk—even as I speak," Jolene said.

27

PRANCER'S ANTLERS LIT UP FOR ONLY A SECOND as the sun filtered through a stand of timber. Moments later, the big deer bolted and leaped across the trail. Tom watched with awe as he saw the white tail disappear into the woods. He stood motionless as three smaller deer bounded in Prancer's direction.

Tom's mind focused on the inquiry notice that appeared in the *Tribune*. Jolene had kept her word and publicly sought another witness to the train accident.

The trail is damp and padded with orange, reddish and yellow leaves, Tom thought. He looked up at the tall trees readying for winter. Only a few leaves remained. The summer birds are all gone. Only the cries of blue jays broke the silence in the forest on that day.

He worried when deer season approached. As usual, Prancer would be a major concern…most deer hunters looked for big racks.

After returning to the house, he reread the notice that Jolene had placed in the local *Tribune*. He felt anxious to talk to her and learn if there had been any responses.

On the way to New Dresden, Tom stopped at the farm of Glen and Lois Sterling, his immediate neighbors to the north. Tom needed permission to place a snow fence on their land. Lois treated him to a coffee and a just-out-of-the-oven cookie. The beautiful black and silver wood cook stove took the chill out of the late October air. Glen had gone to town, but Lois gave Tom the permission to put up the snow fence.

After the third cookie, Tom thanked her and continued on to New Dresden. He rounded *Purgatory Curve* and noticed the flashing lights. Tom saw a state patrol car and a deputy sheriff's car parked off to the side. Two officers stood next to an upside down vehicle. My God! He thought. It's a light colored Toyota, just the kind Jolene drives. I'm afraid to go down there.

He parked the pickup and strode toward the flipped over vehicle. "What happened?" he asked one of the officers.

"Too much speed—some people drive too fast around this curve."

"Who was it? Do you know?"

"Let me see here. A woman by the name of Hunt."

"Geez, was she hurt?" Tom asked.

"She didn't seem to be injured too badly. The ambulance took her away about ten minutes ago."

Tom felt stunned. Jolene is not a fast driver, he said to himself. He quickly returned to his pickup and drove into town. After picking up his mail, he headed for Big Lakes.

TOM CHECKED OUT THE EMERGENCY AREA OF THE HOS-PITAL in Big Lakes and learned that they had only one patient. He convinced the woman at the desk that he was a close friend of the accident victim. She allowed him to pass and enter the suite.

Stopping at the open doorway, he saw that Jolene's bandaged forehead. Her eyes showed pain while the doctor manipulated her left arm.

"You're lucky it isn't broken, but we'll have to keep it in a sling for a couple of weeks," the doctor said.

Jolene looked up at Tom. "Oh, Tom, I've had an accident. Some son-of-a-gun ran me off the road."

"Are you okay, Jolene?

"Yes, I'm fine. A cut in the forehead and a sprained arm, that's all."

"Who ran you off the road?"

"Not sure, but it was a red car. Does that mean anything? Who drives a red car that's been harassing me? Take one guess."

"How did the officers react to your story—getting run off the road?"

"Well, they listened, and a deputy told me that he needed to talk to me before I leave for home."

Tom heard a knock on the doorframe, just outside the room. A deputy sheriff peeked into the room. "When you're ready, I'll be out by the desk, Miss Hunt. I need a statement."

"You'll get one—that's for sure."

"I'll be in the lobby, Jolene. Soon as you are ready, I'll give you a ride. What about it, Doc? Can she go home when you're done?" Tom asked.

"Yes. She'll be fine."

Tom left the room and sat down next to the deputy in the waiting area. "Any idea how it happened?" he asked the deputy.

"She simply lost control when rounding the curve."

"You mean *Purgatory Curve*?"

The deputy laughed and responded. "*Purgatory Curve*! Is that what everyone calls it?"

"That's what I call it. A lot of us have gotten caught speeding there. It's a trap—hiding the thirty sign until the last moment."

The deputy smiled and said, "Big Lakes County needs the money."

Jolene made her appearance, limping slightly and her left arm in a sling. The deputy and Tom watched as she painfully worked her way to the counter. She clumsily signed some papers while attempting to steady them with the fingers of her left hand.

When she came over to sit next to the deputy, he picked up a clipboard. "I'm Deputy Dave Johnson and would like you to tell me what happened."

"Someone ran me off the road, deputy. I wasn't speeding."

"Go ahead, tell me about it."

"I was coming into town on the state highway, going slightly over forty. When I got to the lake, a red car passed me. It was speeding—probably fifty or sixty miles per hour. As I rounded the curve, a car came right toward me—in my lane. I think it was the same one—red. It angled across most of the width of the highway and I didn't have any choice—I got forced off the road. My car rolled at least twice—real steep right there."

After five more minutes of discussion, the deputy rose and said to Jolene, "Thanks. I'll file the report and talk to the sheriff. We'll investigate and hopefully find out who forced you off the road."

The deputy left the room. "A lot of good that will do," cried Jolene angrily.

"Do you think it was Reggie Logan's car?" Tom asked.

"Not sure—just not sure. It happened so fast—but then, who else could it have been?"

28

THE FIRST SUNDAY IN NOVEMBER dawned with a white blanket of snow on the ground. It covered everything, including the row of small pumpkins lining Tom's railing along the sidewalk. All weather is good, really, he thought. Living in Minnesota, you have to expect this.

Traffic on the county highway moved slowly. In the ditch, next to the cemetery, a black pickup truck attempted to work its way back onto the road, spraying a mixture of dirt and snow from its spinning wheels. The flat area next to and below *Purgatory Curve* no longer showed the gouges in the ground created by Jolene's Toyota on the previous day.

The bank robbery that occurred over a month ago no longer got prime time discussion up and down Main Street. Instead, the locals talked about the rollover at *Purgatory Curve*. "These people drive too fast," Tom heard a man say, who wore bib overalls and stood in the entry area of the grocery store. "They've got to slow down— teach 'em a lesson," the man added.

"About half the vehicles coming into town from that direction are going too fast," another person said, a man working a toothpick around his mouth.

Tom walked past them and proceeded up the farthest aisle. An elderly gentleman blocked most of it. He had a list in his hand. "I'm not sure why I came," the man said.

Tom remembered seeing that same man on the sidewalk over four years ago. He was lost then…even more lost now. Scratching his forehead, Tom tried to remember his name…*Reilly*. That's what it is, he thought. Yes, he's the guy known as two-beer Reilly. Tom had herd that Reilly plays cards at *William's Pub* almost every day... and he never has more or less than two beers.

"Lots of parking space on Main Street," Ellie told Tom as she keyed in his grocery items.

"Strange how people are still double-parking, even though there are plenty of places," Tom said. "By the way, Ellie. You had a good view of the bank robbery, didn't you?"

"Yeah, I sure did, right from here. I got down low right there, behind the cash register—real low—awful scared, too."

"Did you get a good look at any of the robbers?"

"Not too good—everything happened so fast—wasn't safe here."

"Did you notice if any one of them had gray hair?"

"No I didn't, why?"

"I just wondered, because it looked to me as if one of them did. I was about the same distance away as you were."

"I was too busy hiding behind the counter to notice much of anything," Ellie said.

"Have you heard anything about the missing robbers? Any news how the state investigation is going?" Tom asked.

"Not a thing."

Tom decided to have an early lunch at *William's Pub*. After putting the groceries into his pickup, he walked to the bar & grill across the street.

After entering, he took a booth and laid his newspapers on the table. He noticed only a handful of people inside. Tom's position allowed a perfect view of Main Street. "What can I get ya'?" a waitress asked.

"A Bud—bottle, if you've got it."

"Don't have bottles, only cans."

"Okay, bring me a can, but also a mug—a frosty."

"Comin' right up," the waitress said and rushed away.

While Tom browsed the newspaper and waited for the beer, he heard loud voices coming from the guys sitting at the bar. Edgar Sandvik appeared to be having a heated discussion with Kyle Fredrickson.

When Edgar got off his barstool, he tossed a handful of change on the counter. All the guys at the bar burst out laughing. Edgar stomped away and headed for the door when he spotted Tom in the booth. He saluted and plunked himself down.

"Edgar, how's it going for you today?" Tom asked.

"Good, except for those idiots over there. They don't have any manners.

"Sit down, Edgar. Take a break."

Edgar waved at a waitress. "Another beer," he yelled.

Tom smiled widely. "Are you doing any more work out at the Talbot's farm?"

"Naw, he don't want me around anymore—the punk."

"Who doesn't want you around any more?"

"Reggie, the nephew—it's probably because he knows."

"Knows what?"

"Knows that I know—he's the one who killed Ralph."

Tom inhaled deeply. He felt shocked by what he just heard. "How do you know that? You didn't say that at the hearing."

"I didn't know for sure then—Ned told me later."

"Ned told you what?"

"That Reggie took the truck out that last time." Edgar gulped down the rest of his beer, got up, saluted and left.

Tom paid his tab and went outside. Edgar had left. Tom drove home.

While Tom put away the groceries in the kitchen, he heard the answering machine beeping.

Jolene had left a message. She wanted to talk about two phone calls that she had gotten concerning her notice in the newspaper.

Tom punched in her number and waited for her to answer. "Hi, Jolene. What's this about two responses to your newspaper inquiry?"

"Tell you what. I'll put some nachos in the microwave. Why don't you come over? I'll tell you all about it," she said.

"Okay. See you in a few minutes."

JOLENE'S EYES SPARKLED WITH EXCITEMENT when she opened the door after Tom buzzed. "Hi. Come on in."

"How do you like that white stuff?" Tom asked while removing his cap and coat.

"Doesn't bother me one bit—excuse the mess. I can't do much with just one hand. At least, my headache is gone."

"So, you've had a couple of calls that responded to your inquiry."

"Yes, I have. One of them is a refrigeration service man. He drove a white van and had just rounded *Purgatory Curve* when the train hit the pickup."

"Did he see anybody?"

"Tom, listen to this! The man's name is Fritz. He mentioned getting a glimpse of someone running toward the elevator right after the train hit the pickup. He had lost sight of the person because of the high bushes on that side of the tracks. He saw someone, Tom! Fritz has agreed to meet me for lunch tomorrow at the *Locomotive*. Will you come?"

"Ah, Jolene, let me think about that. It does sound interesting. What about the second call?"

"It was obviously phony—someone trying to make a buck."

"I had a chat with Edgar Sandvik at *William's Pub* today. He said something interesting, too," Tom said.

"That man is always interesting. What did he have to say"

"He said that Reggie Logan drove the truck that hit Ralph Talbot."

"Well for cripes sake! Why didn't he say that at the hearing?" Jolene said, appearing frustrated.

"That's what I asked him. You want to know why?"

"Yes!"

"Ned Stockwell had told him later, Edgar said—after the hearing. He didn't know then, during the hearing."

"Well of all the! He needs to tell that to McCarthy. Ned's playing games. He should have told the medical examiner—wonder why he didn't?" Jolene muttered.

"Well, you really don't know Edgar. He says a lot—"

29

FRITZ SWIGGUMS HAD BEEN EMPLOYED at Pine Lakes Refrigeration for the past three years. The morning of the train accident, he headed to New Dresden to service a freezer at Stillman's Super Market. After rounding the curve, he had looked at the speedometer and applied his brakes. His memory of a speeding ticket three months ago was still fresh in his mind.

After seeing the flashing red lights at the tracks, he muttered, "Oh, no. There goes ten minutes or more. At least it isn't slowing."

Fritz smoked a cigarette and he had the driver's side window slightly opened. The extraordinary-loud screeching noise drew his attention. Oh, my God, he thought. There's a vehicle on the tracks.

Why is that man running...going the other way? Fritz stopped short of the tracks and watched. Since he couldn't see the wreck, he turned his vehicle around and took an alternate route to get around the train. The next day, he told his boss, Owen, about the accident.

"You're a witness, Fritz. Maybe you should call the sheriff."

"Ah—I don't know—I'd rather stay out of it.

CLOSE TO TWO MONTHS HAD PASSED since the train accident. On a Thursday morning, the office manager handed Fritz a note: *Fritz, come and see me, Owen.*

Fritz stood stoically in front of his boss's desk, and read the inquiry that someone had placed in the *Tribune*.

"Fritz, you are a witness for sure. You definitely should call that woman, Jolene Hunt?" Owen said.

"I'll think about it," Fritz responded.

On Monday morning, Fritz told his boss that he had set up a meeting with Hunt. He asked for extra time at noon. Owen had agreed willingly.

Tom and Jolene waited in the lobby area of the Locomotive restaurant when Fritz arrived. Fritz wore his service uniform that had his first name embossed on his shirt.

Jolene stood. "You're Fritz, the man who called, I assume."

"Sure am."

"Hey, I'm going to buy you lunch," Jolene said.

She pointed at a booth and Fritz sat down. She and Tom sat across from him.

Tom and Jolene listened intently as Fritz told them about seeing a young man running away from the crash.

"Fritz, I'm going to write a letter to the editor of the *Tribune.* Can I use your name?"

"Ah—I guess so. What harm could it do? It's the truth."

After lunch ended, Jolene thanked Fritz for being honest. He smiled when leaving the restaurant.

"Tom, I'm going to do it—the letter to the editor. I hope you don't mind, but I'll be using your name, too."

"Well, like Fritz said, it's the truth."

SHERIFF TORFIN PETERSON SAT AT HIS DESK early Thursday afternoon. One of his deputies knocked on the door. The sheriff gestured with a wave.

"What's up, Dave?"

"Have you seen the letter in the *Tribune*?"

"No, what's it all about?"

"It's about the train accident in New Dresden. This person, who wrote the piece, doesn't think much of our investigation. She claims two witnesses saw someone leave the pickup truck just before the crash."

"Is the name at the end of the letter Jolene Hunt by any chance?"

"Yes—exactly."

The sheriff's face reddened. "Pay no attention. The woman is a radical activist. She's making claims that the dead man, Ben Talbot, was her father—all nonsense."

"Don't you think we should check that out—the second witness?" the deputy asked.

"Hell, I checked out that Hastings guy the day after the accident. He didn't know what he was talking about. Now he's teamed up with the activist. They're after the Talbot money, that's all."

Deputy Dave Johnson appeared disappointed. He had hoped that his boss would react differently. He noticed how red-faced the sheriff had gotten. Turning, he slowly walked out of the office and into the room where the staff hung out. Looking at the schedule, he noticed his patrol route for the day included New Dresden.

Dave thought about his brother, Paul, who had been involved in a series of murders, in the New Dresden area, a couple of years ago. Paul is now a state highway patrolman in the Minneapolis district, he said to himself, feeling proud. Dave had been in college when his brother talked about those harrying experiences…two murders that led to a third…an FBI agent.

Dave has darker hair and is about six inches shorter than his brother. He is also slimmer with a thinner neck and narrower shoulders. Dave's, face is narrow with a pointed chin, his thin lips failing to cover large crowded incisors.

Deputy Dave pulled up at the stop sign next to Stillman's Super Market. He noticed the bank across the street. That's where the big robbery took place, he thought. I wasn't working that day. For some reason, my boss gave me the day off. I was home raking leaves.

He cruised slowly up Main Street and passed the hardware store. After driving through the intersection, he stopped his car in a grassy area just beyond the railroad tracks. From that vantage point, his radar could read the speed of vehicles coming into town. Great spot, he remembered. It's one of the best ticket-issuing places in the county.

The deputy checked his watch. My goal is to monitor the traffic for an hour, he said to himself. He had been parked for only fifteen minutes when a red car came around the curve. Glancing at the radar screen, it showed fifty-five.

Dave pushed the lever that activated the siren and flashing lights. He got out of his car and signaled the speeding vehicle to pull over.

Peering into the car, the deputy said, "You were doin' fifty-five in a thirty zone, sir. Your driver's license, please?"

Deputy Johnson returned to his car and punched in the information, which included the name of Marty Bishop. He noticed the Kansas license plate. After several tries, the deputy's laptop produced a statement: *FBI suspect in a bank robbery.* Suspicion is not enough to hold the guy, the deputy said to himself.

He called in the speeder's license number and found out there weren't any violations registered within the past three years.

Walking back to the red car, the deputy asked, "You're from Kansas, sir?"

"Yes. I'm visiting."

The driver didn't dispute the speeding ticket that the deputy handed him. "Take it easy in the future, sir. Slow down."

30

NED STOCKWELL PUSHED OPEN THE DOOR at *William's Pub.* I haven't had a drink in over five years, but I need one badly, he thought.

"What can I do for you?" The bartender asked.

"I need a beer, any one of those taps over there will do."

Ned finished the first beer quickly and slammed it down on the bar surface. "Another."

After the third beer, Ned's smile widened…beer froth on his lips. He glanced around and saw Reggie Logan sitting in a booth across from a man and woman.

"Hey, Reggie, got any of the money yet?" Ned said loudly.

As he had hoped, his outburst turned Reggie Logan's head. Ned got off his barstool and headed over to their booth.

"Well, Logan. Looks like you're going to have some company,"

Ned drawled.

"What the hell are you talking about?" Reggie asked.

"We're relatives. My wife is your first cousin."

"Why don't you mind your own business? I don't have any cousins. Get lost, you drunk. I didn't invite you over here."

"Just you wait, you young punk. I'll see you at the lawyers," Ned said and staggered toward the door.

REGGIE LOGAN HAD MOVED INTO THE FARMHOUSE that his uncles had lived in all their lives. He didn't like the facility but needed to stay put until the lawyers settled the estate. He expected to inherit everything...farm land, equipment and all the money at the bank.

He planned to hire a realtor to sell the property. If he could sell the equipment and livestock to the same party, he wouldn't need to have an auction sale, he thought. I know there's a ton of cash in the bank. His mind went wild almost every day thinking about the plans he had...one of them to draw out the money and move to California. Dad's going to need some of it, he thought. There should be enough for the both of us.

Reggie glanced at a woman sitting at a table across from him. She's been staring at me, he thought. Yeah, I remember...her name is Judy.

"Who was that nut?" she asked.

Reggie frowned. "Some weirdo—too much to drink."

Reggie felt bored with New Dresden and all the people in it. If it weren't for the money, I'd be long gone, he thought. I wonder when the finance company is going to catch up with me...no payment on my car in four months.

Reggie looked across the table at her. She smiled. Her longhaired friend gazed into space...totally out of it. His ugly un-kept jaw began moving up and down, but no words came out, only garble. What's she hanging around a loser like that for? Reggie asked himself.

"Hey, Judy, I'm heading for home. Do you want to stop by?" Reggie asked softly.

31

ALICE ROSLAND HAD BEEN EMPLOYED at Big Lakes Hospital for twenty years as a medical technician. She finished work at 6:00 p.m. on Thursday and headed out to the parking lot. She shivered and tightened the collar of her black jacket with her gloved hand. Her short red hair clung to the side of her head as she slid behind the wheel of her Honda.

Her dark brown eyes blinked as she felt the bump from the tires hitting the pothole in the pavement while leaving the parking lot. Sure was a long day, she thought. I can't imagine how those parents will deal with that screaming kid of theirs. Just one look at the needle and the little monster lost it. She chuckled and muttered, "I fixed 'em good."

After arriving at her home, she reached up and pressed the garage door remote, carefully driving the car into the garage. I got to clean out all this junk one of these days, she thought.

After entering her house, she kicked off her shoes and switched on the television. The phone rang. She answered and laughed. "Yes, I'll be home. About 10:00 would be fine." Her bright red lips parted as she inhaled and sighed.

Alice had a scotch and water ready when her guest arrived. "Well, hello, Torfin. Did you have a tough day, my baby?"

He threw off his hat and jacket…they landed on the carpet. He gave Alice a big hug. "Hi, doll, how about that drink?"

Torfin Peterson walked out of Alice's house and got into his car at 3:00 a.m. He felt satisfied that she will cooperate, he thought. Just a little switch of a label is all that I need, he thought. That'll get the Hunt bitch off my back.

He looked across the street and saw the shadow of a person through a partially lit window. There's that snoopy Clement again, he thought. Anyhow, he's not smart enough to figure anything out. Even if he did catch on, he knows that I would come after him. I'm not going to worry about Clement…he's harmless.

The Hunt woman is definitely a problem, the sheriff said to himself. Perhaps a little more pressure may discourage her enough to leave well enough alone. Time is against me. The thirty-day deadline for bringing my loan up-to-date will be ending soon. The Talbot's are my only chance. Fathering Reggie is turning out lucky for me.

JOLENE SAW THE SHERIFF'S CAR PULL UP in a space across the street. Today, it's Friday and this evening I have a date with Tom Hastings, she said to herself. She watched as Sheriff Torfin Peterson crossed the street. Gosh sakes, he's coming in here.

She heard the sheriff talking with the receptionist in the waiting room. His voice got loud and drowned out Mary's objection. Jolene heard heavy feet stomping on the carpet. The sheriff didn't knock and entered Jolene's office.

"Jolene Hunt?"

"Yes, you know who I am. Why are you asking?"

"I have a warrant here for your arrest."

"Arrest! What the blazes are you talking about?"

Your blood sample from the accident the other day read one-point-five percent alcohol content. That's way more than enough for a DWI charge."

"What? Does coffee have alcohol? That's all I had before the rollover. You should go after the lunatic who forced me off the road."

"Are you going to come along peacefully or am I going to have to call for assistance?"

Jolene's boss, Craig, poked his head in the door. "What's going on here?"

"Craig, I want you to hear this. This man, Sheriff Peterson, is coercing me with a drummed up drinking and driving charge. It is totally false and I will ask you to be a witness when I sue this jerk."

"Sorry, sir, but this lady was in a car accident and her blood sample was over the legal limit. She has to come with me," the sheriff said firmly.

"Now, wait a minute, sheriff. What do you base your charges on?" Craig asked.

"Blood samples—those at the hospital. The one with Jolene Hunt's name on it contained a lot of alcohol. It's way over the limit."

"It's alright, Craig. I'll go along with this for the moment. I want to see this idiot fall flat on his face," Jolene said.

Jolene felt furious but had to spend a night in jail. She called her attorney Patrick Levitt and asked him to initiate a lawsuit against the sheriff. She asked him to call Tom Hastings and explain what had happened. "We had a date for the evening. He needs to know that I won't be there, at my home."

TOM LOOKED FORWARD to his Friday date with Jolene. He liked being with her and he could feel the warmness between them. Each time they got together, he had more difficulty keeping his emotions under control.

His tractor engine purred right along with the radio that played a Mozart. Tom loved the tractor, which he had purchased as a result of an extremely difficult winter five years ago.

He looked at the bucket out front, heaped with cuttings from three trees, which he had dropped with a chain saw earlier in the week. Most of the snow had melted in the open areas. After dumping his load, he put the tractor in the garage and entered the house.

The answering machine beeped. He listened, confused and disappointed, to Attorney Levitt's explanation of what had happened to Jolene.

His thoughts flashed back to the day of Jolene's accident. It happened only last Saturday, he thought. Tom remembered meeting Deputy Johnson at the hospital emergency room that day. Tom felt certain that Jolene had not been drinking. She must really be one angry woman.

Daylight faded as Tom watched the surroundings from his hot tub spa. The sunset had been spectacular—red and purple colors kept changing in hue and brightness. The thought of Jolene and her plight in jail worried Tom. He got out of the spa, dried and called the sheriff's office. He asked the dispatcher to ring Deputy Johnson. "Give me your phone number and I'll have him call you back," the dispatcher said.

Minutes later, Tom's phone rang. This is Deputy Johnson. What can I do for you, Mr. Hastings?"

Tom told him about Jolene Hunt getting arrested and jailed. "I had nothing to do with that," the deputy responded.

"Do you remember seeing her at the hospital the day of the roll-over?" Tom asked.

"Yes, I do."

"Did she look intoxicated to you?" Tom asked.

"No. I don't believe she did. At least, it sure didn't look that way at the hospital. But apparently her blood sample showed a one-point-five."

"Is it possible that the blood sample could have gotten mixed up?" Tom asked.

"Tell you what, Mr. Hastings. I'll look into it and get back to you. It may not be until tomorrow morning."

"Okay. Thanks a lot for calling. I'll expect your call tomorrow."

INK STAINS ON JOLENE'S FINGERS irritated her as she sat in a cell in the county jail. There isn't much else to do but think and stare, she thought. This has been the most humiliating experience I've ever had. Someone's going to pay. Her attorney had told her the overnight jail stay is part of state law and he couldn't do anything about it, even though the accident occurred at an earlier date.

Patrick had agreed that the sheriff was probably playing with the law and had singled her out for harassment. Patrick promised to discuss the matter with the county attorney the next day. Jolene's attorney did say that they would have to prove the blood sample was deliberately tampered with at the hospital…not an easy chore.

Concentrating on a novel, which the jailer loaned me, is difficult, she thought. Heck, it's impossible. Falling asleep is about the same…also impossible.

My being embarrassed is one thing, but what is my new friend Tom going to think, she asked herself. He could alienate me over this. Tom's already gotten into trouble hanging around me. Jolene winced when remembering the look on Tom's face when they had been forced to get into the sheriff's car at the farm.

She fantasized Reggie leaping from the pickup truck and running away from the train crash scene. She visualized her father as being asleep, not knowing the locomotive bore down on him. Tom saw Reggie leap. Tom's an honest man, she said to herself. He told the sheriff and the committee the truth. He doesn't seem like the type who would make up or imagine things like that.

THE FIRST PHONE CALL TOM RECEIVED on Saturday morning came from Jolene. "Tom, I'm so sorry about missing our date, but you'll never believe what happened to me. I was railroaded–that damn sheriff—he did it again."

"Jolene, your attorney phoned me. He informed me that you couldn't keep our date."

"I'm so relieved that Levitt called you. That lunatic of a sheriff barged right into my office and read me my rights. The nerve of 'em!" Jolene exclaimed.

"Oh, I talked to Deputy Johnson yesterday. He's looking into the possibility that your blood sample was mixed up with someone else's. I'm expecting him to call me today. Let's go out for dinner this evening and we can talk about it," Tom said.

"Okay, Tom. Meanwhile, I'm steaming! I'm meeting with Patrick this afternoon. I'm going to sue that sheriff."

"Have your attorney talk to Deputy Johnson. You'd probably get somewhere with him. He appears to be a straight shooter."

"I'll give that a try. What time are you going to pick me up?"

"Is 6:00 p.m. okay?"

"Yes, that'll be fine. I'll see you then."

Tom hung around the house waiting for the deputy's call. It came at 11:00. "Mr. Hastings, I checked out the hospital. One of the other deputies brought in a guy for a blood test on the same day. According to Mel, the guy was tanked. Well, when the blood sample results came in, they failed to register any alcohol. Mel had to let him go."

"Uh-hah, then there was a mix-up. Jolene's vial got switched with the other guy—the one that was released," Tom said excitedly.

"It appears so. I'll bring the issue up with the sheriff," the deputy responded.

"That's the right thing to do, deputy, but I doubt it will do any good."

32

TOM TURNED OFF THE COUNTY HIGHWAY and headed down the road toward Jolene's house on Saturday evening. While slowing his pickup truck to make the turn into her driveway, he noticed a red car parked on the side of the road beyond her turnoff. After Tom turned, he glanced back and saw it speed by in the opposite direction.

Tom expected Jolene to be furious when she came to the door. Instead, her smile enticed. "Good evening, Tom."

"Hi, Jolene, I'm glad to see that you've cooled off."

"Yes I have, because that crumb of a sheriff isn't worth stewing over. My attorney, Levitt, talked to Deputy Johnson. My blood sample was obviously swapped for one they got from a drunkard late Friday afternoon. It would be tough to prove, though," she said.

"Whoever is doing this to you doesn't know you very well. The more they harass and discourage you, the stronger your resolve gets. Running you off the road at *Purgatory Curve*, if intentional, is certainly a crime. Before something is called criminal in this county, it has to get the okay from the sheriff, so it seems. Somehow, you've got to figure out how to go over the sheriff's head," Tom said.

"Well, let me tell you that I am going over his head. Patrick is working on the county attorney. We are pushing him to request state investigators to take on this case—train accident, farm accident and my harassment by the sheriff."

Tom walked to the window that overlooked the lake. "I wonder how much power the sheriff has over his deputies. We know for sure that Deputy Johnson is a straight shooter. If he was in charge, this would be an entirely different ballgame."

"Yeah, I liked that man. He was certainly sympathetic at the hospital. I'm not going to have to appear in court, you know—about the driving-while-intoxicated charges. They've been mysteriously dropped and I think I know why."

"Why?"

"Because the sheriff knows that I would challenge the charge, which would mean bringing in witnesses. The only evidence he had was the blood sample, which we could have tossed out, according to Patrick. My question is—who in the hospital laboratory has something going with the sheriff?"

"Whew! If that's all true, our county is going to have an upheaval. Well, let's get over to Mary Ann's. Who knows what adventure awaits us there?"

THE CONVERSATION BETWEEN TOM AND JOLENE while driving to Mary Ann's continued to focus on the sheriff and the phony driving-while-intoxicated charge. Tom felt good when they entered the restaurant. He hoped to change the subject…food or drink.

After getting seated in a booth overlooking the lake, Tom said quietly, "Geez, there's the bank robber."

Jolene strained to see who he was referring to. "Do you still think it was him, Marty Bishop—one of the bank robbers?"

"I don't know what to think. There isn't a face–just body mannerisms," Tom replied. "I better be quiet about that. I could be wrong. You would think the FBI would have arrested him by now, if he actually was involved in the robbery."

Oh no. Look who just came in," Jolene said.

Tom glanced and saw Reggie Logan in the foyer, standing with a guy about the same age. "Don't look now, but there's some more fuel being added to the fire."

Jolene and Tom watched and listened as the people with Marty Bishop had gotten louder. The group occupied two of the high tables close to the bar.

Reggie Logan and his friend had sauntered over to the bar. There weren't any barstools available so they wedged into an available space between stools.

Marty Bishop had left his group and headed for the men's room. Returning, he paused after spotting Reggie Logan. He walked over and tapped Reggie on the shoulder. "Hello nephew," he said loudly.

Reggie turned his head and smirked but didn't say a word, ignoring the intrusion. Instead he turned back to his friend.

"Hey, I'm talking to you—to you!" Marty said loudly.

"Get lost, you thief," Reggie replied. "Mind your own business."

"Why, you little jerk—ah heck, you're not worth the time," Marty said and stomped back to his group.

"I don't know if Reggie knows it or not, but he's legally Marty's nephew—I bet he does know—just doesn't want to let on." Jolene said.

Half an hour later, Tom and Jolene finished dinner and they got up from the booth. Reggie Logan had just returned to the bar from the men's room. He stopped. "Well, hello jailbird."

"Why, you little snipe!" Jolene snapped.

"If you would stay out of other people's business, things like this wouldn't happen. Why don't you just leave everything alone?" Reggie snarled.

"Reggie Logan! My father was murdered. What do you say to that?"

"You're nuts. His pickup stalled on the track. You're an idiot!"

"Ah-hah, so you admit he was my father!" Jolene exclaimed.

Tom stood up. "Look, Mr. Logan. I want you to leave us alone. Just get away from here, right now."

"Ah—go to hell. You're an idiot to hang around her, anyhow."

Tom lost his cool. He swatted Reggie across the mouth. The sound of the slap turned many heads in the room. Blood oozed from Reggie's lower lip.

"You want to step outside, old man!" Reggie exclaimed loudly. He stepped closer to Tom, bringing his face within inches.

Using the palm of his right hand, Tom pushed against Reggie's chest, driving him back. I'm bigger than he is, but age isn't on my side, he said to himself. Reggie faked a punch to the head and hit Tom in the stomach. Jolene had gotten up from the booth and lunged at Reggie. Harold and one of the cooks rushed to the scene and pulled Reggie away, pinning his arms behind his back. Tom had bent over and gasped for air.

"Logan, you get the hell out of here or I'm calling the cops," Harold said, angrily.

Another cook, wearing a stained apron, came trotting out of the kitchen. Jeremy, a tall, lean brawny guy, grabbed Reggie by the collar. "Out you go, buddy. The boss says you're leaving," he said.

Reggie motioned to his companion, who continued to stand by the bar and watch, like most everyone else. "Come on Chad. Let's blow this soup joint," Reggie said sneering defiantly.

After Reggie and his friend left, Harold turned to Tom and asked, "Are you okay?"

"Yeah, I'm fine now. The little snipe sure wrecked a nice dinner."

"Tell you what. You and your lady friend leave right now and there won't be any charges this evening," said Harold. "It's all on the house."

Tom rubbed his chin with a finger. "Yup, best we do leave."

After walking into the parking lot, they heard the sound of rubber squealing on pavement of the county highway down below. Tom got a glimpse of Reggie Logan's red car heading south.

33

DEER HUNTING SEASON HAD ARRIVED. Pete's orange cap stood out over the top boards of his deer stand as Tom passed by on his way to New Dresden. The morning felt crisp on a Sunday and patches of frost showed up in open areas of the ground. Two deer hunters stood at the edge of a field as Tom drove onto the township road.

Tom had phoned Jolene earlier that morning. He felt concerned that Reggie's harassment of Jolene could take on a new higher level after the incident at Mary Ann's. She sounded okay when he had called. Tom asked her to look out of the windows and check for strange vehicles. I'm glad that she didn't see anyone out there, he said to himself.

The traffic around Stillman's Super Market had an off-season look on Sunday morning. Only four vehicles parked on that side of Main Street. Tom saw a sports utility vehicle parked next to the stop sign where he had his windshield blown away by the bank robbers a couple of months ago.

Tom parked across the street from the grocery store, half a block away from *Bev's Embroidery* shop. He stopped and studied the red car that he saw parked in front of her store. Is that Reggie Logan's car? Tom asked himself. What would he be doing in the embroidery shop?

He saw two young men stocking up on grocery supplies in the far aisle of the grocery store after entering. Tom didn't see many other shoppers in the aisles. Ellie didn't work on weekends and the smiling young woman behind the counter accepted his check and said, "Have a good day."

Tom picked up his grocery bag and looked up the nearest aisle. Suddenly, he saw Reggie Logan selecting items from the candy shelves. Rather then risk a confrontation, Tom moved out the door quickly.

During the return trip home, Tom pulled onto the road that led to the cemetery. He visited his wife's gravesite and looked out over the valley. The trees on the ridge had lost their colorful leaves and appeared a dull gray-brown. Winter and cold temperatures are on their way, he thought. Another year had gone by for Tom without his wife, Becky. His memory of the delightful life, which they shared, intensified when he visited the cemetery. The sound of a rifle shot coming from the direction of his home caught his attention and he returned to his pickup.

Tom, an ex-deer hunter, drove slowly down the township road and looked for hunters in their orange get-ups. Tom didn't see any until he drove onto his roadway. A deer hunter walked down the road toward his home. Tom stopped and rolled down a window. "Anything I can do for you, young man? You're on posted property, you know."

"We've wounded a deer and the blood trail led us here. Is it okay if we check it out?"

"We? How many hunters?"

"Two of us."

"Sure, but be careful. My house is at the end of this roadway."

Tom felt uncomfortable with a stranger, carrying a gun, on his property. Just before darkness set in, he walked onto his driveway and listened. He couldn't see or hear anything. The deer hunting season had closed temporarily at sunset and wouldn't open again until the following Saturday.

Tom locked the front door and lit a fire in the den fireplace. He experienced the comfort of a warm crackling wood fire on a chilly evening. Tom felt good about the quantity of firewood stacked near the garage.

PETER ERICKSON, THE TALBOT'S ATTORNEY sat at his desk on Monday morning. He had rented a suite on the second floor of a brick office building in downtown Big Lakes. His first meeting regarding the estate of the two brothers had been last week with Reggie Logan. Since there is no will, it is apparent the nephew is going to inherit the entire estate, he thought.

Peter had heard through the legal grapevine that there will be a challenge to the Talbot estate. According to rumors, each of the brothers had fathered a daughter. To complicate the matter further, he had had a conversation with Jack McCarthy, the county attorney.

McCarthy, also a friend, hinted there could be a new investigation into the death of the two Talbot brothers. In Peter's mind, that meant a possible murder charge. He shuddered at the thought. A new investigation could delay estate settlement for a year or longer.

The two documents lying on his desk had been received in the mail yesterday. Both were requests to delay the Talbot estate settlement. One came from Patrick Levitt, attorney for Jolene Hunt. The other from William Sherman, attorney for Beverly Stockwell.

JACK MCCARTHY REACHED FOR THE PHONE. "Will, what's the deal on Beverly Stockwell? Is she for real?" William Sherman's attorney asked.

"Hi, Jack. Yeah, she is. I've asked a judge to issue an exhume order on Ralph Talbot. DNA could prove that he is Beverly's father."

"What did the judge say? Is he going to do it?"

"He's going to rule on it within a week. My educated guess is that he will approve it," William Sherman responded.

"Okay. I'll delay the estate settlement until we hear from the judge. Boy, this could take awhile. Reggie Logan is going to be plenty hot," Jack said.

"This case has the potential to explode. There are a lot of hot collars out there. It could mean a legal war, not to mention the possibility of violence," Sherman added.

TOM DROVE TO NEW DRESDEN ON MONDAY MORNING
and took advantage of senior discount day at the local municipal
liquor store. He selected two bottles of wine and placed them on the
counter. Glancing around the room and into the office through an
open door, he didn't see the checkout clerk. Tom continued to stand
at the counter. And then he heard a noise coming from the doorway
that led to the storage room.

The clerk appeared, standing sideways in the doorway, "Sir,
you're not allowed back here," she said loudly.

A strong voice answered. "Sorry, but no one was around when I
came in. I needed a cart and there weren't any out there. Since you
weren't here to help me, I decided to help myself. Don't you want
my business? I can go somewhere else, you know."

"Mister, you get out of there right now or I'm calling the sheriff."

"Last time I'm ever coming in here," someone in the back room
said loudly. A gray-haired, middle-aged man came out of the stock
room and stomped out the door.

"The nerve of that guy," the clerk said to Tom. "Ever since the
bank robbery last month, we've had an awful lot of odd-ball people
come in here. News of violence seems to attract them like flies."

Tom paid for his wine and headed across the street to *Borders
Café*. He felt disappointed that Henry wasn't at his usual table. Tom
took off his jacket and lay it on a chair where Henry normally sat.
He looked out the window and hoped to see him approaching.

The coffee hawks are gone and the restaurant is empty except for
one couple, he said to himself. They occupied a table in the middle
of the room. And then the front door opened. Tom felt disappointed
that it wasn't Henry. Instead, Edgar Sandvik entered. He quickly
walked to the middle of the room and stopped. Looking around, he
chose to join the couple.

Tom nibbled on a sandwich and read an article in the newspaper
when he heard Edgar say loudly, "But, there was a will. I know, because I signed it. I was a witness."

"You better tell the authorities about that," the woman said.

"Authorities! Who are they?"

A man laughed and said, "The county attorney would be a good start."

"Yeah, and they're going to dig them up—both of 'em!" Edgar exclaimed.

"Edgar, now what the heck are you talking about? They were both accidents."

"You've got that right. Both the Talbot's had an accident. They each had a daughter–someone needs to prove that—DNR, or something like that."

"You mean DNA, don't you?"

"Yeah, I think that's it—the one where they can tell who belongs to who."

Edgar's conversation with the couple deflected Tom's interest in the newspaper. Jolene will be incredibly interested in a potential will and the use of DNA technology on Ralph, he thought. I remember helping Ralph install legal software on their computer. It included a section on the creation of wills. Perhaps Ralph created one for himself and his brother without me. It's certainly possible.

Geez, if Edgar is telling the truth and signed the will…it could be legal. Tom put a hand over his stomach where Reggie had punched it…still tender.

That young punk probably found the will, Tom thought. If so, he surely would have destroyed it…but then, just maybe, the brothers had a safe-deposit box…the bank.

34

THE NEWS ABOUT A WILL AND THE TALBOT BROTHERS spread around the community like wildfire. Tom's visit to New Dresden on Friday included a shopping run to the grocery store. "I hear they're diggin' 'em both up," a bib-overalls shopper at the checkout counter said.

"Don't know," Ellie responded. "It all sounds fishy to me."

"I've known Beverly all my life. I had no idea. She always talk-ed about her family out east," the woman carrying a bag of onions said.

The bib-overall man said, "Then there's that woman that works over in Pine Lakes. She claims Ben was her father. God knows how many more are going to come out of the woodwork. Money talks you know."

Tom felt an itch growing in his mind…to get into the Talbot's computer hard-drive. If no one messed with it, the will might still be there, he thought. I wonder if Reggie Logan knows how to use a computer. If so, he probably would have deleted it. I've got to talk to Jolene.

Things didn't change much at the bank. One of the tellers and a lady customer discussed the Talbot brothers at the teller window. "Is it really true they have a million dollars in here?" the customer asked.

The teller laughed and said, "Sorry, even if I knew, I couldn't let out information like that. You wouldn't like it if I told everyone how much money you have in your account, would you?"

"No, I guess not, but who would care. I will never have enough cash in mine to get anyone's attention," the customer said. She laughed and dropped a paper into her purse and left.

"Good morning, Tom. How are you today?" the woman teller asked as he stepped up to the window.

"I'm fine, but need some cash. Sounds like you're getting all the news right here. There's been lots of talk lately."

"Yeah, there sure has—never a dull moment in this town. How much cash do you need?"

"Forty will do."

JOLENE ANSWERED THE PHONE ON THE FIRST RING. "There's a lot of scuttlebutt in town that the Talbot brothers are go-ing to be exhumed. Do you need anyone to talk to? I'm available," Tom said.

"Yes, that would be great. Why don't you come over this evening? I'll put a pizza in the oven."

"Okay. I'll be there about 7:00."

Darkness prevailed when Tom left his house at 6:30. Tom saw a deer leap across the Lake Trevor road as he headed for Jolene's house. The sky appeared overcast and gloomy that evening. A few minutes later he turned off the gravel road and onto Jolene's paved driveway. He touched his brake pedal a couple of times proceeding slowly down the steep slope and a curve.

As Tom approached Jolene's house, he saw a black SUV parked in front of the garage. It doesn't look familiar, he thought. Tom came to a stop and parked along side. He looked through the vehicle window and saw a holster and gun on the passenger seat. He also saw a police badge clipped to the holster.

Feeling his stomach knot, he feared the worst. Those could belong to the sheriff, he said to himself. Tom felt determined to stay cool, and cautiously approached the front door. Looking through the long window next to the door, he couldn't see anyone. A pair of gloves lay on a small table. Tom knew they weren't Jolene's.

Torn between fear and Jolene's well being, Tom stood in front of the door for a few moments, staring at the doorbell. Instead of pressing it, he pressed the latch and pushed the door slightly open. And then he heard voices…Jolene sounded upset. He heard a man's voice. Tom reached back and pressed the doorbell, resulting in silence inside.

"I've got company. You two lunatics get out of here. Leave me alone," Jolene shrieked.

Tom entered and grabbed a porcelain statue off the tabletop, clenching it in his right fist. Here goes nothing, he thought and burst into Jolene's kitchen area.

He saw Jolene sitting on a chair. Sheriff Peterson, in street clothes, stood in front of her. And then Tom saw Reggie Logan standing close to her, his hands on top of his head.

"What's going on here?" Tom said loudly.

The sheriff's head turned. "Just talking things over."

"Oh, thank God you've come, Tom. These two lugs are harassing me. Please call somebody, the state patrol, anybody."

"Look who we've got here," Reggie said and sneered. "The local warrior has arrived."

Tom took a couple of steps toward the group, raising the statue over his head. "Who wants it first? How about you?" he asked and stepped toward the sheriff.

Reggie quickly moved between them. "Why don't you take me on, old man?" he asked.

"Back off, Reggie," the sheriff said. "Now, Mr. Hastings, take it easy. We're just having a little talk. No one needs to get hurt. This is official business. You best stay out of it."

"It looks one-sided to me and you weren't invited. There are laws against that!" Tom exclaimed, angrily.

Jolene got up from the chair and gave the sheriff a push. "Get away from me."

"Let's go, Reggie," the sheriff said.

Tom continued to hold the statue in striking position as the two intruders stomped out of the house. When the door closed, Jolene rushed to Tom and he held her close.

"You better take time away from work tomorrow, Jolene. We need to visit the county attorney. Are you okay? Did they hurt you?" he asked.

"No, not physically, but Reggie did grab me by the wrist and force me down on the chair."

"Jolene, let's boot the computer. I want you to record everything that's happened. You need to date and sign it. We'll present it to the county attorney. If we don't get anywhere with him, we need to call the attorney general's office in St. Paul. Perhaps your attorney, Patrick, could do that? This is really serious."

Jolene began to sob. "Oh, Tom—thanks for showing up in time. I'm not sure what would have happened otherwise," she cried.

Tom looked out the window at the lake. "I wonder if Deputy Johnson could help you. I'll call him again. Come on, let's sit a bit. I have some more news."

"What—what news?" she asked.

"Edgar Sandvik claims that he signed a will—for the Talbot brothers."

"You're kidding!" Jolene exclaimed.

"That's what I overheard him say at Borders. The story is all over town. But there's more."

"More?" she asked.

"Ralph Talbot's body is going to be exhumed. A judge has given the necessary order—he signed a paper."

"Why?"

"So Beverly Stockwell can prove she is Ralph's daughter," Tom responded excitedly.

"Uh-oh, do you think that I should do the same?" Jolene asked.

"That's going to be up to you. Why don't you talk to Patrick?" Tom asked, his eyes lighting up.

"I have mixed feelings about doing that. On a lighter note, I have a pizza heating in the microwave."

"Smells good," Tom said.

Jolene got up off the couch and she retrieved the pizza and they spent the rest of the evening talking about possibilities.

Two hours later, Tom said, "I've got to get going. Be sure to lock your door and don't open it for anyone—except someone you know and trust."

Jolene said, "Tom, would you go with me tomorrow, to see Patrick?"

"Yes, Jolene. I will."

35

PATRICK LEVITT ATE A SANDWICH and drank a Coke while reading Jolene's computer generated statement. He set the paper down, stood, and put his palms on the desk. "Jolene, I'm going to file a complaint against the sheriff with the county attorney, Jack McCarthy, today. Are you willing to talk to him?"

"Absolutely! Something has to be done."

"What about you, Hastings? You're a witness."

"I sure will. How about contacting the Minnesota Attorney General?"

"Well, that's a possibility. Let's go to Jack McCarthy first. I think he knows what's going on. It's certainly in his jurisdiction."

"What do I do right now? I don't feel safe," asked Jolene.

"Okay. I'll request a restraining order from the judge, including Sheriff Peterson and Reggie Logan."

Jolene placed a finger on her chin. "Patrick, have you heard the news about Ralph Talbot—his body being exhumed?"

"Yes, I sure have. I've been thinking that you might request the same thing with Ben."

"Let me think about that one. Okay?"

"Sure," the attorney said.

"Tom told me yesterday, he had overheard at the local café yesterday that the Talbot's have a will. Have you heard anything? Tom said that Edgar Sandvik claimed he had signed it as a witness."

"Yes, I have, but unless the Talbot attorney, Peter Erickson, comes up with it, there's nothing I can do."

"I wonder if the Talbot brothers had a safe-deposit box at the bank. And if so, who would have access to it under the current circumstances?" Jolene asked.

"Gosh, Jolene, I just don't know. If they do have one, I would think the next of kin would have a right to the box. A power of attorney and an official death certificate is all the person would need. I'll see what I can find out from the Talbot brothers attorney."

During the drive back to Jolene's house, Tom said, "Well that's a start. I've got lots of work to do at my home this afternoon. Will you be okay by yourself?"

"Yes, I don't think those two lugs will bother me anymore. Tom, do you suppose that Reggie Logan has gotten to that safe-deposit box by now?"

"First, you'll have to find out if there is one. Patrick will help you. The will might be in it—the safe-deposit box. There are other possibilities."

"What are those, Tom?"

"It's in the house, or—"

"Or, what?" Jolene asked anxiously.

"Reggie destroyed it—or—"

"What are you getting at?"

Tom clenched his teeth…a snide smile on his face. "Or—it's still in the computer."

TOM CHECKED HIS WATCH. It showed 2:15 p.m. He turned onto the township road after returning from Jolene's house. Down his roadway, he glanced at Pete's deer stand. It's empty as expected, Tom said to himself. The season opens again on Saturday at dawn. Something's down on the roadway. Slowing the pickup, he stared at the object. Geez, it's a deer.

Tom stopped his pickup and stepped out. He approached the deer and noticed it had antlers…a big rack. Oh, no. Please, God, not Prancer. The deer is obviously dead, he thought. Tom noticed a patch of blood just behind the left eye. I better call the Department of Natural Resources.

He managed to drive the pickup around the deer and continue on to his house. After entering, he called the DNR. Explaining what happened and giving a location, Tom listened to the officer say that someone would be out there within a couple of hours.

Later, after almost two hours had passed, Tom got into his pick-up and drove to where the deer laid. The sight of its distorted body churned his stomach. A short time later, he heard a vehicle coming down the roadway. It came into view and stopped. Two uniformed DNR officers got out and approached. "Wow, a big one," one of them said.

The other officer placed his hand on the deer's chest. "It's still warm. This didn't happen very long ago." He grabbed the antlers and twisted. "Hey, Vern, there're two holes in the head. Well, grab my butt. Look here. There's a deep cut in the chest."

Vern examined the hole. "Looks like the heart had been plucked out." He stood and looked toward the grassy, brushy area next to the roadway. "Hey, this deer's been dragged."

Vern said, "Let's follow the trail and see where it leads."

Tom stayed behind the two officers, who led the way through a wooded area and into a clearing. Most of the snow had melted, and they continued to follow the drag trail.

"Up there!" Tom suddenly exclaimed. "The heart—it's perched on a limb."

"Well, look at that," the second officer said. "Uh-oh, there's leaves stained with blood over there," he added and pointed.

Vern said, "Let's get a plastic bag for the heart before we take it down."

After packing the heart in a bag, the two officers and Tom walked back to the road.

"We're going to take the deer and try to find the bullets. Then, we'll deliver it to a meat processor."

After they loaded the deer, one of the officers wrote down Tom's name and phone number. "We'll give you a call if we learn anything."

Tom watched them turn around on the roadway and drive off. He stood there for a few minutes, puzzled. *I wonder…I wonder…is this one of Reggie Logan's tricks? What about his sheriff father, was he in on this, too?*

After parking the pickup in the garage, Tom entered his house. He felt himself getting angrier by the minute. Tromping up the stairs to his bedroom he removed his deer rife, shotgun and pistol from the closet. Taking them downstairs, he laid them on the dining room table. Returning to his bedroom, he came down again with three boxes of shells.

After loading each of the weapons, he carried them to an open area beyond his garage…a greenway, he called it. Tom tested each weapon by firing a couple of rounds. Angrily, he returned to the house and placed the deer rifle and shotgun in the front closet. He went up to his bedroom and laid the pistol, a .32-automatic, on his nightstand.

36

WEDNESDAY MID-MORNING, Tom set out for New Dresden. Rounding *Purgatory Curve,* he slowed and looked toward the railroad tracks, looking for a deputy sheriff's car...none there. His speedometer read slightly over forty. The Main Street in New Dresden looks nearly empty, he thought. Tom parked and quickly got the mail. He felt anxious to hear from the DNR so he bought a newspaper at the grocery store and headed right back home.

As he had hoped, the answering machine beeped. He had a message from the Vern at the DNR. Tom called their office and talked to the dispatcher, agreeing to drive to Big Lakes for a visit right after lunch.

Tom headed for Big Lakes shortly after 12:30. He planned to stop at his vehicle dealer to set up an appointment to service his pickup. He pulled into the parking lot of Bates Motors and noticed flashing lights. He saw two police cars in the parking area and several people gathered directly in front of the show room. Parking his pickup, he approached the scene.

Getting closer he noticed the back end of a red vehicle protruding from the remains of a show room window. Tom saw broken glass everywhere...on top of the vehicle...in the flowerbeds next to the building...in the show room.

"What happened?" Tom asked a bystander.

"Some nut drove his car into the show room. He must have been drunk. The cops have him in a car over there." The bystander pointed.

Tom entered the showroom and walked over to the service counter. He said, "Ron, I need to set up a date to change oil in my pickup."

The attendant nodded. "When do want to come back. I've got some openings on Monday."

Tom remained and watched several guys pick up pieces of glass and drop them into a big pail.

He walked out the door into the parking lot and stopped close to the police car where the driver of the red car sat in the back seat. Tom shook his head when he recognized Marty Bishop. He walked back to his pickup, wishing all his problems would go away. He drove north to the DNR office north of town.

"Hello there, Mr. Hastings. Come on in. I have some news."

Tom followed Vern into an office and noticed a lead slug lying on the desk.

"That's one of the bullets that killed your deer. It's a .38-caliber– came from a .38-special revolver. The buck wasn't likely shot by a hunter because only rifles and shotguns are allowed in the field.

"It's possible that whoever killed the deer dragged it to the road, intending to pick it up with their vehicle. Meanwhile, you arrived on the scene and forced them to abandon their kill–a clear case of poaching."

Tom stared at the bullet. I refuse to believe the dead deer is Prancer, he said to himself. The color of the deer's hide seems different. I'm sympathetic with the officer's view of what happened, but I'm not going to share my view with the DNR officer…it was not poaching…it was a clear message from Reggie Logan and Torfin Peterson.

After thanking Vern for their efforts, he left the building and drove downtown. He needed a new jacket and parked on the street across from a department store. Jaywalking across, he drew a horn. That would never happen in New Dresden, where Jaywalkers have the right-of-way, he said to himself.

Tom browsed the men's clothing section and noticed a woman turn sharply to respond to a clerk. A second woman did the same thing and Tom collided with her, knocking over a clothing rack. It resulted in a domino effect…moments later a total of six racks lay on the floor.

Tom smiled and shook his head. Everyone's got problems, he

thought.

"You need to be more careful, sir," the clerk said, angrily.

Tom lifted his arms. "I didn't do it. It wasn't me."

The clerk scoffed and started picking up the clothing from the floor.

When Tom checked out the new jacket, the clerk behind the counter said, "You've caused quite a stir over there."

"Hey, it wasn't me."

"Oh sure," the woman at the cash register said, frowning.

On his way home, Tom drove slowly down his roadway. He stopped the pickup at the spot where he had seen the dead deer. I was certain the dead deer was not Prancer, he said to himself. Now, I'm not so sure. The antlers were certainly large enough, but the hide was a different color. The dead deer was light brown…Prancer is partially gray.

Tom went to sleep with the .32-automatic by his side. When he woke at 3:00 a.m., he reached over and felt the cold steel of the gun. How could I be going through this again? He said to himself. This should only happen on television.

37

THURSDAY MID-MORNING, Tom arrived in New Dresden and parked next to the bank. He watched a man walk the intersection kiddy-corner. X-walk, Tom called it…only in New Dresden.

Midway up the Main Street sidewalk, he crossed the street to the post office. Tom brought his package-notice card to the main counter. Jerry fumbled amongst a group of packages on the floor and retrieved one. "Here you are, Tom. How's it going today?"

"I'm fuming about a big buck that was shot on my road a couple of days ago–off season."

"Oh, yeah, a little poaching, huh?"

"Not sure what the deal is. The DNR people are investigating."

"Did you hear about Edgar Sandvik?"

"No. What? What's happened to him?"

"He's in the hospital. Someone beat the heck out of him back of *William's Pub*. If they hadn't found him after the bar closed, he may have frozen to death."

"Geez, the poor guy, He's never hurt anyone. What did he do to deserve that?"

"Dunno, but he's got six broken ribs, a broken nose and two pretty black eyes, so I hear."

When Tom walked out of the post office he saw a car pull up and park in the no-parking zone. A blonde middle-aged woman got out of the car. Tom frowned, looked at her and said, "I see you have a good parking spot."

If looks could kill, I'd be dead right now, Tom thought. He smiled and walked down the sidewalk. He thought about the Talbot Will. Did Edgar really sign one? If so, is that why he got beat up? As Tom approached Stillman's Super Market, he looked back at the pub. Edgar does hang around there a lot. He does spout off a lot. He must have said too much…got beneath somebody's skin.

Tom entered the grocery. "Hi, Tom, what's new today?" Ellie asked.

"Have you heard about Edgar Sandvik? Jerry told me he got beat up last night."

"Oh yeah, that's old news. I heard he got drunk, went out the wrong door and fell over a bunch of barrels."

Tom proceeded up an aisle and returned with a basket of grocery items. "How could you have six broken ribs and a broken nose falling over barrels?"

Ellie shook her head. "That'll be fifteen-sixty."

Tom wrote a check and left the store. On the way home he thought about Edgar and what Jolene's reaction would be to the attack. She's going to be very interested.

That evening, he phoned Jolene and told her about Edgar.

"Tom, do you suppose he got beat up because of what he said at the restaurant the other day?"

"About the Talbot Will, you mean," Tom said.

"Exactly! You know, this legal stuff seems to be taking forever.

I've got an idea. Are you willing to listen?"

Tom laughed. "Sure. Go ahead. Here we go again."

"I believe that Edgar did sign a Will. I also believe that Reggie Logan has long destroyed it. Chances are that Reggie doesn't know anything about computers."

"Where is all this leading?"

"I would give anything to check out the hard drive on the computer that you told me about–Ralph's toy. Would you help me? You know the computer."

"How the heck would we ever get permission to do that?"

Jolene exclaimed, "Permission! Who's talking about permission?"

"Whoa! Wait a minute–break into the house, you mean?"

"Not exactly, just visit the house. How about tomorrow evening? I bet Reggie will be out. He's always out drinking with his buddy during the evenings, especially weekends."

"Don't you remember? We got caught last time we tried something like that."

"Ah-hah, but this time we'll do it different. I'll come up with a plan."

"Let me think about it, would you?"

"Just like the first time, if you decide not to help, I'm going it alone."

38

TOM PUSHED THE GLOVE COMPARTMENT CLOSED after placing in the automatic. He had checked the clip earlier to make sure it was full of bullets. Jolene expected him at 7:00. I must be off my rocker to go along with this scheme, he thought. I'm damn mad, though…the dead deer. If I find out it was Prancer, I'm going after that little weasel of a Reggie. Whoa, Tom thought. I need to control myself. The law is eventually going to get 'em…maybe it wasn't him.

He drove slowly up his roadway hoping to see an antlered deer. The night appeared clear, sky full of stars and complimented by an almost full moon. He arrived at Jolene's house, and noticed an additional outdoor light. It lit up the entire length of the driveway. Good strategy, he thought.

He rang the bell. Jolene opened the door and Tom entered. "Are you sure you want to go through with this?" Tom asked.

"Darn right. If the law won't help us, we have to help ourselves."

Jolene wore a pair of dark warm-ups. She had a black stocking cap on her head, pulled down to the top of her ears. "I'm ready. Looks like you are, too," she said while pulling on a pair of gloves.

Tom took a deep breath, realizing that he might be spending the night in jail. "Okay, but I want to hear about your plan first."

"We'll drive by and make sure Reggie's car is gone. Then we'll park at least half a mile away, well off the road, and go there on foot."

"How are we going to get in? It's going to be locked."

Jolene held up a small crowbar. "This is my key."

Tom didn't know why, but he laughed and said, "A couple of old fogies up to no good."

"Not old, and we're not up to no good. We're searching for the truth," Jolene said firmly.

Tom shook his head, amazed that he considered going along with her plan. He walked away from Jolene and looked out over the lake. He thought about Ralph's computer and how he would do almost anything to see what was in there. "Well, okay, I'll do it, even though we may spend the night in jail."

EXCEPT FOR A YARD LIGHT, everything appeared dark at the Talbot house when they drove by...no lights on in the house.

"Looks good," Jolene said.

Tom slowed to forty-five and let a vehicle pass. His headlights flashed across the approach that he had been looking for. After turning into the field, he switched off the lights. The pickup rocked as he slowly drove across the rough, cultivated surface.

Well off the highway, he stopped the pickup and felt an annoying tension in his stomach. What the heck am I doing here? How did I ever allow this woman to talk me into this? He thought about their previous clandestine visit to the farm…an embarrassment for getting caught trespassing by the sheriff.

Jolene got out first. Tom reached across the seat and retrieved the pistol from the glove compartment, placing it into his jacket pocket. He stepped down to the ground and closed the door, making sure it had locked. Jolene walked around the front and stood by the bumper.

"Let's go," she said.

They begin plodding toward the farmstead. Tom stopped a moment and looked back after walking about a hundred yards. He could still see the outline of his pickup. Not too late to go back, he thought.

"Hey, Tom! Are you coming, or not?"

"Sure," he said. I can't go back on her now, he thought. She's got that super-determined look on her face.

It took nearly fifteen minutes to trek across the field and arrive at a stand of trees, which marked the beginning of the farmstead.

After walking along the edge for a short distance, they found a path that led through the trees and into the farmyard. Tom followed her as she stepped softly to minimize the noise that her boots made on the crispy leaves. Stopping at the end of the path, they could see the yard light.

"Let's stay on this side of the house," Jolene whispered.

Tom looked at her and saw the wrecking tool in her right hand. She means business, he thought, while holding back a chuckle.

They approached a screened porch on the north side of the house. Jolene walked over to the door and pulled. It opened. She waved and Tom followed her inside. They stood in the porch for a few minutes, waiting and listening. "Don't hear a thing," she said.

Grasping the doorknob on the door that led into the house, she attempted to turn it. "The door's locked," She whispered and pushed the edge of the crow bar between the door and frame.

Tom said softly, "Stop. Let me check something."

He reached above the doorframe and dragged his fore finger along slowly. "Ah-hah, look what I found." Tom showed Jolene a key. He placed it into the door lock and it turned.

"Very cool, sir, you've done this before, huh," she said, giggling.

Reaching into her jacket pocket, she pulled out a flashlight.

Tom turned the knob and pushed the door open.

"Where is it, Tom? Where's the computer kept?"

"There's an office next to the kitchen over there."

Jolene's flashlight shone on the cream-colored computer. Tom walked over and flicked on a power-surge switch. The computer came on and the monitor lit up. He sat down on the chair and began to work the keyboard. He had no problem finding the legal software folder. Jolene had walked into another room. "Find anything yet?" she asked.

"I'm working on it," Tom whispered.

"Holy Blazes!" Jolene exclaimed. "Someone just drove up. We better get the heck out of here."

TOM HEARD A CAR DOOR SLAM. He got up from the computer just as someone unlocked the front door. During his haste in leaving, Tom crashed into a chair, knocking it over.

"Who's there?" Someone asked loudly.

Recovering from the stumble, Tom followed Jolene into the porch and out the door. They ran toward the trail that led through the wooded area.

"There they go. Let's catch 'em, Chad," Tom heard Reggie Logan yell.

Tom and Jolene had gotten past the wooded area and moved into the field when Jolene fell. Tom stopped to help and heard a twig crack somewhere behind them. "Come on, Jolene. We can outrun those guys. They've likely been drinking."

He helped her up and they continued to trudge the rough cultivated field toward the pickup. Both gasping for air, they stopped to listen. Hearing nothing, they continued. In a couple of minutes,

Jolene said, "I need to rest, Tom. My heart is really racing."

They stopped again, and Tom heard the sound of thudding footsteps behind them. "Hear that, they're still coming," he blurted, gasping for air.

Struggling along for another few minutes, Jolene stopped. "I just can't go any farther, not another step," she said and dropped to one knee.

Tom looked ahead and could see the vague shape of his pickup. "We don't have far to go. I can see my truck."

"Then go on without me. I just can't."

Tom looked left and saw a rock pile. "Give me your hand. Let's get behind those rocks. I'll help you."

He grabbed Jolene and guided her behind the pile where she flopped down. "Listen, I can hear them coming," Tom said.

Their pursuers had drawn even with the rock pile. "Look, there's a vehicle," Tom heard Reggie Logan say.

"I'm fagged out," Chad grunted, his airway hissing and panting.

"It looks like a pickup truck, and I know who it belongs to. Come on," Reggie said.

Tom watched as Reggie Logan and Chad approached his vehicle. He whispered to Jolene, "You stay here. I'll take care of this."

"Oh, Tom, be careful," she whispered.

Tom stepped out from behind the rock pile. He racked the slide, and held the .32-automatic tightly with his right hand. He thought about the deer, which he found dead on his roadway. I've got the gun this time.

"Doesn't look like anyone in there," Reggie said. "I wonder where they could've gone," he added.

Reggie grabbed the door handle and pressed the button. "It's locked."

"Here, I can take care of that," Chad said holding up a rock in his right hand.

Tom pointed the barrel toward the sky and pulled the trigger. Reggie and Chad jerked their heads toward him, freezing in their tracks.

"Drop that rock!" Tom yelled.

Chad continued to hold the rock up by his head. Tom pulled the trigger again…the dirt kicked up about twenty feet from where the two guys stood. Chad dropped the rock.

"Okay, now you guys back off—get out of here," Tom said and advanced toward them slowly.

Reggie and Chad retreated toward the farm. Reggie stopped and turned. He yelled, "You're going to pay for this, Hastings."

Tom returned to the rock pile and helped Jolene to her feet. Together they plodded toward his pickup. Tom unlocked the doors and they got in. He turned the truck around, put on the lights and headed for the highway.

WHEN THEY GOT BACK TO JOLENE'S HOUSE, she brought out a bottle of wine. "I'm sorry, Tom. I got you into this. Let's have a drink. Darn, now we'll never know if there is a will."

Tom smiled and his eyes glittered. "Oh, but we shall. Look what I've got." He held up a diskette. "It's here. I got the copying done just in time."

Jolene walked over to Tom and hugged him. "How the devil? You did it—mission accomplished."

"Start up your computer, would you? Let's see if the diskette is okay."

He replaced Jolene on the computer chair and put the diskette in the drive bay. Moments later, he said, "Yup—its okay."

"Wonderful."

"I can't load the file here, though. You don't have the correct software on your computer. I can do it at my house, but how about tomorrow. I'm just beat."

"Yes, as anxious as I am to see what's in that will, I'm tired, too. A few hours isn't going to make much difference."

39

THE SUN HAD RISEN AND EXPOSED A CLEAR BLUE SKY on Saturday morning. Tom sat in front of his computer. He had successfully copied the Talbot file into his hard drive. A big smile formed on his face when the file loaded...it is indeed a will, a joint one, he thought. Both of the Talbot's have their names at the bottom.

Tom decided not to read it and clicked the *Print* icon. He planned on giving it to Jolene as soon as possible...it's none of my business, he thought. The phone rang and Tom felt certain who called.

"Tom, did you check the diskette—find the will?"

Tom smiled widely. "Yes, I did, Jolene. I'm printing it now. I could bring it over later today or you can come over and pick it up."

"I'll come over. Could you print more than one copy, say three?"

"No problem. When are you coming?"

"How about in an hour, okay?"

"Sure, see you then."

TOM CONTINUED TO WORK ON HIS COMPUTER and saw Jolene's Toyota arrive in his driveway. Nice job, he thought. Jolene had gotten the vehicle back from the auto body shop a couple of days ago. She hurried down the sidewalk. Tom opened the door as she approached. "Come on in. I've got what you want."

"Oh, thanks so much, Tom. I've got a date with Levitt on Monday. He wants to see it."

"This envelope also has the original diskette–the one I used for the copy at the farm house. By the way, have you heard anything from our enemies? They must be livid."

"No, Tom, not a word. I don't think they want me in court. There's sort of a hit-and-run game going on between us and them. Hey, I'll take you out for dinner tonight. That's the least that I can do for you, considering all your help."

"It's a deal. I'll pick you up about 6:30," Tom said.

Jolene gave Tom a hug, grabbed the envelope and hustled out the door. She wasted no time in starting the Toyota and heading up the roadway. Tom watched the brake lights flash after she rounded a curve. Someday, he thought. Things will be better for us.

TOM HAD SELECTED AN ORANGE COAT AND CAP for his afternoon walk. Checking his watch, it read 1:45. Deer season is in progress, and I'm not taking any chances being mistaken for a deer. He strapped on his holster and gun. And then he heard a shot and a dull thud…another shot and another thud.

He stepped out the front door and looked around…listening… he heard nothing, but noticed a splinter of wood on the deck. Tom reached down and picked it up. It's fresh. Looking at the log siding, he could see the gouge where the splinter had fallen from. He saw a small hole in the deep part of the depression.

Someone shot at my house, he thought. Geez, guys! Grabbing his rifle from the front closet, he hurried to his pickup and slowly drove up his roadway. He saw orange in Pete's deer stand. Tom drove slightly past and stopped. He got out and walked slowly along the edge of the trees

"Pete, someone just shot at my house–only minutes ago. Did you see any hunters around here?"

"No, didn't see anyone, but I heard a couple of shots—over there, closer to your place. Come on up. There's another seat here. Maybe we'll see someone moving around. Hmm, I see you have your rifle. Started hunting again, did you?"

Tom handed his rifle up to Pete and climbed the ladder. "No, I'm not hunting, deer that is. Geez, Pete, there's never been a shot fired even close to my house before. You know the guys who hunt this area. They're experienced. They know better than to shoot at a house."

"Yeah, they are, but I've seen some hunters over on Sylvan Tullaby's road. No one lives there right now, you know."

"Has Missy moved?" Tom asked.

"Yeah, she moved out a couple of months ago. It's too bad about Sylvan being forced to move to the city to take on that job at the University. Missy couldn't handle living all alone. I feel great for Sylvan. He earned the promotion."

"Is anyone living there now?" Tom asked.

"Not that I know of—a sign got posted on the township road just the other day. Sabrina King from New Dresden has it listed."

Tom and Pete sat and watched from the stand for another half an hour. I'm going to miss that beautiful sailboat, Tom thought. Sylvan and Missy used to look so gallant standing in the bow, cruising up and down the bay in their boat. Now I know why they haven't been out on the bay lately, he said to himself.

"Pete, I'd like to check for tracks—where the shots came from. Are you game? Want to come along?"

"You bet. Let's go."

The two men got down from the deer stand and crossed the narrow field of harvested corn. Walking at the edge along a wooded area, they came across another deer stand...empty.

They worked their way down the slope that led to the lake. The ice had a light cover of snow. "Look, Pete, I see some tracks," Tom said.

Pete and Tom walked out onto the ice and saw two sets of boot tracks, one in each direction.

"Looks like those tracks came from the direction of Sylvan's place. Do you think we should follow 'em?" Pete asked.

Tom stared at the tracks. "Darn right, let's see where they originated."

They followed the tracks to Sylvan's abandoned house where the dock had been pulled up on shore. Tom looked up. "The tracks head up there, Pete."

After climbing the slope and walking around the side of the house, they came to the driveway area. "Hey, Pete, tire tracks!" Tom exclaimed.

"An all terrain vehicle," Pete said. "Whoever made those boot tracks on the ice parked an ATV right here."

"I'd like to go back and see where the foot tracks go," Tom said.

Pete and Tom walked back down onto the ice and followed the tracks until they turned up the hill. Most of the snow on the slope had melted and the tracks became difficult to follow. Scruffy patches of leaves, evenly spaced apart, guided them.

When they got to the top, Tom stopped and said, "Look, Pete, you can see my house clearly from here."

"Someone stood right there," Pete said, pointing.

Tom carefully stepped to a place where the long grass had been trampled. After sifting through the grass for a few moments, he said, "Here it is, Pete."

Tom had reached down and picked up an empty cartridge casing. "It's a .25-06-caliber, see!" he exclaimed.

They continued to search. "Here's another one!" Pete exclaimed.

"Pete, I'm going back to the house and call the DNR. Thanks for your help. Sorry to disrupt your hunt."

"Glad to help out. We've gone through this before, haven't we?"

"Yeah, we sure have," Tom said and thought about the time they found an incriminating cigarette butt in a field near his roadway during *Blue Darkness* days.

Pete returned to his deer stand, and Tom walked back to his pickup. After returning to his house, he picked up the phone and called the DNR office in Big Lakes. "I'd like to talk to Vern, please."

"Vern is off today, but you can talk to someone else."

"Okay, that'll be fine."

Tom explained the two shots and bullet holes to another agent, who agreed to drive to Tom's home to investigate.

AN HOUR LATER, A CAR WITH A DNR INSIGNIA on the door pulled into Tom's driveway. Two agents got out and approached the house. Tom met them at the door.

"Hi, I'm Tom Hastings. I called about the shots."

"You had mentioned something about a bullet hitting your house," the first agent said.

"Yeah, right over there," Tom pointed.

"Mind if we try digging it out?" the second agent asked.

"No. Go ahead."

The agent produced a knife and began prying.

Tom pointed. "My neighbor and I recovered these two empty casings from the tall grass over there."

He handed them to the first agent.

The agent looked at the rim of each and said, "There both 25-06's."

"I got it," said his partner, and rolled the bullet between his thumb and forefinger.

The first agent asked, "Is it a .25-06?"

"Yes, it is," his partner said.

"Do you know who hunts that land over there, Hastings?" the first agent asked.

"No, I don't, but Pete might. You may have noticed him in the deer stand while driving down my roadway."

"That's a nice looking stand. Tell you what, Mr. Hastings, we'll investigate further and give you a call."

When the DNR vehicle left his driveway, Tom looked up at the bullet hole. While searching a different section of the outside wall, he noticed another one.

"Deliberate," he whispered. *"Reggie Logan."*

40

JOLENE TALKED ON THE PHONE. She looked out the window, and noticed that a narrow band of ice had accumulated next to the shoreline.

"Mary Ann's is where I would like to go, Tom. No way am I going to allow that guttersnipe to affect my decision on where to go for dinner."

"Okay with me, Jolene. I'll pick you up at 6:30."

TOM HUNG UP THE PHONE and sat down on his computer chair. Geez, I'm thinking in pairs, he thought. There were two bullets in the buck's head and two more in the siding of my house. He hadn't heard back from the DNR and didn't expect one until Monday. He had dug out the second bullet and placed it into a plastic bag. Tom made a mental note to call Vern at DNR on Monday morning. Tom wanted to show him the second one.

Tom drove up his roadway and onto the township road after it had gotten dark outside. I feel okay knowing that my .32-automatic is in the glove compartment, he thought.

Feelings of apprehension surfaced when he approached the turn to Jolene's driveway. The last time I drove down there, the sheriff and Reggie Logan had invaded Jolene's privacy. He felt relieved not seeing any vehicles.

Pushing on the doorbell he heard the sound of heels approaching from within.

"Come on in, Tom. Let's have a glass of wine before we go."

"Sure. How was your day today?"

"I had a hard time concentrating at work. That darn legal stuff is sure taking a long time," Jolene answered.

"Making decisions, during investigations, can be like that, Jolene," Tom said.

"I suppose you're right, Tom."

"What are you going to do if Reggie Logan is at the restaurant?" Tom asked.

"I'm fully prepared for just that. If he tries anything, I'm going to stand up to him noisily—let everyone see what a jerk he is."

After downing the last sips of wine, they headed out the front door to Tom's pickup.

"Up you go," Tom said as he assisted her onto the passenger seat.

MARTY BISHOP FELT DEPRESSED AND DISSAPOINTED. His recent doings with Torfin had happened strictly because he needed money. Marty recently had to close his savings account to cover an overdraft. He didn't bank in New Dresden because of an embarrassing incident that forced him out of the community some years ago. He banked in Big Lakes instead.

"How much is in my checking?" he asked the teller.

"Eighty-four dollars and thirty cents," she replied.

Marty walked outside onto the sidewalk. I hate my job, but under the circumstances it's going to have to do, he thought. The chunk of money that I had gotten last month is gone.

After talking to Peter Erickson, the Talbot attorney, I'm seriously depressed because of a delay in the estate settlement, he said to himself. Until now, it was just me and the nephew who would inherit. Half of it could go as high as eight hundred thousand. What the deuce are those two broads delaying the settlement for? They're both illegitimate. What rights do they have to any part of the estate, anyhow?

Marty hated Reggie Logan, but he was willing to share half of the money with him. Certainly, the two broads, Jolene Hunt and

Beverly Stockwell, don't deserve a dime, he said to himself. They aren't part of the family…digging up poor Ralph was the lowest… the two broads have had a whole lifetime to decide…who was who. Even if there is a will, surely Reggie would have destroyed it. It's too bad about old Edgar getting beat up. He had to shoot off his big mouth…serves him right.

He visualized Reggie and that buddy of his, Chad, beating on Edgar in the back alley. What was Edgar doing there? Bet they lured him…probably had too much to drink, he thought. Maybe Edgar is in the will…hmm…he might be…yeah, that's it…that's why he shot off his mouth. The dumb bugger should have kept a copy.

That Hunt woman is meddling big-time, he thought. If there is anything I like about Reggie, it's the harassment that he's inflicting on her. Marty smiled when he thought about the windshield. Her boyfriend got lucky. He could have gotten a face-full of buckshot.

It's a good thing that I had that alibi set up, he said to himself and smiled. No matter how much they tried, the FBI agents couldn't break it down.

Crashing into the show window of the Big Lakes car dealership actually helped me, he thought. The police felt sorry for me. I'm sure everyone there was disappointed that I didn't have any alcohol in my blood. It happened simply because I lost my concentration in the parking lot. Marty smiled when remembering the astonished expression on the face of one of the salesmen…*Kevin* is his name.

Marty walked into Mary Ann's. He looked around and felt glad not seeing Reggie Logan and his henchman. He sat on a barstool and ordered a beer. Glancing around a second time, he saw Tom Hastings and Jolene Hunt suddenly show up at the hostess station.

THE PARKING LOT AT *MARY ANN'S* is nearly full, Tom thought. Not unusual since it's a Saturday. He walked with Jolene toward the front door when she said, "There it is—looks like the guttersnipe's car. See that red one?"

"Yup, I see it."

They entered and saw Harold greeting his customers in the foyer.

"Well hello, you two. I've got a table for two in back, very romantic corner."

"That is so nice of Harold," Jolene said after they got seated. She looked around and Tom could tell by her relaxed facial expression that she hadn't seen Reggie Logan, yet.

"Jolene, there are a couple of things that have happened that you probably don't know about, but may find interesting."

Jolene leaned forward, an expression of anxiety on her face.

"First of all, someone shot a deer on my property and dragged it onto my roadway and just left it lying there."

"Really, what do you think that means?" Jolene said.

"*Reggie Logan*, that's what that means! What's unusual is that the bullets that killed the deer came from a pistol, not a deer rifle. Also, whoever killed the deer cut the heart out and hung it up on a tree."

"Wow! Did you report it?"

"Sure did. The DNR is checking it out. And there's more."

"Yes?"

This afternoon, someone took a couple of shots at my house. The DNR pried out one of the bullets from the siding. I found the second one later."

Jolene appeared startled. She moved to the edge of her seat. "Good God!"

"I got Pete to help me look for tracks. We found the shell casings," Tom continued.

"You know, Tom, I'm sorry that I got you into all this. It's my fault," Jolene responded contritely.

"No, it's not your fault. You didn't pull the trigger. I've got a new idea. On Monday, besides visiting with the DNR guys, I'm going to try to get hold of Deputy Johnson. I liked him when we first talked, and he appears to be an independent thinker. Perhaps he can be of some help to us."

"Maybe we should call the state criminal agency," Jolene said.

"You know, all we've got so far isn't much more than a fender bender—two apparent accidents; you-said, he-said harassments; an alleged vial switch; and an unidentified shooter of my house. Considering the sheriff has thwarted you at every turn, I can't imagine the state being the slightest bit interested—unless of course."

"Unless of course what?" Jolene asked, anxiously.

"We have positive evidence that the sheriff is breaking the law," Tom said, his upper and lower teeth coming together tightly.

"Does it surprise you that Reggie did not report us breaking into the Talbot house?" Jolene asked.

"No it doesn't. I don't think Reggie Logan is in any position to complain about anyone. The will, Jolene, did you learn anything about the will?" Tom asked anxiously.

"Yes, I sure did. First of all, Reggie Logan is down to inherit fifty thousand dollars. But get this—it can only be spent on college or an alternative educational program."

Tom smile. "Wow, a couple of wise men, the Talbot's"

"I'm down for a hundred thousand. So is Bev Stockwell. The rest of the cash goes to various charities, including the New Dresden baseball team, one of the churches and the city."

Tom's thought about what they had discussed earlier…calling the state criminal agency. "Jolene, there's possibly one more thing we could do."

"What's that?"

"Talk to the FBI agents that were here investigating the bank robbery."

Jolene shook her head. "I doubt that would do any good—this isn't their territory. They're only interested in the bank robbery."

Tom nodded. "Yes but, it's possible that one of our tormentors was a part of the robbery."

"Amazing—amazing," Jolene said.

"Amazing what?" Tom asked.

"All this law enforcement—we're surrounded by it—and the guttersnipe is still running around loose."

"Jolene, except for the sheriff, I think everyone else is doing their job. This is a very unusual circumstance," Tom replied.

After finishing dinner, Tom and Jolene left the main dining room and headed for checkout. Jolene stopped to pay the bill as Tom gazed far and wide into the bar area, but couldn't spot either Reggie Logan or the guttersnipe's buddy Chad.

As Tom pulled up in front of Jolene's garage door, he asked,

"Are you afraid to be in the house by yourself?"

"No, I'm not, Tom. If they wanted to hurt me physically, they could have already done so. I'm likely a lot safer here in my house than I am on the highway. *Remember Purgatory Curve.*"

41

SUNDAY MORNING, Tom decided to attend church services in Big Lakes. The denominations of the churches in New Dresden didn't match his inherited religion. More snow had fallen overnight covering his driveway with a mass of white. He looked back at his boot tracks while the garage door opened. Deer tracks will really show up for the hunters today, he thought.

As he headed up his roadway and passed by the beginning of the greenway, he glanced into his woods. Standing next to a huge oak tree he saw a deer...a very large buck. Tom stopped the pickup...the deer didn't move. It's Prancer, Tom said to himself, feelings of elation building. My special deer isn't dead after all. Tom opened the door to spook the deer, making sure it didn't cross the roadway and break into the open and get shot.

Even though Tom had a great deal of respect for Pete and the deer stand, he didn't cherish the thought of Prancer dying in the snow. Pete's orange cap, as expected, showed up just above the highest board when Tom drove past.

Tom smiled and shook hands with a greeter as he entered the church. After sitting in a pew, he admired and enjoyed the music that he heard before the service started. Eventually the huge room became silent...the time had arrived for the sermon. Sitting with others on a hard oak pew, Tom thought the sermon too long and con-fusing...repetition after repetition. How many attempts at a message does one need to make a point? He asked himself.

Tom's thought about the big deer...Prancer. I thank God that the dead buck found on my roadway was not Prancer. He looked up at the high ceiling and fantasized that the priest would mention Prancer in his sermon.

After returning from Big Lakes, Tom made breakfast and settled down on his couch with the Sunday newspapers. He noted the television schedule listed a Vikings game at noon. Tom looked forward to the couch and a beer. Before the game started, he called Jolene. "Glad to hear you're okay," Tom said.

The Vikings played very well except for numerous penalties and turnovers. They lost again…a common occurrence during the past two seasons.

Donning his orange coat and cap, Tom strapped on his gun and left the house for his evening walk. He stayed close to the edge of the tall trees bordering the greenway. After getting near the small cultivated field, he saw movement at the edge of the woods to the north. Tom became alarmed, seeing two orange clad hunters? What the heck are they doing there? No one's asked me for permission… They're only about a hundred fifty yards away, he thought. Didn't they see the no-hunting sign at the beginning of my roadway?

Tom drew back to the edge of his woods and stood next to a tall aspen tree and thought about walking over to find out who they are…perhaps they're lost.

"Ka-boom!" The explosive sound of a rifle shot startled him, and he quickly slipped behind the aspen tree. Tom expected to see a deer running across the greenway, but saw nothing.

"Ka-boom!" Another shot…a sprinkling of leaves, from a small branch above his head, landed on his shoulder.

Tom yelled, "Hey, you guys! I'm not a deer!"

Peeking around the tree, he couldn't see anyone moving. Tom assumed that whoever had fired the shots left after hearing him yell. Minutes went by and the stillness became frightening and nerve-wracking. Moving from his hiding position, he advanced into the clearing.

"Ka-boom! Zing!" Tom dove back behind the tree.

He unsnapped the holster strap and pulled his gun out. He racked the slide and pointed the gun in the direction of the intruders. Tom anxiously watched and waited. He felt his heart beating at an intense pace as darkness approached. I need a decision and right now, he said to himself…at least I'm not hit.

Tom felt a surge of anger. Damn-it anyhow, he thought and fired off a volley of four shots high into the trees with his automatic. Taking a deep breath, he released his finger from the trigger and waited…no sound, except for his rapid heartbeat.

Suddenly: "Ka-boom!"

And then another: "Ka-boom!"

Tom's body jerked back and he snuggled tighter to the tree. No doubt it's a deer rifle shooting at me, he thought anxiously. I could retreat deeper into the trees and make my way to the house.

He heard the sounds of someone running. Whoever it is over there may be leaving, he thought hopefully. Tom remained still for a few more minutes.

Quiet is good, but it's killing me, Tom thought. Under the cover of partial darkness, he quickly moved along the trees back toward his house. Tom entered and shut off all the lights. Grabbing his deer rifle from the front closet, he dashed upstairs, picking up a flashlight along the way. After finding a box of .32 shells in the closet, he re-filled the pistol's clip. Placing it into his holster, he grabbed his deer rifle and moved to a window that overlooked his driveway.

After feeling more secure, he picked up a phone and punched *911*. He explained what had happened to the dispatcher at the state patrol station. Tom described his location and hung up.

"I'll get someone over there as soon as possible," the man said.

The next hour passed agonizingly slow. Tom spent it in the dark, continually monitoring the lighted area around his house. He felt thankful for the outdoor pole lights. Tom had mixed feelings when seeing a set of headlights approach his driveway. He felt gigantic relief when noticing the plastic bubble on the roof of the car.

TOM LEANED HIS RIFLE AGAINST THE WALL and hustled down the stairway, striding quickly toward the front door. Returning his pistol to its holster, he flicked on the light switch.

Suddenly, the front door crashed open. "Freeze!" the officer yelled.

Tom couldn't believe his eyes. He saw Sheriff Torfin Peterson crouched just inside the room and a deputy next to him. Tom shockingly stared at the barrels of two guns.

"Down on the floor!" The sheriff yelled.

"Wait! I'm the one that called 911!" Tom exclaimed.

"Down! Now!"

Tom lowered to one knee. The sheriff moved quickly and brutally pushed Tom, knocking him to the floor. Tom could feel his gun being yanked from his holster.

"Put the cuffs on 'em, Frank," the sheriff told his deputy.

"Hey, you've got it all wrong! Two deer hunters shot at me. That's why I called 911," Tom said desperately.

"Shut up! Two deer hunters filed a complaint. They said you opened fire on them. They shot back in self-defense."

"That's an outright lie. They fired on me first," Tom stammered.

"We'll let the judge decide that," the sheriff said. "Empty your pockets and take off your watch. Lay the stuff right there," he pointed, his eyes dancing with excitement.

"Geez—geez," Tom muttered with disgust and obeyed the sheriff's order.

"Now turn around and stick out your hands!" The sheriff yelled.

"What! Handcuffs! Are you nuts or what?"

The sheriff's eyes narrowed, one partially covered by a puffy red cheek. I better do as he says, Tom thought. I'm sure glad someone is with him.

The sheriff grabbed Tom's right hand and jerked it across the back of his waist. For the first time in his life, Tom felt metal around his wrists.

Tom saw the deputy place his .32-automatic into a plastic bag… his watch and the other things that had been in his pocket got put into a separate bag. The deputy helped him up and led him up the sidewalk to the sheriff's car. Tom got pushed into the back seat. He sat quietly and sorted his thoughts.

"Where are you taking me?" Tom asked.

Neither the sheriff nor the deputy talked as the car drove up

Tom's roadway, the township road and onto the county highway. In fifteen minutes, the car stopped in front of the county jailhouse. "Okay—out!" the sheriff yelled.

Tom glared at the sheriff. "I want a phone. I demand to exercise my right to call an attorney."

"Now you get your butt out of that back seat, or we'll pull ya' out."

Tom got escorted into the building and took a seat next to a small counter. A deputy watched the sheriff write something on a small form. The sheriff came up behind Tom and removed the handcuffs.

The deputy lay down Tom's driver license next to a second form. He filled in three lines and began reading. "In compliance with the Minnesota Government Data Practices Act, I'm required—"

Tom rubbed his bruised wrists and didn't listen very well as the deputy droned on, "to inform you—the answers which you supply— if you choose—your release from the facility may be delayed."

When the deputy finished reading, he laid the form on the counter next to a pencil.

"Read those two lines," he said.

Tom looked at the paper. The deputy had his pencil planted at the beginning of the first line. Tom read: *Do you understand what I have read to you?*

The second line read: *Will you answer my questions now?*

"Answer those two questions and sign on the line below," the deputy said firmly.

Tom picked up the paper, glanced at it and said, "Before I sign this, I need to call my attorney. A phone book, please."

"You sign this first and then you can call your attorney."

"No! My attorney comes first—ever heard of the American Constitution!" Tom exclaimed.

"Just a second," the deputy said and he got up from behind the counter and went through a door at the other end of the room.

Tom fidgeted and continued to rub his wrists. He noticed the handwritten scrawl in the third line: *Felonious use of a firearm.*

Good God, this is really horrible. I got shot at and they have arrested me for defending myself, Tom thought, outraged.

After the deputy returned, he planted a finger on the document and said, "Sign there, right now!"

"What if I don't?" Tom asked bitterly.

"Look, signing this only means that you understand what I have read to you, and also that your phone call may be monitored."

"Yeah, okay—give me your stupid form."

After Tom signed the form in two places, he said, "Now! My call!"

At last the deputy handed me a phone, he said to himself. He punched some numbers and waited. "Jolene, thank God you're there."

"What's the matter, Tom? You sound stressed."

"I'm about to get thrown into jail."

"Jail! What the heck happened?"

"It's a long story, but to make it short, our buddy the sheriff is framing me. Would you get hold of your attorney? I need to hire him to get me out of here."

"Oh my God, I'll call him right away. Hopefully, he's home."

"Do the best you can. I'll behave and await his arrival—thanks."

AFTER THE PHONE CALL, the deputy pulled Tom's arms behind his waist again and snapped the cuffs back on. The officer said, "Follow me."

Tom begrudged, walked behind the deputy down a long corridor. The officer snapped open a jail door and pushed Tom inside. Before leaving, the deputy removed the cuffs. The sickening sound of a jail door closing behind me is one of the worst things I've ever experienced, Tom said to himself.

He sat down on the bunk and put his head in his hands. I might as well rest and wait for Levitt, he thought. Geez, I hope he's home.

Minutes later, he lay down on the bunk. There's got to be a way to stop that monster, he thought. The county attorney better do something about this or I'm going to the State Attorney General's office for sure.

Sometime later, the clanging of the door awakened Tom. He

opened his eyes and saw a deputy's face poke through the partially open jail door. Tom sat up and saw Patrick Levitt and Jolene behind the uniformed officer.

"Oh, thank God, you've come," Tom said, relieved.

Jolene rushed into the cell and asked, "Are you okay, Tom?"

"Yeah, I'm fine except for the humiliation and anger—big time!" he exclaimed.

Jolene placed a hand over her mouth. "Tom, your arm is bruised. It's bleeding!"

"Ah-hah, bruises and blood" Levitt said.

Tom took off his shirt and held up his right elbow. "Right there—I got that from being shoved onto the floor in my house—by that brute of a sheriff."

"Tom, the sheriff originally charged you with a felony, felonious use of a firearm. I put a couple of hard questions to him and he has backed down—reduced it to a misdemeanor," Levitt said.

"What does that mean?" Tom asked.

"It means you don't have to spend the night in jail or post bail."

After getting his bag of personal belongings, Tom checked to make sure the items in his billfold were untouched.

"Come on, Tom. Let's head over to the emergency room. I want a doctor to examine and document your bruises," Levitt said.

On the way to the hospital, Tom asked, "What is that clod of a sheriff charging me with?"

"Shooting at a deer after dark, after the season closed," the attorney said softly.

"We've gone through this before, huh, Jolene."

"Sure have."

42

WHILE DRIVING TOM HOME FROM THE HOSPITAL, Jolene said angrily, "Let's hope that Patrick can talk some sense into the county attorney."

"If not, surely he'll get somewhere with the Bureau of Criminal Apprehension. I wonder what would happen if I complained to the state patrol?" Tom asked.

"From what I hear, they don't mess with arrests that have been originated by the sheriff's department."

"Well, I'm going to give this a week. If nothing happens, I'm driving to St. Paul to see the Attorney General," Tom said firmly. "Damn, the sheriff still has my gun. I'm going back there to fetch it tomorrow. I'm going to call Deputy Dave Johnson. Maybe, he'll get it for me. Besides, I think he'll listen."

MONDAY EVENING, NED STOCKWELL VISITED *WILLIAM'S PUB*. He saw Edgar, the salute-man, in the bar, talking a mile-a-minute. Later, close to 11:00 he saw Edgar go to the men's room. Ned didn't see the salute-man come out and wondered what happened to him. He checked out the men's room...no one there. Ned walked out onto the outside deck and saw Edgar arguing with Reggie Logan. Logan and another guy begin to push Edgar around.

One thing led to another and Reggie punched Edgar in the stomach, and then threw him to the ground. Reggie began kicking Edgar.

Ned had had enough. He came up behind Reggie and spun him

around. Using his right arm, he drove a fist into his face. Reggie fell backward against a stack of garbage cans. Ned just stood there with his arms hanging down, daring either Reggie or his pal to take him on.

Ned had checked on Edgar and made sure he was breathing. Then he went back inside and had the bartender call the sheriff's office. "Better call an ambulance, too," Ned had told him.

Ned felt glad that the Talbot's will disappeared, likely, my wife, Bev, wouldn't be in it anyhow, he thought. This way, if there is no will, and she can prove to be Ralph's daughter, she will get her share...better this way.

WIND AND COLD WEATHER HAD MOVED into the area during the night. Tom went downstairs just before daylight and started a fire in his wood burner. Walking back up the stairs, he paused by a window. After looking out, he moved quickly to a light switch and turned it off. Someone could see me in here, he thought, anxiously. Geez, I better watch it. I've already been shot at twice.

Returning downstairs, he sipped coffee and nestled close to the fire while watching daylight emerge on Monday morning. The sky looked peaceful and serene as the upper rim of the sun showed through the tree tops.

His mind drifted away from his horrendous experience that occurred the past evening, and he thought about his children, Brad and Kris, and the upcoming holiday. He had invited both of them and Brad's spouse for Thanksgiving dinner. They all agreed to drive over a week from Wednesday.

Tom had received e-mail from his cousin Maxine. She had been doing family genealogy research and passed on a long story about their great grandfather Thomas Hastings. Tom became interested and looked forward to the day he could visit the site of his American origins in western Missouri. His great grandfather was a survivor of the Civil War and its peripheral lawlessness.

Mid-morning, he called the county sheriff's office and asked for Deputy Johnson. Tom learned that the deputy wasn't currently available, but the woman dispatcher agreed to give him the message. Tom repeated his phone number and hung up.

After backing the pickup out of the garage, he returned to the house to retrieve his deer rifle, remembering that his automatic remained in the hands of the sheriff. *I wonder what the rock would have done to my pickup out in the field the other day if I hadn't had the gun along. Also, what would have happened if I hadn't fired back last night? I might be dead.*

Parking his pickup on his roadway, he stepped out with his rifle and headed for the area where he had seen the intruders on the previous day. Across the greenway, he could see the tree, which he had hidden behind during the shooting.

Searching the ground thoroughly, his eyes focused on an object. Stooping, he picked up a shell casing...a .25-06. *It's the same caliber that I found on the other side of the road,* he thought. Tom spent another five minutes looking for more casings. He placed the one that he had found in his shirt pocket and walked back to his pickup and headed for town.

Tom saw Ned Stockwell in the mailroom when he entered. *Big Ned uses up at least half the space in this small room,* Tom said to himself. He had never officially met Ned.

"Good morning," Tom said.

Ned didn't reply and headed for the door. While passing through, he caught the pocket of his jacket on the doorknob. Ned cursed and jerked the jacket loose, causing some change to fall and roll around on the floor. Ned got down on one knee and began retrieving the coins. Tom noticed that the knuckles of his right hand had severe bruises...*ah-hah, I bet the guttersnipe had something to do with those,* he thought.

Tom bought a newspaper at the grocery store and hustled home, hoping to have gotten a message from Deputy Johnson. At 12:00, the phone rang, but it wasn't the deputy. Jolene called to inform Tom that the judge needed her and Tom's testimony before ruling on a restraining order.

Attorney Patrick Levitt had arranged a time when they would meet with the judge. It had been set for Wednesday at 1:00 p.m. Tom agreed to accompany Jolene to the meeting. *It'll give me a chance,* he thought, to plead my case with the county attorney about last night, too.

Immediately after Tom's lunch hour, Officer Vern from the DNR called. He expressed interest as to where Tom and Pete had found the empty rifle casings. The DNR officer agreed to stop at Tom's home at 4:00.

Half an hour later the phone rang again. Deputy Johnson said, "I'm returning your call. What's on your mind?"

"This is Tom Hastings. Do you remember the case of a woman who got arrested by the sheriff by mistake—her blood sample got mixed up with a drunk driver?"

"Yup, I remember her well—someone had switched blood vial, right?"

"Right."

"So what can I do for you?"

"I would like to meet with you privately. It has to do with the two Talbot deaths and their nephew, who is harassing my friend, Jolene Hunt.

"Well actually, it's also about your boss, Sheriff Peterson. He's also been harassing Jolene, and wait until you hear what he did to me last night.

"Sounds like you need to go talk to the county attorney," the deputy said.

"We've already done that."

"We?" the deputy asked.

"Yes, Jolene Hunt and I. She's my—the woman who's being harassed by the sheriff and Reggie Logan."

"Tell you what. Tomorrow, I'm coming out that way. Why don't we meet at *Borders Café* for lunch, say, at 12:00 noon?"

"Great! I'll be there."

After hanging up the phone, Tom thought about the attention they would get at the café. Oh well, any perceptions the people draw from our meeting could actually do some good, he thought.

TOM WORKED ON HIS COMPUTERS and looked up at the clock. It read 4:00 p.m. He watched a DNR vehicle enter his driveway and stop. Two officers got out of the car, and Tom recognized Vern, who had investigated the dead deer on his roadway.

"Hello again, Mr. Hastings. This is Al, my partner."

"Hi, Al, I'm Tom."

"Okay, first let's have a look at where the bullet hit the house."

"Two bullets—there were two," Tom said.

Agent Vern puckered his mouth. "Two! I thought there was only one."

"I found a second hole after the other officers left," Tom added.

Tom showed them the two holes. He went into his house and brought out the plastic bag that contained the second bullet. He handed it to Vern.

"Okay, now show us where you found the casings."

Tom led the officers across the barbed wire and through the long grass. "I found it right there where the grass is trampled."

Officer Vern turned to look at the house. "This doesn't look right. Either we have a very stupid hunter, or someone deliberately shot at your house.

"Our enforcement division has checked out all the hunters that had been in this area that day and no one saw anything. Some of them heard the shots. Your neighbor, Pete—he heard the shots. I understand he assisted you in finding the casings."

"Yes, he did."

"I think this is a case for the sheriff," Vern said.

Tom looked at him doubtfully and shook his head. He considered holding back information and agreeing. Suddenly, he became angry. I hate this…justice is gone! Tom settled down and spent the next five minutes explaining to Vern his negative experiences with the sheriff.

The DNR agent shook his head and opened up his arms. "Tom, this is not the first time I've heard complaints about our elected official."

Tom felt so relieved he felt like giving the agent a hug. "Thanks for understanding, Vern.

"I'll consider what you said and think about going a different direction on this one," the agent replied.

"Yes, would you do that? Thanks so much."

They walked back to the DNR vehicle. "Nice place you got here," Vern said and extended his arm. They shook hands.

Feelings of hope overcame Tom as he watched the vehicle leave his driveway.

NED STOCKWELL SAW A DEPUTY and Tom Hastings enter *Borders Café* just before noon on Tuesday. It's one of the two deputies that had come to *William's Pub* after Edgar's beating, he thought.

I had avoided him and the other deputy, because I didn't want to get involved, he said to himself. It felt much more comfortable out on the back deck after the sirens brought an ambulance and a sheriff's car. I could have stepped forward and talked to the deputies that night…no way.

TALKING HAD CEASED MOMENTARILY WHEN TOM ENTERED *BORDERS CAFÉ* with Deputy Johnson. Most of the eyes followed them as they selected the far corner table. Tom sat with his back to the other pats so his voice wouldn't carry.

"I got to know your brother quite well about four years ago. We actually had lunch here and sat at this exact table."

"Yeah, he told me about the Ranforth murders. So that was you—right in the middle of it all."

The waitress interrupted and they ordered lunch. Tom had a coffee and the deputy drank water.

"So, what's on your mind, as if I didn't already know?" the deputy asked.

Tom explained his first experience with the sheriff, not being believed after the train accident. He told him about discovering the sheriff and Reggie Logan in Jolene's house, harassing her. "Torfin Peterson is doing everything he can to preserve the Talbot estate for his illegitimate son, Reggie Logan."

"That's a serious accusation, Tom. I've known Torfin for a long time. He's a good sheriff—a good boss. The people in the county have a lot of respect for him. This doesn't sound like him at all.

"However, the business of someone deliberately switching blood samples at the hospital got my attention, for sure."

The deputy narrowed his eyes and looked out the window. "Since the charges against Miss Hunt were dropped, I didn't pursue the matter any further.

Tom took a sip of coffee and waited for the deputy to continue.

"If Torfin was behind it, then it's another matter. But we'd have to find proof that he was, and there isn't any so far. Heavens help our department if your suspicions are right, Tom," the deputy added.

"There's more, Deputy Johnson," Tom said softly.

The deputy sat with his mouth agape when Tom told him what had happened on Sunday evening. "Here's one of the casings," Tom said and reached into his shirt pocket.

"This is extremely serious, Hastings. Tell you what I'll do. I'll talk to the county attorney. Meanwhile, I'll check on what happened to your gun. Whew!"

The couple sitting at the table behind Tom stopped conversing. The deputy looked past Tom, placed his hand above his mouth and softly said, "I guess this isn't the best place to be talking about these things. Tell you what. My brother told me all about the nice place you have. I can't do it today, but how about if I came out, say tomorrow after work?"

"Sure, Dave, that'll be fine."

The deputy and Tom finished their lunch and left the restaurant. While walking across the street, Tom felt the stare of all the eyes in the room.

NED STOCKWELL SAT IN HIS PICKUP across the street. He watched as the two men parted. He brought the knuckles of his right hand up to his lips. The bruises felt warm and he feared they might be infected. It is well worth it, he thought. What a great feeling it was to see that little runt flying into the garbage cans. Ned cleared his throat and laughed roughly.

REGGIE LOGAN HAD JUST PAID FOR TWO BOTTLES of Cola at Stillman's. He paused at the door and watched the deputy and Hastings cross the street. "Damn-it, I don't like the looks of this," he whispered. Reggie wore sunglasses even though there wasn't any sun. The skin around both eyes got blackened from the blow he had received from the fist of Ned Stockwell. He glared at the pickup where his attacker sat. I'll get even with that gook, thought Reggie vengefully.

MARTY BISHOP STOOD IN THE MAILROOM of the post office. Marty anxiously expected his first unemployment check He had just fished out his mail from a box, mostly bills and junk, he thought and felt disappointed...no check. While sorting the mail on the counter by the window, he saw the deputy and Tom Hastings move in different directions after crossing Main Street. I wonder what that Hastings guy is up to.

His boss had dismissed everyone for the season except for a skeleton crew. There would be no work until spring.

The only hope I've got for another source of income is the up-coming meeting I have with the big guy–the one he had met at the casino.

I could blow the whistle on 'em, Marty thought. Of course, then I would go to jail...the money wouldn't do me any good. I'm probably going there anyhow...it's just a matter of time...for real this time. Marty laughed nervously. I'll stand right up in front of the judge and admit that I did it. The look on TR's face...it's going to be worth it.

TOM SAW PETE IN THE DEER STAND when he drove by. Another glance exposed a second person... two orange caps. In a few hours the season will be over, and Prancer will be safe for another year, he said to himself.

When Tom passed the place on the roadway where he found the dead deer, he visualized Reggie Logan standing in his woods waiting for Prancer to come by.

43

JUDGE GLAVINE SAT AT HIS DESK, reading glasses resting on the tip of his nose, when Tom and Jolene entered the room with Patrick Levitt.

He looked up and said, "Good afternoon, folks. Have a seat."

The judge added. "Counselor, I've looked into your request to issue a restraining order by Jolene Hunt for Reggie Logan and Torfin Peterson. Before making a ruling, I have some questions for Miss Hunt."

Pat Levitt pointed with his finger. "Judge, that's Jolene Hunt sitting over there. Beside her is Mr. Tom Hastings."

The judge nodded and looked directly at Jolene. "Miss Hunt, your attorney claims that Reggie Logan and Torfin Peterson harassed you at your home on Monday evening, the eleventh of this month. It also says Reggie Logan harassed you at *Mary Ann's* restaurant the previous Saturday evening, the ninth. Would you tell me in your own words what you mean by harassment?"

Jolene leaned forward in her chair...her eyes dancing with excitement.

"Relax, Miss Hunt," the judge said.

Jolene took a deep breath and went on to explain to the judge about the intrusion by the sheriff and Reggie Logan on Monday evening. Then she told him what Reggie had said to her at the restaurant when she and Tom were out for dinner.

"Mr. Hastings, I understand you are a witness to those happenings. Is that true?"

"Yes, your honor. I totally agree with what she said. Well, actually I didn't get to Jolene's house on Monday until later, but the two men were still there. I overheard some of the conversation."

"Very well, Levitt, I'm going to sign this paper. It is a restraining order against Reggie Logan and Torfin Peterson. However, it applies only to Torfin Peterson if he's a civilian. If he is on duty and in uniform, it does not apply."

"Your honor, there's another matter. My client was forced off the highway leading into New Dresden last Thursday. Her vehicle rolled and she was injured and taken to the hospital.

"The next day, while at work, my client was arrested for a DWI by the sheriff. I have witnesses that claim Jolene Hunt was not drinking at that time. The sheriff had based his arrest on a blood sample taken at the hospital. He forced my client to spend a night in the jail. The very next day, the sheriff dropped the DWI charges."

"Who are your witnesses that said your client wasn't drinking on Thursday?"

"First, there is the investigating officer, Deputy Dave Johnson. He investigated the accident and was present at the hospital. Secondly, there is Mr. Hastings who was also there."

"Mr. Hastings, when and where did you see Miss Hunt?"

"I saw her, on the evening of the accident, in the emergency room, your honor. I'm no expert, but she absolutely didn't appear to have been drinking."

Attorney Levitt continued. "Another deputy had brought in an obvious drunk on the same day of Miss Hunt's rollover. The very next day, the drunk's blood sample showed no alcohol content. Your honor, I believe that the blood samples were tampered with—switched by someone."

The judge stared thoughtfully down at the paper. He cleared his throat and asked, "How about the examining doctor and nurse?"

"Your honor, I have here a copy of the doctor's statement. As you can see for yourself, there is no mention of alcohol."

"So, let's see now. Miss Hunt wasn't charged with DWI until Friday, the next day, by the sheriff."

Levitt nodded his head. "That's right, your honor,"

The judge peered at the document. "Mr. Levitt, my decision on the restraining order stands as stated earlier. My advice to you would be to take the issue of the sheriff's DWI charge up with Mr. McCarthy, the county attorney."

"Yes, your honor."

This meeting has ended," the judge said.

"There's one more thing, your honor."

The judge looked irritated. He looked up at the attorney and asked, "What's that, Levitt?"

"Mr. Hastings was jailed illegally by Sheriff Peterson last Sunday. He was out walking on his own property and was shot at by someone. He fired back and eventually called 911. The sheriff came out and arrested him."

"Sounds like you have your work cut out for you, Levitt. Please take that matter up with McCarthy. I have work to do."

"Thank you, your honor," Patrick Levitt said and turned to leave.

AFTER THE HEARING, Jolene's attorney Levitt told her that he felt pleased with the judge's decision. "It will make a difference. Mr. Torfin is going to hear about it. He can't afford negative publicity… election next year, you know.

"I've been studying the Talbot's will, Jolene. Since it hasn't been signed, it might be difficult to sell it to the judge. I didn't want to bring it up to him right now. I've sent a copy to the Talbot's attorney, Peter Erickson. I'm sure the computerized version will have its day in court when the estate hearings are held."

During the drive to Jolene's home, Tom said, "I'm wondering what caliber the Talbot's rifles are—perhaps .25-06."

"Why?" Jolene asked.

"The bullets that the officers and I pried out of my house were both .25-06—so were the casings, which Pete and I found in the tall grass across my roadway."

Tom could still hear the ringing in his ears, even though the shooting had occurred only three days ago. I need to look for the rest of the shell casings in my woods, he thought. The shooters may have been using more than one type of rifle.

DEER SEASON HAD ENDED. Tom took along his deer rifle and anxiously wandered around his property after returning from Big Lakes. He spent some time studying a large beaver pond. Tom examined an aspen tree, which had a deep chewed-out area in its trunk. It's being held up by a thread, he thought. The slightest breeze is going to take it down. Look at those fresh pilings of sticks and branches on top of the beaver house. They weren't there the last time that I visited here.

Later, while sitting at his computer desk, a pair of headlights shone across his driveway. As Tom had expected, the vehicle had a deputy sheriff's markings. Two men got out. Tom recognized the tall blond man dressed in street clothes. Geez, it's Dave's brother, Paul Johnson, Tom thought. He had left the sheriff's department in Big Lakes County two years ago, and became a state highway patrolman.

They're sure built differently, Tom thought. He met the two men at the door. "Come on in. Hey, it's really good to see you again, Paul."

After a warm handshake, Tom said, "Thanks for coming, Dave."

Paul Johnson, as a deputy sheriff, had played a major role in the capture and arrest of a renegade CIA Agent on the Hastings's property over two years ago during Tom's *Blue Darkness* days. The deputy became one of the prime investigators, and spent a lot of time at Tom's home. Paul currently resides in the St. Louis Park suburb of Minneapolis, Tom said to himself.

The conversation eventually drifted to the current frustrations that Tom and Jolene have had with the sheriff and Reggie Logan.

Paul asked Tom, "When you saw the person jump just before the train hit the pickup, did the person appear light or dark? Let's assume it was a male."

"Dark."

"Was he wearing a hat—or cap?"

"A cap, I think."

"Did he appear agile—young rather than old?"

"Agile and young. You know, Paul, I would have felt a lot better if Sheriff Peterson had asked me those same questions."

"Now, what's this about getting shot at?" Dave asked.

Tom repeated the story about the gun battle. His voice trembled explaining getting knocked down by the sheriff. "Right there," he pointed. "Oh, this is one of the casings that I recovered from the shoot-out. It appears to be the same caliber as the two retrieved earlier—the house shooting."

The discussion continued for close to an hour. "Well, brother, I've got to be getting home. Our wives are expecting us home by 7:30."

There is something about the tall patrolman that makes me feel more secure, Tom thought while watching their vehicle drive off.

44

A *MASTER TRUCK LINE'S* SEMI-TRUCK SLOWED to forty as it rounded *Purgatory Curve* heading into New Dresden on Thursday morning. Steve Steiger drove and he thought about money and his mother. Even though she was on Medicare, the medical bills had been piling up.

He slowed down to twenty-five before crossing the railroad tracks. During his last visit to *William's Pub,* he had overheard a conversation: *The Talbot's have a huge chunk of money in the bank, in cash–safe-deposit box.*

As he was parked his truck in the vacant lot across the street from his mother's house, Steve thought about the news, which his mother had passed on to him yesterday.

Steve had spent the whole day with her, and they sat at the kitchen table having coffee. His mother looked up at him and said, "I hoped that this day would never come, but it's time."

Steve frowned and asked, "Time for what?"

He watched as his mother walked over to her small built-in desk in the kitchen. She brought back an envelope.

After sitting down, she opened it and pulled out a document. "This is your birth certificate, son. I've never showed this to you before. Please don't think little of me, because I've done the best that I could."

Steve's heart throbbed as his mother began to cry. After setting the document down on the table, he started reading. Steve remained motionless when he came to the Parents section.

Mother: Edna Steiger.

Father: Ben Talbot.

Steve, felt stunned, continuing to stare at the document.

"There's more, Steve."

His mother stood and his eyes followed her.

"Jolene Hunt is your half-sister. Have you ever met her? She lives in a cottage on Trevor Lake."

"No, I haven't."

That's the shocking news I got yesterday, he said to himself. His mind had been running wild all day long, thoughts of money and his half-sister. As the day wore on, he formulated a strategy. He could not let another day pass without contacting his half-sister, Jolene Hunt.

Steve grabbed his bag and stepped down to the ground. He looked across the street and surveyed the small house that he had lived in his entire life.

After greeting his mother, Steve opened a drawer and, pulled out a phone book. He scanned the *"H"* listings, and drew a line under *J Hunt, 34204 West Trevor Lake Drive*. After typing a note on his computer, he printed it.

"Mother, I'm going out for awhile. Be back in an hour."

He drove his rusty blue pickup uptown and parked on Main Street. Entering *Borders Café,* he ordered coffee and signaled his waitress, who he had been flirting with for the past ten years. Steve asked her, "Do you know where Jolene Hunt works?"

"Yes, in Pine Lakes, I think it's the title company on Main Street."

"Thanks," Steve said and left a dollar tip, even though he had had only one cup of coffee.

Steve found West Trevor Lake Road and placed the note in Jolene Hunt's mailbox. As he drove off, he felt confident that she lived there.

After returning home, he thumbed through the phone book, and found only one business under the heading of *Title Company.* Jolene must work at *Midwest Title Company,* he said to himself.

45

THURSDAY MORNING, TOM HAD STOPPED at Byron and Eva's farm home on his return trip from New Dresden. The location of their house is very strategic, he said to himself. They could see right down the township road. He was well aware that they spent a lot of time looking out the window.

"Sorry, Tom, but I don't have any cookies today. Byron ate them all."

"Eva, I really wasn't expecting any today. I mainly stopped to hear if either one of you saw an all terrain vehicle on Rocky Point Road Saturday afternoon—did you by any chance?"

"Yup," Byron said. "I saw two of 'em—one late in the morning, and another later, sometime during the afternoon, about 2:00. Why do you ask?"

"Someone took a couple of pot shots at my house on that day. Whoever did it left the scene with an all terrain vehicle."

"Oh my," Eva said, holding a hand over her mouth. "Someone got careless."

"What color was the one you saw last—about mid-afternoon?"

"Ah—I think the first one was red—the second one sort of gray-green. You know, like camouflage."

"Do you see many on the township road?"

"No, not many. Most all terrain vehicles, which I see come by here, are in the box of a pickup."

"Did you see what direction the second one took when it got to the highway?"

"Ah, no, I didn't—sorry—not paying enough attention."

"By, you used to hunt with Ben and Ralph Talbot, didn't you?"

"I sure did, for many years."

"Do you remember what kind of rifles they used? What caliber?"

"Yup, both of 'em had .30-06s. Why do you ask?

"Well. The bullets that came from the log siding of my house were both .25-06-caliber–it couldn't have been their rifles, then."

Eva gasped. "Why in the world would anyone be shooting at your house?"

"Eva, that's what I'd like to find out. I have no proof, but I believe that the Talbot's nephew is responsible. He does have access to their rifles."

"Uh-oh, that sounds like trouble. I've heard some rumors, too. About the nephew—they aren't good," Eva murmured.

After leaving the Schultz farm, Tom drove to the home of Bill and Mary Jones. They had sold South Shore Resort when Tom lived in Minneapolis. Their new house burrowed into a height of land where they also had a good view of the township road...like the Schultz's, he thought.

Mary answered the door. "Well, hello stranger."

"Hi, Mary, hi, Bill. Wow, what a nice house."

"Sure cost enough," Bill said as he extended his hand.

His hands appeared calloused, Tom thought as they shook. This is a hard working guy.

"Oh, the price wasn't too bad," Mary said. "We got a bargain," She added.

"Mary, I see you look as young as ever. A couple of years haven't made any difference at all. As a matter of fact, I think you look even younger."

"Flattery will get you nowhere, Tom. You know that," she responded. "But, do it anytime you want." Mary set a cup on the table for Tom and filled it with coffee.

"Well, Tom, I hear that you're right in the middle of more trouble," Bill said.

"Yup, you're right. That dark cloud continues to follow me around. Have you heard about the shots fired into the siding on my house?" Tom asked.

"Yeah, we did. I hunt farther east of your place, so I don't have a clue as to who could have done it."

"Did either or you two—mainly you, Mary see a green-gray all terrain vehicle on the township road last Saturday afternoon, about 2:00, perhaps?"

"Now that you mention it, Tom, I did see one," Mary said. "I was sitting in the living room watching—ah, my soap on television and I walked outside to stretch. This noisy thing came roaring up the gravel road from your direction."

"Where did it go?" Tom asked.

"It turned onto the county highway and headed toward New Dresden."

"Had you ever seen it before, Mary?"

"No, I don't think so. Why is that important?"

"Whoever was driving that ATV was likely the person who shot at my house."

"Whoa, that's getting pretty close to home," Bill said. "Did ya' hear about the bank robber?"

"No, what happened."

"The FBI caught another one of them."

"Do you know who it was?"

"No, never heard the name before."

Tom chose not to share his scary shootout experience with Bill and Mary.

"I gotta go—have things to do. Thanks for the coffee," Tom said and he headed out to his pickup.

Tom left the Jones's home and turned onto the township road. He saw two horseback riders approaching from Rocky Point as he approached his turn off. Tom recognized Becky Anderson, who was the owner of Shady Acres Resort on the opposite shore of Borders Lake. Tom admired her horses.

He stopped the pickup and got out. Becky waved as they approached.

"Hi, Tom, what 'cha up to today?" Becky asked.

"Patrolling—keeping an eye on the neighborhood."

"This is my friend, Marlene, Tom," Becky said.

"Nice day for a ride. Say, Becky, you weren't out here about two o'clock last Saturday afternoon, were you?" Tom asked.

"No, I wasn't, Tom. Why?"

"Someone shot my house twice—about that time."

"Oh, for heavens sakes, it wasn't me. I was in Big Lakes."

Tom smiled. "The shooter drove up Sylvan Tullaby's roadway in an all terrain vehicle—a green-gray one. Did you see one like that around here yesterday?"

"No, sorry, Tom, I didn't."

"I did," her rider friend Marlene said.

"You did, where?"

"I had just made the turn onto the county highway, coming from Pine Lakes, and this ATV came toward me from this direction—really going fast. They're not supposed to drive on the road, are they?"

"No, they're not. Did you see what color it was?"

"Yup, just like you described—gray-green."

"Did you get a look at the driver?"

"I sure did. The guy appeared quite young and had dark hair. I should've reported him."

"Thanks. Well, I've got to go. Have a good ride."

TOM PAUSED AT HIS FRONT DOOR after walking down the sidewalk. He stood and stared at the two bullet holes. Tom thought about what Byron had said...the Talbot's hunted with .30-06-caliber rifles. The two holes in my siding were made by 25-06's. I wonder if either Ben or Ralph had more than one rifle.

The phone rang when he entered his house. "Hello," Tom said.

"It's Jolene. How about meeting me for lunch at the *Locomotive?* I know its short notice, but there's a lot to talk about."

"Sure. See you there in about half an hour."

Closing the front door carefully, he looked forward to his lunch date with Jolene. During their most recent get-togethers, Jolene had warmed towards me, he thought.

When Tom got back into the pickup, he opened the glove box. He thought about his pistol, which was still in the hands of the sheriff. I'm getting careless, he thought. I should take my rifle with me wherever I go…as long as Reggie Logan and his father-sheriff are on the loose.

On his way to Pine Lakes, Tom slowed while passing the Talbot's farmstead. He looked for an all terrain vehicle, but didn't see one. There weren't any vehicles parked in the farmyard.

Tom smiled when he passed the site of the rock-pile confrontation. If I hadn't intervened when the rock was up in the guy's hand, I would've been seeking glass service and perhaps some bodywork for my pickup. Perhaps another windshield…whew, my insurance rates would've really gone up. Thank God I had my gun along that night, he thought. Geez, they could've hurt Jolene, too.

As he drove down the road, Tom glanced down on the passenger seat and felt reassured when seeing his rifle.

Tom got seated at the *Locomotive* and waited for only a few minutes before Jolene arrived. After she entered and approached, Jolene's dancing eyes gave her away, he thought. She must have some news.

"Hi, Jolene, have a seat," Tom said as he stood to help with her coat.

"It's warm in here. Oh, maybe it's just me," she muttered.

"You know, I've been thinking, Jolene. After all the discussions you've had with lawyers and officials, we haven't gotten anywhere. The chances of the county initiating action against the sheriff are slim to none. Peterson is obviously in control and no one dares challenge him."

"You're right, Tom. You know, I really appreciate what you are doing, putting your neck on the line." She put her hand on his arm. "I'll never forget this, you know. So do you have a plan?"

"Not right now, but it seems to me we have to bait the sheriff and set a trap. I had an interesting visit yesterday. You remember Dave

Johnson, the deputy, don't you?"

"Yes, he investigated my accident—if you can call it that. It was a lot more than an accident."

"That's the problem, Jolene. All those harassing things they've done to you don't mean squat to the county attorney. We have to find or create some solid evidence."

"Okay. I'm all ears. What do you suggest?" Jolene asked, taking a sip of tea.

"Well, I'm not fixed on anything, yet, but I've been thinking strategies."

"Like what—what strategies?"

"You could call Torfin Peterson and offer him a deal."

"What kind of deal?"

"You could offer to drop your investigation for a chunk of money."

"Are you kidding?" Jolene asked, irritated.

"Ah-hah, but we would have a tape recorder running. If the sheriff fell for our plan, we'd have 'em. The county attorney would be forced to go over his head, perhaps to the BCA—*Minnesota Bureau of Criminal Apprehension.*"

"That sounds interesting, but I have another apple to throw into the bag," said Jolene as she put her hands on the table and leaned forward."

"Geez, Jolene, what's happened now?" Tom.

"I picked up my mail on the way to work this morning and look what I found," she said and lay a piece of paper down in front of him.

Tom read the note, his eyes darting back and forth.

Hello, Sister Jolene,

You've never met me before, but we have the same father, the late Ben Talbot. You don't know who I am, but I know who you are. When the time is right, we will meet.

Your brother, Steve.

"Is someone playing games or what?" Tom asked.

"I don't know what to do, Tom. I think I'll just sit on this for a day or two. If Steve really is my brother, I will accept him with open arms."

"I heard that another one of the bank robbers got caught. Only one left to go," Tom said.

"Wow! It wasn't Marty Bishop, was it?"

"Naw, I don't think so. My neighbors across the county highway said they saw the name. They would have recognized the name of Bishop, I think," Tom said.

"Let's get together at *Mary Ann's* this evening and we'll talk about it. Okay?"

"Sure, I'll be ready by 6:30."

While heading down the state highway on his way home, Tom glanced at the Talbot farmstead as he passed. There was one vehicle parked next to the house, a red car. Over by the gray metal machinery building, he saw a sheriff's car. We need a winner for a plan, he thought. This won't be easy.

As he drove by, he glanced back and saw a gray-green all terrain vehicle. He saw it parked around the corner of the house. The distraction nearly caused him to drive into the ditch. After grabbing the steering wheel tightly with both hands, his pickup undulated before steadying and returning to the lane. *The weasel has got an ATV...he did shoot at my house. I bet he and that Chad guy were the trespassers, who shot at me across the greenway, too.*

What is it that Jolene calls him? Tom asked himself...a guttersnipe.

MARTY BISHOP PAUSED AT THE ENTRANCE. He shivered and looked up at a sky full of cold looking stars. Not only did he feel the chill, but he wasn't looking forward to the meeting. Our strategy didn't go well, he said to himself. We should've gotten a lot more money...TR won't be pleased.

Marty opened the door and frowned when seeing a set of concrete steps heading down to another door. The debris that littered the corners had been there for a long time, he thought.

After moving down the steps, he opened the door below to the sounds of a pool table. After stepping in, he looked to his left, and saw the pool players. A young man with hair hanging to his shoulders leaned over the table, lining up a shot.

Glancing to his right, he saw cigarette smoke rising from a group of tables. A man wearing a cowboy hat sat alone. Marty recognized the ruddy face, which reflected light from a small greenish lamp. I hoped that TR wouldn't show up, he said to himself.

Marty looked away when the big man's thumb and forefinger tugged on the brim. He walked straight ahead to the bar and ordered a beer. Setting down a five dollar bill, he took two long pulls from the bottle while waiting for his change. Striding over to the tables, he pulled up a chair across from the big guy.

"Well! How much ya' got for me?" the big man asked.

"Nuthin'—"

The big man tugged at his hat. "I might have known that you'd screw it up somehow. Damn it, didn't I tell ya'—the safe doesn't unlock until 1:00."

"No you didn't—you told me 11:00."

"Oh for Christ's sake, Marty, did ya' need for me to take you by the hand? Ya' knew that you were gonna have plenty of time. The deputies were miles away, and normally the troopers don't patrol that area."

Marty finished the rest of his beer. He wiped his lips with his hand and said, "TA, I'm going to need a chunk from the Talbot cash or else I'm gonna sing to the cops."

The big man glared at Marty. "No, you're not gonna talk to anybody. You're good as dead if ya' do!"

"So I'm dead. If that happens, the letter gets mailed. The cops will find out, and you'll go to jail."

"You're bluffin'. Besides, no one would believe ya' anyhow. Now, get the hell outta' here before I get mad."

46

JOLENE FELT PLEASED THAT HER FRIEND WENDY, who worked at the bank, had called earlier. Wendy announced she had the day off and wanted to have lunch in Pine Lakes. Jolene told Wendy she would be delighted to join her at the *Locomotive* on Friday at noon.

"Well, hi. How are you?" Jolene asked and gave Wendy a big hug.

"Just fine, how are you?"

They ordered lunch and chatted. When lunch was almost finished, Wendy said sternly, "Jolene, I know that this isn't ethical for me to say, but there's something that you should know."

"What?"

"All the Talbot certificates of deposit have been converted to cash. The cash was initially placed in a safe-deposit box. Well, what happened was—someone removed all the cash. All that's needed is the key, a death certificate and a power of attorney document. I think it was Reggie Logan."

"Was it a lot of money?"

"Yes, it was, over seven hundred thousand dollars!"

WENDY HAD GONE BACK TO HER CAR. Jolene walked across the street and entered the Midwest Title suite. She wasn't sure what to make of Wendy's startling news about the Talbot cash. It really doesn't affect me directly, she thought. My main and only purpose is to have justice served on my father's killer.

She sat at her desk drinking a glass of water when she noticed a man crossing the street. There is something about the walk and demeanor that drew my attention, she thought. Oh well…back to work.

A couple of minutes later she heard a light knock on her door. "Come in," Jolene said.

A man stood in her doorway. Jolene didn't know the person. I may have seen him before, not sure where, she said to herself. His face is bearded but neat. He remained standing and filled most of the doorway. Ordinary looking guy, she thought.

"Yes, can I help you?" Jolene asked.

"Jolene—Jolene Hunt?"

"Yes?"

"I—I'm your brother, Steve."

Jolene didn't respond. She rose and just stared for a few moments. Waves of mixed feelings radiated through her body. Sitting there and looking at him, she knew and said to herself, that man is my brother.

Jolene's throat became dry. Her words came out distorted. "Are you the one who left a note in my mailbox?"

"Yes, I sure am. I thought it would be best that way–to break the news before meeting."

Jolene cleared her throat. "What's your name and how do you claim to be my brother?"

"My name is Steve Steiger. My mother's name is Edna. She showed me my birth certificate for the very first time only two days ago. It showed that Ben Talbot was my father."

"Sit down, Steve. I don't know what to say—just don't. How did you know that Ben Talbot was my father?"

"My neighbor, Martha, told my mother."

"If what you say is true, are you involved in the Talbot estate settlement?"

"Not yet, but I will be. I've showed the certificate to my attorney and he's probably already contacted the Talbot attorney."

"Steve, I'm not after the money. I only want justice for Ben Talbot's death. I strongly believe that he was murdered."

"Murdered! The newspaper said that it was an accident."

"The paper has it wrong. Someone else drove his pickup truck before the train hit, Steve. Whoever it was jumped out—just before—"

The skin on Steve's forehead creased, his eyes narrowed. "How do you know that? Why aren't the cops doing something?"

Jolene chose not to share any other information with Steve Steiger. After all he could be an impostor, she thought. "Steve, I can't say any more right now. It's too complicated. I've got to get back to work. If Ben Talbot was your father, then we shall be seeing more of each other."

"Yes, we will," said Steve and he extended his hand.

Jolene held it for a moment and let it drop.

"Goodbye, Jolene. Here's my phone number if you need to reach me."

Steve walked to the door. Before leaving, he looked back and smiled. Moments later he disappeared.

Jolene watched out the window as Steve walked across the street, and got into a rusty, blue pickup.

47

CONCENTRATING ON HER WORK for the remaining hours of the workday, after Steve had left, is next to impossible, Jolene thought. She sat at her desk looking out the window. She kept thinking about the latest news...I have a brother.

Her emotions turned to anger. I've been cheated all these years, she thought, dejected. First I find out who my father is, and now Steve shows up. Shortly after 5:00, Jolene left work and headed for home.

Jolene slowed her vehicle when approaching the drive to the Talbot farm. As she drove by the farmstead, she saw four vehicles in the farmyard. There are two red cars parked near the house, she thought. Over by the gray metal machinery building, Jolene saw a blue pickup and a sheriff's car.

The blue pickup looked like the one that Steve had driven into Pine Lakes, she thought. Two miles down the road, she slowed and turned onto a field approach. Darkness approached. Tom is picking me up at 6:30. Do I have the time? Oh, what the blazes. It looks like a family reunion–I'll join it. Jolene backed her car up onto the highway, her anger growing. She turned back toward the farm.

Confidently, mainly because of the number of vehicles in the farmyard, she drove in and parked next to the vehicles by the machinery building. Jolene's memory of being caught by the sheriff when she was with Tom angered her even more.

The large building appeared rectangular with the narrower part running north and south. There was no door in the far wall, near the hog barn. Two large machinery doors and a regular door could be seen from the highway. The door near the corner of the building, nearest the house, led into an office. There are two small windows in the office, she said to herself, one near the door and another in the north wall.

The spacious interior is wide open, most of it being used for storing machinery. Next to the office, a room had a shop bench with an enormous assortment of tools. The office and shop area are connected by a door.

JOLENE HAD NOTICED A LIGHT IN THE OFFICE WINDOW earlier after she shut off her headlights. As she opened the car door, she noticed someone in the window. After stepping out, Jolene realized that coming here at this time could prove to be a huge mistake.

The rusty blue pickup parked beside the sheriff's car is my safety net, she thought. My half-brother must be in there. It's the same one that Steve parked across the street earlier. I'm positive, she said to herself.

She turned the knob on the office door and pushed it open. Jolene inhaled and gasped while staring at a pile of green bills stacked on a table. Wendy wasn't kidding about the cash taken out of the safe–

deposit box, she thought. I've never seen so much money.

"Come on in, Hunt. Get a good look," Torfin Peterson said, who sat on a chair, his knees tucked tightly under the tabletop.

Jolene entered and saw Reggie Logan standing in front of the door that led to the shop.

"Well, look who we have here, Miss Snoopy," Reggie said sarcastically.

The door behind Reggie opened and Ned Stockwell entered. "What's she doing here?" he asked.

"We have another visitor, Ned. She probably wants a piece of the pie," Torfin said as he lifted a glass to his lips. Jolene continued to stare at the money. Next to the stack of green bills sat a bottle of whiskey and three glasses.

"Where's Steve? What did you do with him?" Jolene asked angrily.

Reggie sneered and said, "He's busy right now. Your meddling could get you hurt, you know. You've been stupidly lucky so far."

"Look, you little guttersnipe! I know it was you in that pickup truck that my father got killed in. You set it up. I have a witness!" Jolene exclaimed. "Furthermore, I'm going to call the sheriff's office right now. If they're not interested in what's going on here, I'll call the state patrol."

Jolene turned and hurried out the door. She was about to open her car door when an arm grabbed her around the neck. "You're not going anywhere, lady."

"Stop it. You're choking me," Jolene screamed, feeling pain. She became nauseated by the smell of whiskey coming from her attacker's breath.

She felt a strong arm around her waist, and struggled to stay on her feet as her attacker dragged her toward the building. Jolene's attempt to escape his grasp became futile. Ned succeeded in getting her into the office, and through the door leading to the machinery storage area.

The darkness frightened here, especially after a dim light exposed the supine body of Steve Steiger. His wrists and ankles appeared tied together, and a rag covered his mouth.

"Hey, out there—Reggie—Torfin, I need some help," Ned yelled.

"She's a real tiger."

Jolene heard footsteps approaching, and caught a glance of Reggie with a coil of rope in his hands. She gasped for air as Ned tightened his grip on her neck. Her arms, which had been futilely beating on the body of Ned, got pulled behind her back. She felt the burn of the rope as Reggie tied her wrists together.

Jolene felt pain in her back when Ned forced her down on the concrete floor. He dragged her across the room, and dropped her down on the floor next to Steve.

After tying her ankles together, Reggie said, "This'll keep you quiet for a while, you bitch."

Jolene scowled at him as he placed a rag over her mouth and tied it behind the back of her head.

"Have a nice evening," Reggie said and laughed.

48

TOM LOOKED AT HIS WATCH. He saw 6:15 and time to leave for his date. His headlights shone on a fox, which had stopped in the middle of the gravel road leading to Jolene's house. He had slowed the pickup, and kept advancing until the fox ran off into the woods.

Geez, why aren't there any lights in the house? He asked himself while driving down her driveway. After parking, he walked to the front door and pushed the doorbell button. His concern deepened as he waited and got no response from inside. A minute later, he pushed the button a second time. Getting no answer again, he walked around the back of the house. "Jolene isn't home," he muttered

Slowly walking back to his pickup, he tried to remember when he and Jolene had decided on a time. Yes, it was in Pine Lakes at the *Locomotive,* just yesterday. Jolene has never even been late for a date, much less forget one, he thought.

Tom hung around her driveway for another five minutes, anxiously watching the gravel road above for a sign. After giving up, he got into his pickup and drove toward his home, planning to phone and hoping to hear an explanation from her answering machine.

There was no message from Jolene, and Tom felt tension building in his stomach. Not sure what to do next, he drove back to Jolene's house. Nothing had changed. Getting back in his pickup, his mind became flooded with possibilities as he drove toward New Dresden. Stopping at the state and county highway intersection, his pickup truck and mind searched for a solution. Turning sharply left, he drove onto the state highway.

He thought about the Talbot farm and its convenient location regarding Jolene's route to-and-from work. Tom slowed his pickup as he approached the roadway to the farm. There were two vehicles near the house and three next to the machinery building. "Geez, one of those by the metal building looks like Jolene's," he muttered.

Tom continued past the farm and turned onto the first field approach…the same one used during his and Jolene's raid on the Talbot computer. Turning his pickup around, he drove past the farm again and looked for a field approach on the other side of the farmstead. He found one about half a mile away. After driving into the field he looked toward the buildings and could clearly see the yard light.

Getting out of the truck, he reached behind the seat, and brought out his deer rifle. After locking the pickup doors, he began walking across a meadow toward the farm buildings. Attempting to cross a barbed wire fence, at the edge of a narrow grove of trees, he stumbled and fell, dropping his rifle.

Wincing, he got up and stooped to pick it up. Noticing a patch of dirt and grass at the end of the barrel, he removed the bolt mechanism, and checked the inside of the barrel against a bright star. It looks okay, he thought.

Tom remained in the shadows of the machinery building as he approached the north end. When he got around the corner, he could see a splash of light on the ground. It's coming from that small window in the office, he thought.

Pausing, he thought about the location of the doors. Jolene and I had entered through a door in the south wall, he thought. I think there's another door that goes into the office near the northeast corner. The three vehicles are parked in front of it.

The yard light, near the middle of the farmyard, illuminated a part of his face as he sneaked along the north wall. He looked toward the hog barn and appreciated the odor. Hesitating near the small window, Tom ignored the yard light and looked inside.

His world exploded. On a table in the middle of the office lay a pile of stacks of green bills. Torfin Peterson and Reggie Logan sat there, apparently counting and sorting the bills. Where's Jolene? He asked himself, his mind panicking, and not being certain of what to do.

Tom visualized his drive-by, wondering if he really did see her car parked by the building. I'm sure there was a gray Toyota parked there, he said to himself. What if it wasn't hers'?

His confused mental state debated between the wisdom of charging in there with his rifle or coming up with another plan. There is a trained police officer inside, he said to himself. I think calling 911 on my cell phone would be the best thing to do. Maybe Darrin will send out an army.

While Tom debated his next move, he didn't hear the footsteps that had come up behind him. Suddenly, he felt pain in his arms as they were grabbed and pinned behind his back. His rifle dropped to the ground. I'm really stupid, he thought disgustingly. Wrenching his body from side to side, Tom attempted to break free.

"Hey, guys. Come on out. We have a visitor," his attacker yelled into his ear.

Tom had heard that voice before…Ned Stockwell.

"Well—well, another money monger," Reggie Logan said as he came around the corner. Tom wanted to hit him, but his arms remained pinned behind his back…locked in a vise.

"What's going on out there, Reggie?" Torfin shouted from inside the office.

"We have ourselves another prisoner," Tom heard Reggie answer, as he gave up his attempt to free himself from Ned's grasp.

Tom got forced through the door, into the office, and through the other door, which accessed the shop and machinery area. He got tied up, gagged and pushed down on the floor against the far wall.

Tom heard a groan and sensed that someone else is on the floor close to him. As his eyes adjusted to the dark, he saw the outlines of two forms sprawled nearby. At that moment, he knew that he had found Jolene. I bet the other one is Steve Steiger, he thought.

49

TORFIN, NED AND REGGIE HAD RETURNED TO THE OF-FICE. Reggie and Torfin continued counting and sorting. Ned stood by the shop door, watching them anxiously. When they had finished, Torfin said, "Let's see, that's a total of seven hundred and eighty thousand."

He looked up at Ned. "I'm offering you twenty thousand of this. That's not bad for one night's work."

"Twenty—why you cheap bastard. I want a lot more than that. After all, my wife is a part of the family."

Torfin reached down, and brought up his gun. Holding it up in the air for a moment, he set it down on the table with a bang. "Ned, you better take the twenty and run." He lifted a glass and drew in another swig of whiskey, watching Ned closely.

Ned glared at Torfin. "I think you'd be smart to give me more. I could talk you know–you'd be in deep trot—how about forty?"

"You get your butt out of here, Stockwell. Remember you're into this as much as we are. Keeping your mouth shut is in your best interest. Besides, no one is going to believe an idiot like you, any-how," Torfin said, snarling.

Ned threw his glass against the far wall, breaking it and splatter-ing whiskey all over the floor. Torfin grabbed his gun from the table and pointed it at Ned. "Get otta here—now!" he exclaimed.

Ned didn't move, and Torfin stood. "There's twenty grand in that stack—take it or leave it! Last chance, Ned."

Ned glared at the man for a few moments. He walked over, grabbed the money, and headed out the door.

Torfin looked up and smiled at Reggie, when he heard wheels spinning and gravel spraying against the metal building.

"LOOK WHAT'S COMING, PAUL," Deputy Dave Johnson said to his brother. The deputy sheriff's car parked close to the railroad tracks in New Dresden on Friday evening, watching *Purgatory Curve.*

"Holy smokes. Fifty-eight in a thirty zone!" Paul Johnson exclaimed. He had been visiting his brother Dave and his family during the weekend. Dave had talked him into a ride-along that evening.

'He's not slowing down one bit. Well, here goes," the deputy said as he pushed the button to activate the flashing lights.

"Look at that, Dave, he's speeding right through Main Street. We better get him stopped before he kills somebody."

"Uh-oh, he just went through the stop sign," Dave said.

Cautiously, but hurriedly, Dave guided the deputy sheriff's car through Main Street and paused at the stop sign. Catching the speeder is important, but not enough to cause a collision at the intersection, he thought. Heading toward Nabor's, he noticed the speeding vehicle had already made the next turn and might be heading out of town.

"We gotta catch this guy, and quick," Paul said.

"Look at that bugger. He's trying to hide. See him turn into that driveway," said Dave as they rounded the corner.

The deputy sheriff pulled up behind the car as the garage door rumbled upward. Dave quickly got out and unbuttoned his holster strap. Before Paul opened the car door, he unsnapped the shotgun from the holder overhead. After stepping outside, he racked the slide.

Cautiously, Dave approached the driver's side door. He removed an asp from his belt with his left hand and wrapped on the window, keeping the fingers of his right hand on the handle of his Berreta automatic. The driver didn't respond and remained sitting. Paul had jerked open the car door from the other side and yelled, "Hands over your head!"

The driver put one hand over his head and opened the door with the other. Dave had his gun pointed at the speeder. "You're in big trouble, guy. I clocked you at fifty-eight in a thirty zone, plus resisting arrest. Your driver's license, please."

"Sorry, officer, but I got confused," slurred the speeder and struggled to get his license out of his billfold, bumping against the car door with his elbow. The license fell to the ground.

"Pick it up," ordered the deputy as he backed away a step and waved a hand across his nose. "You've been drinking!" the deputy exclaimed.

"So I had one drink, officer. What's the big deal?"

"Do you have any objections to a breathalyzer test?"

"Yes, I sure as hell do. I don't believe in those things. It's against my rights."

"Not if you've broken the law, it's not against your rights," the deputy responded angrily. "Hey, Paul, would you reach in and grab the keys?"

"Keys—hey—what the hell! You leave my keys alone," the speeder said and made an attempt to get back into his car.

Deputy Johnson grabbed him from behind. "Better help me, Paul, this guy is strong."

Paul came running around from the other side of the car. He grabbed the perpetrator around the neck and wrestled him to the ground. The speeder got up and took a swing at the off duty state patrolman...Paul ducked and avoided the blow. Dave pulled out his asp and flicked it open. He swung and struck the speeder across a knee. The speeder screamed with pain and fell to the ground.

Dave got down beside the man and pulled an arm around his back. He snapped on a cuff. "Turn him over a little, Paul. I need to grab the other wrist."

"Whew! This guy is something else," Paul said.

The speeder lay on his stomach, his hands locked behind him. "Keep an eye on him, Paul. I'm going to check 'em out on the radio." Dave walked toward his car.

Paul leaned into the speeder's car and pulled out the keys. "Whoa, what do we have here?" he asked, after spotting a pack of green bills on the seat.

When Dave returned and saw Paul holding up a greenback, he asked, "What ya' got there?"

"Dave, take a look in the car—on the passenger seat."

The deputy stuck his head in and whistled. "Holy smokes, there's a pile of money in here."

"Yeah, there sure is. What's this guy's name?" Paul asked.

"Ned—Ned Stockwell," the deputy said. "No previous record."

"Okay, Ned. Where did you get the money?" the deputy asked sternly.

"None of your business, fuzz."

Beverly Stockwell made an appearance from inside the garage. "What the heck is going on out here?" she asked anxiously.

"Sorry ma'am, but this gentleman is giving us a lot of grief. We clocked him at fifty-eight miles per hour in a thirty zone on the other side of town. He's been resisting arrest. Is he your husband?"

"I'm ashamed that I have to say yes."

"Ned! What's the matter with you?" Beverly said, placing her hands over her face.

Ned grunted and said, "You can take these off now. I won't give you anymore trouble."

Paul helped Ned to his feet. Dave said, "Mr. Stockwell, you'll need to explain about all that money. Where did it come from? Did you steal it? Huh!"

"Money, what money?" asked Beverly anxiously.

"In there, on the seat. There's a big wad of bills in there," Paul said. "Real big wad," he added.

"Can I see?" Beverly asked.

"Sure," the visiting patrolman said.

Beverly looked into the car. "Ned, where did you get all that money? What's going on?"

"Ah—it's for back wages at the Talbot's."

"The Talbot's—back wages—what are you talking about? Who at the Talbot's paid you all that money?"

"Reggie, the nephew. He's in charge now, you know."

"Paul, would you help me get this guy into the back seat? Sorry, ma'am, but we're going to have to take your husband with us."

"With you, where—where are you taking him?"

"Well, for starters to the county jail. I don't know if you realize it, but he's been drinking and has refused a breathalyzer test. He's guaranteed at least one night in jail. Also, we're going to confiscate the car. I'm calling a tow truck."

Beverly began to cry. "Do you have to do that, officer?" she sobbed.

"I'm afraid so, ma'am."

"I'm going back inside—don't want any part of this," she said.

After Ned got placed into the backseat of the deputy sheriff's car, Paul got in on the passenger side. Dave punched some numbers on a phone and talked to a towing service. After he had finished, he turned toward Ned. "Mr. Stockwell, you're in serious trouble. The speeding and drinking is one thing, but the money could be even a bigger problem. We need to know where it came from."

Ned stammered, "Like I said before—I got paid."

"Your wife doubted you, didn't she? I doubt you, too. I think you're lying. If the money is part of something illegal, you're only making matters worse by not coming clean. Do you understand?"

"Ah, go to hell."

"Did you just come from the Talbot farm?" the deputy asked.

"It's none of your business, fuzz."

"You damn right it's my business. I've been hired to enforce the law in this county. One last time! Where did you get the money?"

"I got it at the farm, so what? It's my money," Ned said sarcastically.

"The Talbot farm!" the deputy exclaimed.

"Yeah, the Talbot farm."

"Who gave it to you?"

"Reggie."

"Reggie who?"

"Reggie Logan, the nephew. It's his money. He can do with it what he wants—none of your damn business."

"Who else is at the farm?" the deputy asked.

"A couple of other guys."

"What other guys?"

"Oh—just some guys."

"Paul, I'm calling for backup. We're headed to the farm."

"Okay, Dave."

50

STATE PATROLMAN TODD BUCHOLTZ closed in on the final half-hour of his work day.

His car phone rang. "Todd, Darrin here."

"Yeah, what's up?"

"I've a call here from the county sheriff's office. They're requesting backup. Where ya' at?"

I'm about fifteen miles to the south. Where do you need the backup?"

"New Dresden."

"What, another bank robbery?"

"No, not this time. One of the county deputies called. Do you know Paul Johnson?"

"Yeah, but he's in the Minneapolis district. You must mean his brother Dave."

"Paul is riding with his brother Dave. They've stopped a guy for a speeding violation. The guy was drinking and had a pile of money on the seat. They're heading out to the farm where the money came from. Better prepare for hostility. I'll give you his number. Would you give 'em a call?"

"Okay. Ten-four."

"LOOKS LIKE A CONVENTION OVER THERE," Deputy Johnson said as he turned onto the Talbot roadway and noticed the number of vehicles in the farmyard.

"Isn't that a police car over by the big building?" his brother

Paul said. "See the red and blue reflections from the yard light?"

Dave pressed the brake bringing the car to a stop. He turned the ignition and headlights off. His phone rang.

"Bucholtz, state patrol. Darrin says you need backup. I'm not too far away."

"This is Dave Johnson, Todd. How ya' doin'?"

"Fine, where you at?"

"We're approximately five miles beyond New Dresden, up the state highway toward Pine Lakes. We're parked on a roadway, just off the highway."

"You're not alone?"

"No, I have my brother along. Perhaps you know him, Paul Johnson."

"Sure do. I'll be there in minutes."

"I've also got a traffic violator in the back seat. We suspect something illegal is going on at the farm. We suspect there are armed and dangerous people there. I'll stay put until you get here. Keep your radio on, and we'll talk," the deputy said calmly.

Trooper Bucholtz flicked the switch that opened the scanner channel for Big Lakes County.

"PAUL, DO YOU THINK WE SHOULD WALK IN?" Dave asked. "I mean after Todd gets here," he added.

"Going in on foot, rather then driving up, makes sense. Who knows what we'll find in there? Buckholtz should be here any minute."

"Thirty-two fifty. Are you there, twenty-nine ten?" The deputy asked, talking into the mike.

"I've just gone through New Dresden. Would you flash your lights in a couple of minutes? I should be able to see where you're at."

"Better not. It may alert someone…put us at a disadvantage. I'll open the car door instead."

"Okay."

The deputy kept glancing at the highway to the west until he saw headlights. He grabbed the door handle and pushed the door open. The vehicle on the highway slowed and pulled in behind. Dave was relieved to see that it was a state patrol car.

51

TORFIN PETERSON HAD FINISHED STUFFING THE BILLS into two canvas bags. He had shoved his gun back into his holster.

"What are we going to do with those guys in there?" Reggie asked pointing toward the shop door.

"We can't afford to let 'em go. Sooner or later, someone is going to believe 'em," Torfin said.

"The building could have an accident–a gas explosion, perhaps," Reggie said.

Torfin looked up at his son and frowned. "You've had a lot of ideas in the past that have scared the pants off me—this one being about the worst."

The sheriff sneered and added, "However, we may not have any choice. I did notice an LP gas tank outside."

"It's not going to look good if they're found all tied up," Reggie said. "We could let some gas out until they become unconscious, then untie them before we blow it."

"Let me think about that. You're right, we've got to make this look like an accident."

The sheriff visualized himself investigating the fire. Of course, I would have to call in a state fire marshal, he thought. I know of several, he said to himself grinning. I think the gas heating units are high up on the west wall.

"Reggie, would you go into the shop and find a crescent wrench and a ladder?"

TOM HAD BEEN WORKING ON THE STRANDS OF ROPE
that bound his wrists. He had crawled over to a four-wheeled trailer,
which had a sharp edged angle I at the end of the pole-hitch. Even
though his wrists bled, he desperately moved them back and forth.
Minutes later, after the rope strands gave way, Tom worked on the
bindings around his ankles. After getting them untied, he jerked the
rag away from his mouth.

He became startled when Jolene uttered a sound. It appeared to
come from her nostrils. Her head motioned toward the office door.
She's trying to tell me something, he desperately said to himself.

Somebody is coming, he feared, and quickly replaced the rag
over his mouth. Sitting down next to Jolene, he clumsily laid loose
strands of rope over his wrists.

Reggie Logan had come through the office door and walked to
the bench across the room. An overhead bench light came on, and
lit up a corn picker parked between them and the other wall. After
watching him rummage, Tom saw him stick a wrench into his back
pocket, and walk over to a ladder. What the devil is he up to? Tom
asked himself as Reggie grasped the ladder and approached.

Feelings of panic radiated through Tom's body as he watched
Reggie place the ladder against the wall. Looking up, he saw a heating unit attached to the wall just short of the ceiling. Reggie had
placed the ladder right next to it. Geez, is it electric or gas? Tom
wondered, his mind going spastic.

Reggie started to climb the ladder, and when he got close to the
unit, Tom saw him grab the wrench from his hind pocket. Good
God, he's going to loosen a gas line, he thought. They're going to
blow us up.

Tom threw off the loose strands lying on his wrists. He shook
his head, and the rag dropped to the floor. Silently, he stepped over
to the ladder, grabbed the bottom, and yanked it away from the wall.
The ladder plunged and Reggie yelled as it came crashing down
onto the concrete floor.

MY LIFE IS RUINED, NED STOCKWELL THOUGHT. My wife is going to throw me out for sure. I don't have any money, and it looks like the cops may keep the twenty thousand, especially when they find out where it came from.

I don't want to spend the rest of my life in prison. Running into Ralph Talbot with the truck wasn't my idea. I shouldn't have listened to them. "Money and inheritance," they said. "I would get my share." Liars! That's who they are, he thought disgustingly.

Jesus, my wrists are hurting. He thought of Beverly and the look on her face when she came out of the garage. Ned's eyes began to water.

STATE TROOPER BUCKHOLTZ STOOD by the open car window of the deputy sheriff's car. "What's the deal, Dave?" he asked after glancing at Ned in the back seat.

"That guy sitting back there has the answers," Dave said and turned toward Ned. "Let's have it—what's going on in that building? Who belongs to those vehicles?"

"Okay, I'll tell you, but you have to promise to give me a break later—with the judge."

"Stockwell, you better talk and right now. Your cooperation could make a difference—it will be mentioned—you have my word," the deputy said. "Whose vehicles are those over there by the shed?"

Ned didn't answer.

"Well—whose?" the deputy asked again firmly.

"The sheriff is there—also Steve Steiger and the Hunt woman—Hastings and the nephew, Reggie."

"So what are they doing, sitting around a table and chatting, playing monopoly?" the deputy asked sarcastically.

"No. Three of 'em are tied up on the floor in the big part. The sheriff and Reggie were in the office counting the money when I left."

"Paul! We better get our butts in there and fast," the deputy said and pulled on the door latch.

The trooper backed away from the door and rushed to his car. He returned moments later carrying his M-16 rifle.

"Do you know if the sheriff is armed?" the deputy asked anxiously.

"Yeah, he sure is."

"How many doors go into that building?" the deputy asked.

"Two. There's one on this end that goes into the big part, and another where the cars are parked. It goes into the office."

"Is the door on this end locked, and what's in the big part, any machinery?" the deputy asked.

"The door isn't usually locked, but I don't know for sure. Inside, there's a tractor and a truck. They're by the big doors on this end. There's a wagon beyond the tractor. Then there are some smaller things further down, near the other end."

"Where is the shop bench?"

"It's on the wall by the cars, next to the office."

"Where's the light switch for the big part of the building?"

"They're in the office by the door."

"Okay, Paul, what do you think?" his brother asked.

"Best we approach from the field and stay away from the yard light. Maybe two of us should go through the door on this end...how about it, Todd?"

"I'll go in through the office," the trooper said.

"Be careful, Todd. Ned, you're staying right here. Don't try anything stupid," the deputy told him.

"Would you take these cuffs off? They're hurting like hell."

"Don't have time—later," the deputy responded anxiously.

Paul had gotten out and held the shotgun in one hand.

The three officers hurried across the ditch and onto the farm field. They moved silently and quickly, and were within thirty feet of the building when they heard a loud clanging crash.

"What was that? We better get in there and fast!" Dave exclaimed. "We'll kick the door open if it's locked."

"Okay, guys, I'm headed for the other door," the trooper said as he racked a shell into the chamber of the rifle. He got a glimpse of the deputy turning the door knob as he rushed by the corner.

TOM DESPERATELY LOOKED FOR SOMETHING RESEM-
BLING A WEAPON. The limited light exposed a short length of
two-by-four leaning against the wall. Reggie had gotten to his knees
and attempted to stand. Tom rushed toward him, holding the piece of
lumber like a baseball bat. He saw Reggie turn his face toward him,
blood dripping from his nose.

Tom pulled back the two-by-four and was about to swing when
he heard the sheriff yell, "Drop it! Okay, Hastings, get back down on
the floor or I'll fill ya' full of holes."

Tom stood there, and slowly lowered the two-by-four to his side.
He saw Reggie get up off the floor. Tom wanted to strike the snipe
in the worst way, but when he looked over at the sheriff and saw the
gun, he didn't dare.

He saw Reggie stand and glare at him and say, "You're going to
get yours for this, Hastings. Start saying your prayers."

Tom expected the worst. The sheriff's gonna shoot me, he
thought. Should I make a run for it? Suddenly, he heard a yell, which
came from somewhere beyond the truck.

"Drop the gun Torfin! Now!"

Tom saw the sheriff point his gun toward a flashlight beam and
pull the trigger. The blast sounded deafening. He saw the barrel jerk
upward when the sheriff fired again. An acrid smell reached his nostrils, and sickened his stomach.

Tom felt pain in his ear drums, and scrambled to hide behind
a trailer wheel. He looked at Jolene and Steve, feeling remorse–
nothing I can do at the moment, he thought.

He saw that the sheriff had gotten behind a stack of tractor tires,
next to the office wall. A panel of light coming from a slightly opened
office doorway reflected off the sheriff's gun barrel. The lights in the
office went out.

"Torfin, we've got you surrounded. Give it up," someone yelled
from the darkness on the other side. Tom recognized the voice–it
belonged to Dave Johnson. The deputy's plea resulted in vain as
another horrendous blast came from behind the tires.

"I'm hit!" Tom heard the deputy shriek.

Tom saw Reggie grab a pipe that had been leaning against the
wall. "Your time is up, old man!"

Reggie approached. Tom had dropped the two-by-four when he had sprinted to the wheel. He glanced around, desperately searching for another weapon. From the darkness behind him, he felt a nudge on his shoulder.

"Stay down," someone whispered.

He looked up and saw a big guy with a shotgun. Turning his head, he saw that Reggie had continued to advance toward him. Suddenly, Reggie stopped–his eyes enlarged–his mouth agape.

Reggie's attempt to protect himself by covering his head with his hands was for naught. The big guy slammed the barrel of the shotgun against his head, sending him reeling backwards. The pipe that Reggie had been carrying clattered to the concrete as he fell.

"Stay down, everyone. Lay down flat," the big man said.

At that moment, Tom recognized the voice of former deputy Paul Johnson—one that Tom had heard so many times before.

Tom muttered, "My two friends are lying over there by the wall. They're still tied up. They're helpless."

Feelings of relief flooded Tom as he watched Paul Johnson crouch and advance along the wall towards Jolene and Steve. He saw the officer position himself between them and the stack of tires.

Suddenly, blitz! The overhead lights in the entire building came on. Tom felt totally startled, and temporarily blinded for a moment. Squinting, he saw a state patrolman crouching by the office door. He sucked in some air and tried to yell a warning as the sheriff peeked around the tires and pointed his gun at the trooper.

"Ka-boom!" Trooper Paul Johnson had pulled the trigger of the shotgun. The sheriff's body got driven back against the tires, his gun clattered to the concrete floor. The trooper stood and dodged one of the tires that had slid off the top of the pile. It rolled toward the office door and lost its momentum. The sound of the tire settling to the floor ended, followed by a moment of silence.

"He's down, Todd!" Paul yelled.

Tom saw the two officers rush the tires. He could hear Sheriff Torfin Peterson groaning and gasping. The bloody mass on his chest looked awful, and Tom turned his head away.

"Keep an eye on him, Todd. I'll check on Dave!" Paul yelled.

Tom watched the big man rush past the bench. "Geez, I hope that

Dave is okay," he whispered.

"Where are you hit, Dave?" Tom heard Paul ask his brother.

"In the chest, under the right arm—I think, I'm okay—breathing is a little tough, though," the deputy said, coarsely.

"Todd!" Paul yelled across the room. "Call an ambulance."

TOM WORKED HIS WEARY FINGERS TO RELEASE JOLENE from her bondage. "There you go, Jolene, I'll try to get the ropes off Steve."

After Tom succeeded in freeing them, they huddled together.

"Is it safe over there?" Tom asked the trooper.

"Yup, it is. If you guys can walk, head into the office."

Tom had his arm around Jolene's waist and he guided her through the door. She sobbed intensely as Steve came around the other side of her and put his hand on her shoulder.

"It's all over, Jolene, we're safe," Steve said.

Tom saw two bags on the table, one of them open, exposing a package of bills.

Tom left Jolene and Steve in the office, and rushed to where Deputy Johnson laid.

"Geez, how does it look, Paul?"

"Dunno for sure. Looks okay for now, but we need help fast."

Tom walked over to the door and looked outside. He could see flashing lights on the state highway. "They're coming, Paul," he said loudly.

The trooper said, "Hastings, would you help me move the vehicles off the roadway?"

Tom followed him out of the building and they rushed to the vehicles parked near the highway. As they approached, Tom noticed a pickup truck parked behind the patrol car.

He saw the trooper run over to the pickup and say, "Hey, we need to clear the road. Get your butt out of here—now!"

As Tom opened the driver's door of the deputy sheriff's car, he looked back and saw the face of Edgar Sandvik through the windshield of the pickup.

Tom turned the key–the car started, and he drove it into the farm-yard and parked under the yard light.

New Dresden Rescue arrived at the scene. Two crew members rushed through the office door. Tom felt weak inside. He worried about Deputy Johnson. A few minutes later, an ambulance turned into the yard. Tom watched as they removed the wounded deputy from the building onto a gurney.

"God speed," Tom whispered.

He reentered the office to join Jolene and Steve. More sirens… another ambulance arrived. Sheriff Torfin Peterson's body appeared covered by a sheet as two crewmen rolled the gurney through the doorway.

Tom, Jolene and Steve sat in silence. Flashing lights accumu-lated in the farmyard. Two more patrol cars and a deputy sheriff's car had arrived. Tom had gotten up off his chair. He stepped outside, and returned moments later with his rifle. After laying it down by the wall, he said, "They know where to find us. Come on, Jolene, Steve. Let's go home."

EPILOGUE

Sheriff Torfin Peterson died in the machinery building from the shotgun wound received at the hands of state patrolman, Paul Johnson.

Deputy Dave Johnson spent three weeks in the hospital recovering from the gunshot wound. A bullet had been removed from his right lung. He returned to his job and eventually got elected sheriff of Big Lakes County.

State Trooper Todd Bucholtz got promoted to Lieutenant and continues to serve the Big Lakes district.

Ned Stockwell is currently serving a thirty year sentence in a federal penitentiary. He was convicted of killing Ralph Talbot and conspiring to defraud the Talbot estate. His wife divorced him before his trial began.

Reggie Logan was tried and convicted of the murder of Ben Talbot. He was also convicted of attempted murder and other felony charges. Reggie was sentenced to life in prison.

Peter Erickson, the Talbot attorney, took charge of the money that was delivered to him by the sheriff's department…the bags from the office of the machinery building. He had officially counted seven hundred and ten thousand dollars. Supposed to be seven hundred and sixty, he said to himself and sighed. There's fifty thousand dollars missing.

According to the will that the computer had generated, Jolene Hunt, Beverly Stockwell and Steve Steiger each received one hundred thousand dollars. The New Dresden baseball team, as did Our Savior's Lutheran church, each benefited, by fifty thousand dollars. Ten thousand dollars was donated to miscellaneous charities. Certificate of Deposits were purchased with the remaining two hundred thousand dollars. Steve Steiger felt the money would be needed for farm equipment purchases.

Steve Steiger quit his job as a truck driver and took over the operations of the Talbot hog farm. He is currently a co-owner along with Jolene Hunt and Beverly Stockton.

Edgar Sandvik occasionally works for Steve Steiger on the farm, especially during the harvest. However, he isn't allowed to drive the truck. Every day, Edgar can be seen driving down Main Street of New Dresden in his new pickup truck. He had purchased the club-cab unit shortly after the shootout at the Talbot farm.

He crisply salutes Ellie at Stillman's Super Market after he pays for his groceries. She continues to speculate where he got the money to spend two winter months in Florida.

Marty Bishop felt devastated after his last meeting with Torfin Peterson. He had remained in his apartment and knew he wouldn't free much longer. As Marty expected, FBI agents eventually knocked on his door. He got charged with first-degree bank robbery and is currently serving a ten-year term in the state penitentiary.

Tom Hastings continues to play tennis frequently and go for long walks in the woods. He spends a lot of time researching his great grandfather, Thomas Hastings, who grew into manhood during the Civil War in western Missouri. Tom stops at the cemetery often and looks over the valley, thinking about peace, and his departed wife Becky.

Closing the wrought-I gate carefully, he had mixed feelings regarding his upcoming date with Jolene–Mary Ann's restaurant is where they decided to go. Jolene had hinted during their last date that she was thinking about moving back to Kansas City.

After arriving at his home, Tom opened the letter from Julie. He felt happy to read that she had moved back to St. Paul.

AUTHOR'S NOTES: Tom Hastings has survived again. He drives to New Dresden every single day for the mail except on Sunday. He keeps busy reading about his famous great, great grand father who played a major part during the Civil War in western Missouri.

Gray Riders, a western-historical-fictional novel, flashes back a hundred and forty five years to Tom Hastings's ancestors, a farm family located in western Missouri. Hastings is a 13 year old boy on a farm when the Civil War breaks out. Please join him, his family and his neighbors as they fight there way through the historical conflict.

Sleep Six is another mystery-suspense novel. It follows *Purgatory Curve*. New Dresden builds a four story apartment complex. Tom Hastings meets fours of its new tenants who are all middle age women. One of them, Birdie Heck, has returned to the small community to attend the funeral of her mother.

While going through her mother's things at the retirement home, she discovers evidence relating to six men who drank too much beer one evening, invaded her home and abused her mother.

Birdie was only six years old when it happened, but her memory returns and her *inner soul demands* **revenge**.

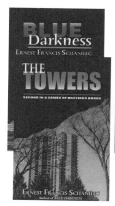  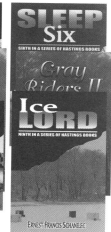

$16.95 EACH
(plus $3.95 shipping & handling for first book,
add $2.00 for each additional book ordered.
Shipping and Handling costs for larger quantites available upon request.

PLEASE INDICATE NUMBER OF COPIES YOU WISH TO ORDER

_____ BLUE DARKNESS	_____ GRAY RIDER
_____ THE TOWERS	_____ SLEEP SIX
_____ DANGER IN THE KEYS	_____ GRAY RIDERS II
_____ NIGHT OUT IN FARGO	_____ ICE LORD
_____ PURGATORY CURVE	_____ RIO GRANDE IDENTITY

Bill my: ❏ VISA   ❏ MasterCard   Expires _____

Card # _____

Signature _____

Daytime Phone Number _____

For credit card orders call 1-888-568-6329

OR SEND THIS ORDER FORM TO:
J&M Printing • PO Box 248 • Gwinner, ND 58040-0248

I am enclosing $_____   ❏ Check   ❏ Money Order
Payable in US funds. No cash accepted.
SHIP TO:

Name_____

Mailing Address _____

City _____

State/Zip _____

Orders by check allow longer delivery time. Money order and credit card orders will be
shipped within 48 hours. This offer is subject to change without notice.

THE HASTINGS SERIES

Blue Darkness
(First in a Series of Hastings Books)
This tale of warm relationships and chilling murders takes place in the lake country of central Minnesota. Normal activities in the small town of New Dresen are disrupted when local resident, ex-CIA agent Maynard Cushing, is murdered. His killer, Robert Ranforth also an ex-CIA agent, had been living anonymously in the community for several years. Stalked and attached at his country home, Tom Hastings employs tools and people to mount a defense and help solve crimes.
Written by Ernest Francis Schanilec (276 pgs.)
ISBN: 1-931916-21-7
$16.95 each in a 6x9" paperback.

The Towers
(Second in a Series of Hastings Books)
Tom Hastings' move to Minneapolis was precipitated by the trauma associated with the murder of one of his neighbors. After renting a high-rise apartment in a building known as The Towers, he's met new friends and retained his relationship with a close friend, Julie, from St. Paul. Hastings is a resident for less than a year when a young lady is found murdered next to a railroad track, a couple of blocks from The Towers. The murderer shares the same elevators, lower-level garage and other areas in the highrise as does Hastings. The building manager and other residents, along with Hastings are caught up in dramatic events that build to a crisis while the local police are baffled. Who is the killer?
Written by Ernest Francis Schanilec. (268 pgs.)
ISBN: 1-931916-23-3
$16.95 each in a 6x9" paperback.

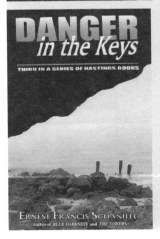

Danger In The Keys
(Third in a Series of Hastings Books)
Tom Hastings is looking forward to a month's vacation in Florida. While driving through Tennessee, he witnesses an automobile leaving the road and plunging down a steep slope. The driver,

a young woman, survives the accident. Tom is totally unaware that the young woman was being chased because she had chanced coming into possession of a valuable gem, which had been heisted from a Saudi Arabian prince. After arriving in Key Marie Island in Florida, Tom meets many interesting people, however, some of them are on the island because of the Guni gem, and they will stop at nothing in order to gain possession. Desperate people and their greedy ambitions interrupt Tom's goal of a peaceful vacation.
Written by Ernest Francis Schanilec. (210 pgs.) ISBN: 1-931916-28-4
$16.95 each in a 6x9" paperback.

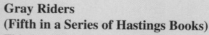

Purgatory Curve
(Fourth in a Series of Hastings Books)

A loud horn penetrated the silence in New Dresden, Minnesota. Tom Hastings stepped onto the Main Street sidewalk and heard a freight train coming and watched in horror as it crushed a pickup truck that was stalled on the railroad tracks. Moments before the crash, he saw someone jump from the cab. An elderly farmer's body was later recovered from the mangled vehicle. Tom was interviewed by the sheriff the next day and was upset that his story about what he saw wasn't believed. The tragic death of the farmer was surrounded with controversy and mysterious people, including a nephew who taunted Tom after the accident. Or, was it an accident?
Written by Ernest Francis Schanilec. (210 pgs.) ISBN: 1-931916-29-2
$16.95 each in a 6x9" paperback.

Gray Riders
(Fifth in a Series of Hastings Books)

This is a flashback to Schanilec's Hastings Series mystery novels where Tom Hastings is the main character. Tom's great-grandfather, Thomas, lives on a farm with his family in western Missouri in 1861. The local citizenry react to the Union calvary by organizing and forming an armed group of horsemen who become known as the Gray Riders. The Riders not only defend their families and properties, but also ride with the Confederate Missouri Guard. They participate in three major battles. Written by Ernest Francis Schanilec. (266 pgs.) ISBN: 1-931916-38-1
$16.95 each in a 6x9" paperback.

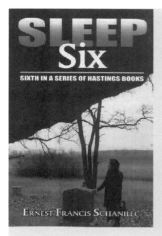

Sleep Six (Sixth in a Series of Hastings Books)
Revenge made Birdie Hec quit her job in Kansas City and move to New Dresden, Minnesota. A discovery after her mother's funeral had rekindled her memory of an abuse incident that had happened when she was six years old. An envelope containing six photographs, four of them with names, revealed some of her mother's abusers. Birdie moved into an apartment complex in New Dresden, using an anonymous name. She befriended three other women, who were all about the same age. While socializing with her new friends, Birdie scouted her potential victims. She plotted the demise of the four men whom she had definitely recognized...
Written by Ernest Francis Schanilec (250 pgs.)
ISBN: 1-931916-40-3
$16.95 each in a 6x9" paperback.

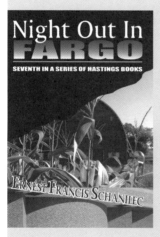

Night Out In Fargo
(Seventh in a Series of Hastings Books)
Tom Hastings property is within view of the senator's lake complex, and once again he is pulled into the world of greed and hard-striking criminals. Hastings is confused, not only because of the suspenseful activities at the senator's complex but also the strange hissing sound in the cornfield next to his property. Armed guards block him from investigating the mystery at the abandoned farmstead. Why are they there, and what are they hiding? Written by Ernest Schanilec.
ISBN: 1-931916-44-6 (280 pages)
$16.95 each in a 6x9" paperback.

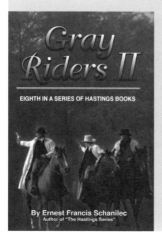

Gray Riders II
(Eighth in a Series of Hastings Books)
The Gray Riders are in the saddle again, battling the Union in Western Missouri and protecting the folks of Tarrytown from ruthless jayhawkers. But their biggest threat comes from within - when an albino mountain man named Bone Erloch sets his sights on Sarah, Tom Hasting's pregnant wife. Gray Riders II brings back Grady, Justin Haggard, and all of his saddle mates. There is no shortage of new arrivals to spice up life in Tarrytown. So saddle up, it's time for a wild ride.

Written by Ernest Schanilec. ISBN: 978-1-931914-50-5 (276 pages)
$16.95 each in a 6x9" paperback.

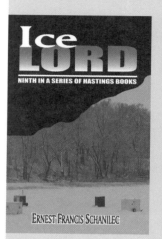

Ice Lord
(Ninth in a Series of Hastings Books)
Tom finds himself up against a killer who haunts the fishing houses on Border's Lake. Tom spots the first burning house from his back deck, and is forever sucked into a world of vengeance and greed where it will take all his wiles to stay on top of thieving thugs, wisecracking bullies, two women who want his love, and a solemn murderer who believes he is carrying out God's will. The January ice will never feel so chilly again. Written by Ernest Schanilec.
ISBN: 978-1-931916-56-1 (264 pages)
$16.95 each in a 6x9" paperback.

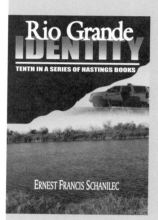

Rio Grande Identity
(Tenth in a Series of Hastings Books)
It sounds too good to be true. Ten percent return on your investment, guaranteed. Or so claims Rio Grand Development Corporation, a Texas firm that has Texas retirees lining up to plunk down their hard earned savings. Tom Hastings and his friend Samantha are at the head of the line with check books open, just as excited as the others.
But then the questions arise. Why is a mysterious car parked outside their apartment in the evenings? Why does the neighbor's apartment burn down right after they give Tom a mysterious package for safe keeping? Why does the firm's director have to enter Texas crossing the Rio Grande on a creaky rowboat in the dead of the night?
Written by Ernest Schanilec.
ISBN: 978-1-931916-66-0 (288 pages)
$16.95 each in a 6x9" paperback.